M000311523

A
FRIEND
IN THE
DARK

AN AUDEN & O'CALLAGHAN MYSTERY

GREGORY ASHE
C.S. POE

This is a work of fiction. Names, characters, places, and incidents either are the product of the authors' imagination or are used fictitiously, and any resemblance to actual persons, living or dead, business establishments, events, or locales is entirely coincidental.

A Friend in the Dark
Copyright © 2020 by Gregory Ashe, C.S. Poe

All rights reserved. No part of this book may be reproduced in any form, stored in any retrieval system, or transmitted in any form by any means—electronic, mechanical, photocopy, recording, or otherwise—without prior written permission of the publisher, except as provided by United States of America copyright law. For permission requests and all other inquiries, contact: contact@cspoe.com

Published by Emporium Press
https://www.cspoe.com
contact@cspoe.com

Cover Art by Reese Dante
Cover content is for illustrative purposes only and any person depicted on the cover is a model.

Edited by Tricia Kristufek
Copyedited by Andrea Zimmerman
Proofread by Lyrical Lines

Published 2020.
Printed in the United States of America

Trade Paperback ISBN: 978-1-952133-21-3
Digital eBook ISBN: 978-1-952133-20-6

I would rather walk with a friend in the dark than alone in the light.

CHAPTER
ONE

At 2:45 p.m. Rufus O'Callaghan stood outside the freight entrance of 619 West Thirty-Eighth with nothing but a burner phone, a lifted pack of spearmint bubblegum, and a certain sense of dread in his gut.

At 2:46 p.m. it started to rain.

Rufus grabbed the handle of the heavy door, yanked it open, and stepped into a long, narrow hallway. The pseudoalley was like a hotbox. Dumpsters lined the right-hand side, the stink of uncollected garbage overwhelming in the late-July heat that'd been cooking New York City. To the left was an elevator, likely utilized by building staff and delivery services. The doors were caked in enough dirt and grease to leave a tag on. Water *drip*, *drip*, *drip*ped from somewhere overhead, writing an urban symphony as it echoed against asphalt and bare brick.

Rufus pulled his phone from the pocket of his jean jacket, entered the passcode, and scrolled through a short list of text conversations. He stored no names in the address book, just memorized the necessary 212s and 917s.

619 W. 38, 7 Fl

3:00

Pickup job JB

Pocketing the burner again, Rufus approached the elevator and used his knuckle to jab the Up button.

The rain picked up, *ping*ing off the tin roof overhead. Thunder cracked and muffled the sounds of Midtown like a television heard through the other side of a motel wall. Taxis honking, jackhammers and shouts from the construction crew across the street, dogs barking, startled pedestrians caught in the storm—they all clotted together and formed a throbbing headache at the base of Rufus's skull.

The elevator door slid open, metal grating against metal. The fluorescent light in the car flickered wildly, which didn't instill much confidence in routine maintenance being performed. Rufus stepped inside, once again used his knuckle to press the button for the seventh floor, then leaned back against the wall as the door groaned shut. Someone had taken a key to the metal interior at some point in the past. The word vaguely resembled *FUCK*. Rufus hoped the little shit hadn't dropped out of art school to pursue a street career, because he was no Banksy, that was for certain.

Through the scratchwork and tacky residue, which was as prominent on the inside of the car as the outside, Rufus's reflection stared back behind cheap plastic sunglasses. He was a tall kid. A skinny kid. But most importantly—not a kid. Rufus was thirty-three, but the carrottop red hair he hid under the frayed and worn slouch beanie still got him carded. At least, he figured the hair had something to do with being asked—more times than he could remember—if he was old enough to hold that bottle of gin. There had been a study published by Erasmus University in Rotterdam that suggested the mutation of the MC1R gene—responsible for his hair and self-evident nickname, *Freckles*—*did* also contribute to the younger appearance of gingers.

The elevator lurched to a sudden stop.

Rufus straightened. He took the sunglasses off and hung them from his T-shirt collar while shifting from foot-to-foot as he waited for something to happen.

His gut was dropping the same way it had when Alex Mitchell, the thirteen-year-old bully who'd been held back a year, had called Rufus an ugly little pussy and pushed him down the stairs of PS14, causing him to break his arm. It was that same sick lurch of being airborne, of gravity taking hold, of the *pop* and *snap* of bone. But Alex had been shipped off to his grandmother's somewhere upstate after seventh grade when Children's Services intervened. Rufus never saw him again. So he took a deep breath and reminded himself that it was Jake who had texted him, not the ghost of a bully long since passed, and when Jake texted, Rufus came.

No matter what.

Because in this city of nearly nine million, Jake had been the only one to give Rufus the time of day in over a decade. Had been the only one who talked to Rufus like he had half a brain. And Jake had been the only one to notice that the mouthy redhead ate Maruchan ramen for dinner and that 190 calories didn't go very far for a six-foot adult male.

The elevator door noisily opened onto the unlit seventh floor.

So if it was only Jake, and Jake was safety and security,

why did Rufus feel like he was about to upchuck?

Rufus took a step forward, angled his body to be shielded by the call button panel, and peered into the dim expanse. There was a scattering of abandoned furniture—outdated office desks, a chair listing to one side on broken wheels, and a few obsolete Apple computer monitors. The floor was littered with the garbage of a hasty office move—pencils, crumpled papers, dust bunnies, a stray power strip. Rufus got down on the floor of the elevator car in order to see beneath the small gaps of erratically placed desks.

No one hiding.

He sat up on his knees.

No one waiting.

The elevator door began to close. Rufus thrust his hand out and forced it back.

Rain pelted the bay windows on the right. Gray shadows, fragmented and erratic, crept about the floor in time with the clouds rolling across the sky.

The elevator door tried to shut a second time. It let out a loud beep when Rufus blocked it. Getting to his feet, Rufus took a cautious step into the unoccupied space.

The door groaned shut behind him, leaving Rufus alone.

Except that was a problem.

Because Jake had texted him.

Where was he?

Rufus tilted his head and studied the linoleum at an angle. Whatever business had vacated the seventh floor had done so recently. There hadn't been enough time for dust to settle and pick up any sort of shoe tread impressions after the fact. No splotches of wet either, which meant Jake had arrived before the rain.

Right?

4

Rufus walked on the balls of his feet toward the only visible door—back right—faintly illuminated by the overhead windows. His Chucks, so worn out, didn't even leave a whisper in his wake. He counted the windows as he moved—one, two, three—six in total. Rufus pressed himself against the wall as he reached the far corner and studied the crack under the door.

No light.

And no living sound except the beating of his own heart in his ears, and to be honest, Rufus was only half-alive on his best days.

He felt that suspension in his gut again. That brief weightlessness and freedom again. Then the world grabbed Rufus by the throat and threw him to the asbestos-ridden linoleum of PS14 again and he was sobbing and vomiting and cradling a broken arm.

Rufus took a deep breath, wiped his palms on his jeans, then pushed down on the door handle with his knuckles. It opened noiselessly. He nudged the door with the toe of his shoe and peered into the darkness within. The initial smell to waft out was that of chemicals and waste, like sewage backing up into a safety shower. But then Rufus was hit with a stink that, once experienced, could never be mistaken for anything other than the inevitability of mortality.

Rufus's hand shook as he felt the inside wall for a light switch. Finding it, he flicked it up.

Jake was sprawled in the basin of the emergency shower, his head reclining where the corners came together at a ninety-degree angle. His face was a mess of broken bone and torn tissue—entrance the third eye, exit the entire fucking back of his head. A bright splatter of blood and brains painted the wall, giving Rufus a rough idea of how Jake had been sitting before a trigger was pulled.

Rufus dropped into a crouched position to hug his

knees. "*Jesus Christ*," he choked out.

Jake was dead.

Just like that.

A finger snap.

Here and gone in the space of a breath, a heartbeat, a crack of thunder over Manhattan.

Rufus gasped and shuddered, inhaling a soggy breath. Heavy tears burned his eyes. His hands shook too much as he tried to wipe his face.

I know you're smart, Rufus.

That's what Jake would say. And Rufus could feel the other man beside him—not dead in that basin—but squeezing the back of Rufus's neck with one of those big, capable hands. Jake would move his hand a bit lower, settle it between Rufus's bony shoulder blades—that contact searing through his jean jacket and T-shirt, offering a starved body barely enough touch to survive another episode.

I need you to take a breath. I need you to be smart.

Pallor mortis, Rufus thought. That was the first onset of death. It occurred within the first thirty minutes, as a result of the collapse of capillary circulation in the body, and led to *livor mortis. Livor mortis* was Latin. It meant "bluish death." Named for when blood settled in the body and discolored the skin. It typically wasn't visible until a few hours postmortem.

Forensic Pathology, Third Edition, copyright 2008, Richard Stewart, M.D.

Rufus had checked out the textbook from the New York Public Library last summer. It'd been 618 pages on determining cause of death in sudden, violent, or suspicious circumstances. In the same visit, he'd also checked out *The Three Musketeers* and *Huge F*cking Tomatoes: Grow Your Own Damn Garden.*

Jake had laughed at him.

Death, justice, and tomatoes.

One of these is not like the others.

And sure, maybe the tomato-growing techniques weren't really relevant at the moment, but Dr. Stewart's text was. Jake was slumped on his back—T-shirt yanked up—and there wasn't any sort of bluish discoloration where blood would naturally pool. That gave Rufus a timeline.

Jake had texted him to meet—*a pickup job*—at 12:25 p.m. So naturally he'd been alive when sending that message. If afterward he'd, what, *shot himself?* There'd be, at most, two hours for nature to set in and begin the breakdown process. But there was no sign of *livor mortis*.

What happened next?

Rufus closed his eyes and referenced Dr. Stewart again. *Rigor mortis.* But that generally occurred between two and four hours after death and began with the stiffening of muscles in the face and neck.

The face.

Rufus's eyes snapped open and he was staring at the fucking hole in Jake's face. His vision blurred again, and he felt hot and cold all over as the panic set in.

Be smart, Rufus.

Something about this was wrong.

All sorts of wrong.

Jake had had a pickup for Rufus. Pickups were important. And so Rufus had arrived on time—early, even. But from what he could see, there was nothing in the stinking closet that would have been related to Jake's request. Which meant Jake *needed* something picked up. And he'd likely meant to supply the details in person.

But now he was dead. And who the fuck shoots themselves in the middle of the forehead? If Jake was looking to tap out on the travesty called Life, he would have put the gun to the side of his head or swallowed a bullet, like any other person.

Where was the gun?

Rufus scooted forward on his knees and took a more careful look around the shower stall—around Jake—but there was no weapon. What'd the pistol do, get up and walk away? For that matter, why were Jake's knuckles puffy and glossy with fresh blood, like he'd been in a scrap recently? Rufus knew those hands. Had long ago memorized every scar, every crease, every tendon. Never once had Jake used his fists on another person. That's what made them such attractive hands.

He fought.

Rufus felt the hairs on his neck rise. His underarms began to sweat.

It's a trap.

He got to his feet, stumbled as he tried to work his numb legs, and fell against the doorway. The shot that followed was loud, like a canon had blown up in Rufus's face. The wooden frame exploded in a shower of splinters, nicking his cheek like a dull razor pulling on whiskers.

"Motherfucker," a man shouted, and then another shot clipped the frame.

Thirty-three years of staying alive kicked Rufus into overdrive, and he ducked down low while moving away from the threshold. The anemic tungsten light spilling out of the closet behind him cast a dim and dirty landscape before him, and *there*, getting to his feet from behind an aluminum work table lying on its side, a man.

Thick neck. Thicker arms. Baseball hat. Fuck—a goddamn Yankees fan. The illumination hadn't been strong enough to reveal more minute details of the shooter, but in the half-second Rufus spared to analyze him, he'd thought black, or maybe dark brown hair.

But then Rufus was running. He didn't even consider waiting for the death-trap elevator as a third shot cracked the air like the thunderstorm had been invited inside through the bay windows. He ran to the right of the elevator and slammed his hands down on the safety bar of the staircase door.

No alarm wailed.

Down, down, *down* seven flights. Rufus came out on the ground floor, his lungs bursting, his long legs stumbling as he overreached. He ran past the dumpsters and out the freight door into the hot summer rain. Rufus pulled up the collar of his jacket, hunched his shoulders, and quickly made his way to the corner of Thirty-Eighth and Eighth. He removed the burner phone from his pocket, tossed it into a trash can, and vanished into crowds.

CHAPTER
TWO

The ticket from Bald Knob, Arkansas, to the New York Port Authority on Eighth Avenue cost a little shy of two hundred bucks, basically a steal. Sam always kept five hundred in the lining of his jacket; he didn't like ATMs, didn't like marking himself on a map, not if he could help it. He'd run down too many stupid sons of bitches that way, and he didn't like to think of the same happening to him. He worked the loose thread in the seam, pulled out the cash, and bought the ticket.

The woman who sold it had her blonde hair in a do that Mrs. Brady would have been proud of. Sam figured he breathed a few pounds of hairspray just in the short time it took to buy the ticket. Then, because some women seemed to have a sixth sense for strays, she asked him if he needed a place to stay for the night. Her church, clean cots, breakfast but no showers. Sam did what he always did: he waited until she ran out of things to say, and then he thanked her and sat on the bench until the bus was ready to leave.

Travel time: thirty-six hours and seventeen minutes. It should have been less, but they got stuck at a railroad crossing outside Memphis, and then again when the Greyhound's engine started overheating.

Thirty-six hours and seventeen minutes to think about Jake.

Sam was a traveler. A walker, by preference. When walking wasn't enough, a bus. Or hitching. Or a train. Travel meant time, an abundance of it. And, usually, quiet. Time and quiet were the things he had bartered everything else for.

He had figured out a lot of ways to use that time and quiet. First, he played back Game 7 of the 2016 World Series, Cubs 8, Indians 7. He didn't have all of it, not perfectly—he'd only seen it the one time—but he could remember most of the at bats, the ninth inning tie at 6-6, the compacted energy he could feel even from a thousand miles away when the rain hit and the delay built into explosive pressure, then Zobrist scoring Almora, then Montero hitting a single and Rizzo crossing home plate. It was a good game. A great game. Sam had grown up in Morgan Park, the Southside Chicago neighborhood. When he was sixteen, he'd thrown away all the Sox gear his dad had bought him since he was a kid and worn a Cubs hat to dinner. His dad had put a chair through the wall. In 2016, watching Rizzo's dusty feet hit the plate, it felt worth it.

When he'd finished with Game 7, he went for music. He had earbuds, and he put them in, but he just turned the MP3 player to a white noise track with ten hours of run time. The world was too noisy in general; the bus was too noisy in particular—at least, sometimes: the engine revving up, the thrum of the huge tires, voices competing to be heard. The earbuds were an escape. It was like having the ocean in an aluminum case; he could drift into it, get lost. In his head, in the cocoon of white noise, he played Blind Willie McTell, then Howlin' Wolf and Muddy Waters. He even played a joke on himself and listened to some Eric Clapton that was hanging around the back of his head.

From time to time, he watched a blond kid two rows up. The kid kept looking back, giving Sam the eye. He had to be nineteen, maybe twenty. Probably on summer vacation. Maybe doing a gap year, which was a nice new way of saying your kid was jerking off on your dime. He had one of those Herschel bags Sam had seen college kids toting; he wore pink shorts that barely came to the middle of his thigh and a banana-colored tank. He obviously shaved. Everywhere. Sam gave him the eye right back.

The Greyhound made its next rest stop somewhere in Ohio, a travel plaza with its lot full of semis and about a million pumps, all in use. Sam got his ruck and moved toward the front of the bus. The kid was still in his seat, playing something on his phone. Sam squeezed the back of his neck as he passed, once, just hard enough that the kid knew who was in charge. Sam didn't look back; he didn't need to.

He rented one of the showers, which were more like private bathrooms, dropped his ruck inside, and then waited in the hall until the kid showed. He looked younger under the fluorescents. His hair was buzzed down on the sides, longer and styled on top, and he had his arms across his chest like the air-conditioning was too cold.

"Hey," the kid said with a goofy grin.

Sam raised an eyebrow.

"Uh, I'm Nicky."

From down the hall, pings and dings came from the

video arcade.

"What's your name?"

Sam shook his head. "No names."

"Yeah, cool, I just—"

"No talking."

Red splotched the boy's neck and chest, visible under the banana tank.

With a shrug, Sam stepped into the shower room.

The kid came through the door a moment later.

Sam didn't waste any time. He kissed the kid, flipped the lock, and kept on kissing. He maneuvered the kid toward the sink, hard kisses, bruising kisses, and the kid was whimpering. Sam caught him by the throat and squeezed once.

"Be quiet."

The kid nodded; Sam thought he probably would have nodded if Sam had told him to jump off a bridge.

Sam fucked him, a business fuck, over the sink. After, while he pulled out and tossed the condom, the kid finished himself off with his hand, letting out a loud cry.

"Holy fuck," the kid kept saying, head on his arm, looking like the sink was the only thing keeping him up. "Holy fuck."

Sam stripped out of his clothes: jeans, a white tee turned inside out, socks turned inside out. He tossed them in a pile near his ruck.

"Holy fuck," the kid said again, pushing himself up with shaky arms, looking at Sam in the mirror. "You are one hot fuck."

"What'd I say about talking?" Sam said, and then he jerked a thumb at the door.

"Hey, you want to shower, maybe grab something to eat before we—"

"No."

"Cool, but maybe—"

"No." Another jerk of his thumb. "Out. I want to clean up."

"What the fuck is wrong with you?"

Sam counted down; he started at fifty-seven this time. He had his hands flat against the wall because the shakes were getting going again.

"You don't have to be an asshole about it," the kid said. The offended dignity was ruined by the fact that he was trying to pull up his shorts while he talked.

"Apparently," Sam said, wishing for a smoke, for quiet, for soap and hot water so he couldn't smell the kid on him anymore, "I do."

The rest of the bus ride, the kid pouted and shot angry, wounded looks back at Sam. Sam ran through the first two *Die Hard* movies in his head and watched the whole world go by in high summer, green and gold and brown. Once, a hawk swooped at the bus and swerved at the last minute, tumbling away on an updraft of hot air. Once, they drove for a stretch of twenty-seven miles of soybean fields at dusk, and against the setting sun, the silhouettes of a doe and her fawn. *Like paper*, Sam thought. Like the targets they hung at the range. Five meters. Fifty. A hundred and fifty. Three hundred. He closed his eyes and pressed his hands against his thighs; the air-conditioning was barely cold enough to keep him from sweating.

At the end of the thirty-six hours and seventeen minutes, New York rose like a blister. That was when Sam started reading the e-mails Jake had sent, every one of them printed on the inside of his skull. Every e-mail since the first time they'd fucked, every e-mail Jake had ever tossed off late at night, drunk, when his guard was down. Even after Jake had left Fort Benning. Even after Jake had gotten out of the Army. Even after Jake joined the

NYPD, got a girlfriend, had a whole new life. The e-mails Jake might not even remember sending from inside the blackouts where he couldn't lie to himself anymore. The last e-mail, the one that had come two days before Jake's death blipped on the CBS affiliate in Bald Knob, Arkansas. And by the time the Greyhound was pulling up at Port Authority, Sam knew where to start.

CHAPTER
THREE

Rufus had been walking the perimeter of Hell's Kitchen for the last hour. He paced up and down Ninth Avenue between Forty-Ninth and Fiftieth Street twice, noting the flyers for Leaping Ladies Ballet, Pointe, Barre, Pole Dancing. All Ages and Sizes Welcome. Yes, Ladies, We Mean You! that someone had liberally distributed across the sidewalk and which the rain had partially dissolved and the July sun baked into place. He noted the guy with his dog, jingling coins in a Starbucks cup. German shepherd mix, big tongue lolling because dogs couldn't sweat and it was fucking July in fucking *Hell's Kitchen* and didn't the guy have any sense of responsibility? He noted the wonky fire hydrant with a RESIST bumper sticker on the ribbed metal. He noted, most of all, Jake's apartment building:

four stories of red brick, a fire escape hanging uneasily off the front. Maybe the fire escape needed those pole dancing lessons; it looked like it was clinging on for dear life.

Rufus slowed as he approached the cross-streets of Ninth and Forty-Ninth for a third time, watching the front door to Jake's building open. A petite blonde in yoga pants, a tank top, and sunglasses straight outta Lady Gaga's wardrobe stepped outside. 4D. And 4D made a repulsed expression as the heat and humidity of the day body-slammed her—enough that she seemed to be second-guessing her plans. But after a moment of internal deliberation, she squared her tiny shoulders and left the doorway, walking away from Rufus and toward Fiftieth. Rufus rushed across the Leaping Ladies and slipped inside the building before the door could shut and automatically lock.

He tapped Jake's mailbox—3C—on the wall in the vestibule as he walked toward the stairs. He hadn't forgotten. It was just a habit. Mailboxes grounded him. They were a tangible reminder of where he was, who he knew, what was real.

Tap.

Rufus took the stairs two at a time, quick and quiet on the balls of his feet, to the third floor. The building was clean and well maintained by the super, but its age showed. Water radiators hissed and sputtered in winter, landlord-white paint had been slapped on a little too thick in the hallways, and the apartments had ancient doorknobs that Rufus had picked on more than one occasion to make a fucking point to Jake that his home security was shit.

The third floor was silent. Then again, it *was* a Wednesday afternoon. With the exception of Yoga Gal out front, most people held regular day jobs—Rufus not being one of those people.

He stopped outside 3C and removed a thin metal tool

from inside his jacket pocket. Rufus used to time himself, shove the door open, and loudly announce his new best time for breaking and entering.

Jake had never thought it was funny.

Rufus put the tool away, straightened, and leaned his shoulder on the door. It gently fell open and he slipped inside.

The studio was too warm. The curtains had been drawn open the morning Jake left for work and never came home. Rufus's underarms immediately began to sweat as he stood in a ray of sunlight that cut across the floor.

He was alone.

Alone but for the ghost of Jake. And that hand on the back of his neck grew more and more distant as each day passed. Soon it'd be gone entirely. Rufus would have only memories and heartbreak and… little else.

To the right of the room was a queen bed, unmade. The television mounted to the wall was off. The basic kitchen looked as if it'd never been used. The closet door opposite the bed was shut. A bachelor pad in every sense, except that Jake hadn't been a bachelor. He had Natalie. And when Rufus learned that tidbit, it'd been… a revelation. And not a welcomed one either.

Focus.

Rufus sucked in a deep breath through his nose, then let it out slowly through his mouth. He tugged his beanie off, took a step forward, and after an initial check in all the limited spaces the bogeyman could have possibly shoved himself into for hiding, Rufus set about methodically searching every square inch of Jake's apartment.

Because he'd been asked to handle a pickup.

And someone had *murdered* Jake.

It might have been because of what the job entailed.

So Rufus owed it to Jake to at least find a scrap of

information worth bringing to the NYPD and say: *Here*. This was the assignment and this was the man I saw—the one who took away the only person I had worth living for.

CHAPTER
FOUR

Already the city was too much for Sam; for a moment, it paralyzed him. He had rented a locker and stowed his ruck, and now he stood just outside Port Authority bus station in the alcove under the crossed I-beams and the grillwork and then the finer meshwork that, he realized after a second look, was probably designed to keep pigeons and bats from taking up residence behind the metalwork. The hot air of the city felt compressed, ultradense with humidity, the stink of piss mixing with what Sam thought had probably once been a falafel sandwich broiling on the asphalt a few feet away. More smells: rubber, exhaust, sweat. When he leaned against the wall, taking deep breaths, focusing on the cool lick of air-conditioning against his back when the doors opened behind him, a layer of soot and dust left a black crease on the sleeve of his white tee. He hated this place, hated every fucking inch of it.

He thought about Jake.

The map inside the terminal had been useful. Several times Jake had included his address in the blackout e-mails, inviting Sam to visit, to take him up on a place to stay for a few weeks. Nominally, the couch, but it was easy to crack Jake's code. Jake had been playing straight too long. Jake was getting thirsty. And maybe Jake didn't want to risk his career, his reputation, his girlfriend by trawling the gay clubs or cruising Grindr. Jake wanted take-out dick. No, delivery dick. Jake just wanted Sam to sleep on the couch. Yeah, right.

A quick look at the map showed Sam where he was and where, more or less, he thought Jake's apartment ought to be. Less than a mile. And, not far from the apartment, the precinct station house where Jake had worked. In the Army, even though Sam hadn't been infantry, he'd rucked a lot of miles. And after leaving Benning, Sam had walked more. He'd walked thirty-some days. Forty, when the weather was nice, when he knew he could hit the next town by nightfall, when he needed as much fresh air and open sky as he could take in. A mile, even in a city—what the fuck was one mile?

Well, he thought, taking those slow, deep breaths, hands tucked in his pockets because the shakes were going. Well, when you were too fucking overwhelmed to take a single fucking step, a mile started to look a lot longer.

He thought about taking a cab. Thought about how fucking ridiculous that was, and the sheer weight of his own scorn got him moving again. He pushed off, grimacing at the second neat, black crease on his white tee, and started walking.

Counting the blocks, the street numbers ticking down, Sam focused on things he could control: the movements of his body (well, more or less, no thanks to the fucking tremors), the rhythm of his breathing. But New York City hit him like a typhoon: horns blared; a woman jogged past with a stroller, bumping Sam from her path; ahead, a digital billboard flashed Dear Evan Hansen Critics' Must-See over and over until Sam had the words burned on the back of his skull. Halfway through his count, he ducked into a pharmacy—Duane Reade, who the fuck had ever heard of that?—and pretended to look for razor blades until he could count twenty steady breaths.

On his second try, he did better. He caught the tempo of the bodies on the sidewalk. He was a fast walker, tall, taking long strides with long legs, and this time he was the one passing people—although one skinny lady with her hair up in locs, probably two feet shorter than him, shot past like a burning arrow, and Sam had to admit he didn't stand a chance. He turned on Forty-Ninth, jogging the last half of the crosswalk as a taxi blatted at him and tried to cut him off. Sam gave him the finger; every inch of his body prickled with adrenaline, threat response, the need to unholster the M9 he had under his arm. When he came up on the sidewalk, he met eyes with a woman who had to be eighty, built like a Star Destroyer and wearing a motley of animal-print spandex. She gazed at him with disgust and then flicked her hand under chin. *Why would anybody live here*, Sam wondered. *Why didn't they all run away screaming?*

Two more blocks. They were semidecent, which for Sam meant relatively less crowded. One had active construction proceeding, so Sam had to detour off the sidewalk and follow a plywood maze under metal scaffolding. And the last one had what Sam thought might be intended to pass as a playground: asphalt and basketball hoops, low cement walls with chain fencing, orange-and-white plastic traffic dividers snugged up against the walls like they were in storage. Two teenagers were playing basketball. One of them, obviously older, dunked the ball and came after the other kid, shouting down into his face.

Fuck. Men everywhere, every age, were always spitting the same fucking macho bullshit. Sam never thought about women, but maybe he needed a change just so he could have a fucking conversation.

Sam wandered two more blocks, cutting up, back, up again, until he spotted the massive brick-and-stone building of the station house. The yellowish stone, the slight irregularities of the bricks, even the arch windows with green trim—they all combined to date the building, a turn-of-the-century construction that had weathered a lot of bad. Someone had stuck a Banksy sticker to the window, and Sam wondered if it was still there because of negligence or if it was new and somebody would scrape it off by the end of the day. Hard to tell in a place like this.

When Sam went inside, he found himself in a lobby where worn linoleum was peeling back to expose the original tilework, every inch of the place smelling like microwaved popcorn and body odor. Two girls sat in wooden chairs, one doing up the other's braids. On the other side of the room, a skinny white guy was scratching his neck, skin already raw and bleeding in a few spots.

Behind a massive wooden counter sat an ancient woman with a cap of white curls, her uniform bulging in places it had probably never been meant to bulge. She was flipping through sheets on a clipboard, occasionally pausing to scribble something out with a ballpoint. Sam was surprised she didn't have a quill.

"Excuse me," Sam said.

The ballpoint stuttered and she looked up. "Yes?" Short and curt. Welcome to *New York fucking New York.*

"I need to see Detective Anthony Lampo."

"Who's asking?"

"Sam Auden, ma'am. It's about Detective Brower."

Her pinched expression relaxed, then drew together again. "Ah. *I see.* Let me just—" She set her pen aside in favor of the telephone receiver and dialed an extension. After a pause, she spoke loudly, "I have a Sam Auden requesting to speak with you, detective. He says... ah, he says he's here about Detective Brower." She nodded absently to the garbled response, said goodbye, quietly set the receiver on the cradle, then looked at Sam again. "Detective Lampo will be right down."

The guy picking at his neck chose this moment to scream, "What about the fucking movie rights, man?" Then he laughed to himself.

Jesus Christ, Sam thought. *They ought to burn the whole island to the ground and try it again.*

A door opened, and a middle-aged man with a bad comb-over stepped out into the lobby. The cheap suit he was wearing had obviously come off the rack at whatever the New York City equivalent of Marshall's was, but he had a nice watch, and Sam wondered what this guy drove, where he lived, what he did on the weekends. The guy glanced around, and his eyes fixed on Sam.

"Mr. Auden?"

"That's me."

Lampo shot Movie-Maker a look when the guy started bitching about his rights again, but then he motioned for Sam with a come-hither gesture. "Let's talk in private."

Sam followed Lampo up a flight of stairs, down a hall hung with bulletin boards announcing meetings for retirement planning, sign-ups for the precinct softball team, an oologically-minded sales pitch regarding the health benefits of goose eggs, ask Rita Johansen for more information, and on and on. Lampo led him past a squad room, continuing down the hall, and then threw open a door. Two-way mirror, battered table, chairs. Sam had been in interview rooms before.

"Sorry about the accommodations," Lampo said as he walked inside first. He pulled out a chair and settled into it. "Not many places in a building full of cops we can have a moment to… discuss Jake."

"I knew Jake in the Army," Sam said. "What can you tell me about his death?"

Bad comb-over and equally bad suit aside, Lampo's gaze was smart and sharp—shining like a buffed and polished diamond. "You read the newspaper? Watch the news?"

"I know people are falling over themselves to say it was suicide."

Lampo's mouth twitched a little and he grunted. "Yeah. That's what the ME ruled." He nudged the leg of the second chair with his foot, pushing it back in invitation.

No sound penetrated the interview room, and Sam knew that was standard, knew that was intentional, but the silence had a kind of ringing energy to it as he dropped into the seat opposite Lampo.

"That's not exactly the same as saying you believe it was suicide," Sam said slowly.

Lampo didn't look away—his gaze followed Sam as Sam sat down. "I think the city does its job. I shouldn't have to second-guess the investigation." He leaned forward on the scratched surface of the metal table and folded his hands together. "I think Jake could have had his reasons."

The tremors were starting again; Sam rested his hands on his legs, resisting the urge to sit on them. "From what I can tell, the city does fuck-all. There is no way Jake killed himself."

Lampo frowned a little at Sam's words. Only a little. "I think Jake was dealing with some personal shit. That's between you and me. Maybe he wasn't dealing as well as I thought. Some folks wear a great mask."

"Ah," Sam said after a moment. "Fuck that. Jake knew how to handle his shit. All his shit. I didn't come here for your Baruch-fucking-evening-class psycho-talk. I want to know what you have—I'm talking forensics—that says this was a suicide."

Lampo was still staring at Sam. He leaned back, looking uncomfortable in the chair. "How long did you say you knew Jake?"

"Eight years," Sam said. "Four deployments." The tremor was worse now, and Sam slid one hand down to clutch the back of his thigh. "And I... knew about his personal shit, as you call it. Fuck. I was his personal shit."

Lampo's eyes, dark and unblinking, burrowed under Sam's skin like some sort of beetle—made him want to scratch at an itch that wasn't there. "I see," he finally murmured, followed by blowing out a breath. "Jake was shot in the middle of his forehead." Lampo raised a hand to indicate as such. "Not typical of suicides."

"No," Sam said. "Not fucking typical."

"ME reported no gunshot residue on his hands."

"I know I'm new here," Sam said, "but how fucking typical is that?"

"*Not*," Lampo said, with another twitch at the corner of his mouth. A smile that tried and gave up, maybe. "Pretty damn hard to shoot yourself and not have evidence on your hands."

"And what are you doing about it?"

"Jake's death is an open-and-shut case, Mr. Auden," Lampo replied, but at some point, he'd begun gripping his hands together and now they were so tightly clasped that his fingertips blanched. "Did you plan on telling me how to do my job while you were here?"

"Not really, but apparently I need to. Jake Brower didn't kill himself. I know it. You know it. Why doesn't your ME know it? What's going on here?"

Lampo opened his mouth, but a knock at the door interrupted. Before he could call a response, it swung open. A small woman—her mousy brown hair pulled back into a simple ponytail and wearing a pantsuit and a nude shade of lipstick that didn't flatter her—poked her head inside.

"Lampo."

"Ma'am," he said, sitting as straight as a lightning rod.

"Something going on?" Her gaze met Sam's, then returned to Lampo.

"No." Lampo quickly stood and wiped his hair with one hand, despite it still being in place. "Having a chat, is all."

She studied Lampo for another beat, looked at Sam again, and then said, holding that gaze, "Your phone's been ringing off the hook."

"Right. Sorry. We're done," Lampo answered with a quick, automatic smile. He waited until the woman retreated before looking down at Sam. "We'll have to call it here, I'm afraid."

Sam listened for voices from outside the interview room, the sounds of a squad room in a city that never slept; he would have settled for a coffee maker percolating. Instead, he got nothing, and he lined that up with this woman coming in here, the way she had known, somehow, the way she had asked, *Something going on?*

"I'll be around for a few days," Sam said, "if you want to trade war stories."

Lampo just nodded. The woman, when Sam moved for the door, waited until the last minute to move, and then Sam had to squeeze past her or risk knocking a cop on her ass.

Once outside the station house, Sam consulted the

mental map in his head, found the whole thing fucked to shit by the interview—shot in the center of the forehead, no fucking GSR, and they wanted to pretend it was a suicide when every cop everywhere knew the first rule was no cop died by suicide—and had to pull out his phone and open the Maps app.

After that, it was smooth sailing. Sam headed uptown, counting streets, navigating the same obstacle course he'd faced on the way to the station house, only now in reverse. Eventually, though, he spotted the apartment building across the street. It was brick with a patina of soot and dirt and dust, an iron fire escape with paint flaking away to expose rusted gouges, and it had the number stenciled on the door in gold letters, peeling now, that Sam was looking for.

He started to jog across the street and pulled up sharp at another blaring horn. Fuck this fucking city. Give him Montana again, where he could walk twenty miles down the middle of a state highway and the only living thing he'd troubled was a lost cow.

Pulling back, Sam waited for the street to clear. The door to Jake's building swung open, and a woman stepped out, yoga pants and massive sunglasses. A skinny guy in a beanie slipped past the woman; she didn't even seem to see him as he caught the door before it could shut and lock. Sam wasn't a city boy, but he wasn't a dumbshit either. The skinny guy wasn't his focus today, though. His focus was getting inside Jake's apartment and figuring out what had happened. The truth, please. Nothing but the truth.

When an opening appeared in the traffic, Sam sprinted. He reached the opposite side, leaned up against the wall—trying not to think about the crosshatch in black that would cover his back—and got out his phone. He held it to his ear, pretending to talk. He had to wait almost thirty minutes before he could duplicate the skinny guy's trick, but he had to give credit: it worked like a charm. An aging hippy wearing a serape in spite of the weather, his beard knotted with beads, drifted out of the building, high as a kite, and Sam caught the door with his elbow. He took the stairs two at a time to 3C.

Sam didn't like the idea of knocking; the building was too quiet, and, anyway, Jake was dead. If anybody was home—Jesus, the girlfriend? No, Jake had said they weren't living together, come stay on the couch, thirsty little bitch that he was. So knocking wasn't on the agenda. Sam settled a hand on the doorknob, lightly. He wanted to see how it felt first—if it was as old and rattly as it looked, he could probably get past it with a decent chisel and mallet from a hardware store. But if it was in better condition, he'd have to figure out something else.

When he tested the knob, though, it turned. Sam let out a slow breath. His heart beat quicker, like an internal fuse was lit. He had only a little time before the shakes started acting up, bad, and if somebody was in there, Sam would be fucked. He unholstered the M9, leaned into the door slowly until he was sure there wasn't a chain, something that might catch it, and then he threw it open all the way, bringing the M9 up a third of the way but still mostly pointed at the ground.

The skinny guy with the beanie, the one Sam had spotted slipping into the building, was sitting in a chair, watching the door. Eating tortilla chips. He raised his light-colored eyebrows and asked with no particular inflection in his voice, "Who the fuck are you?"

Sam brought up the M9. "Get on the ground. Drop the fucking chips and get on the fucking ground."

The guy shoved a few more chips in his mouth and crunched loudly. "You don't live here."

"But I've got the gun, fuckwad. Get on the ground. Let me see your hands."

The skinny kid dropped the bag unceremoniously.

Crumbs littered the hardwood at his feet. He licked salt from his fingers and then wiggled them. "Here they are."

Sam felt a moment of panic; he could feel the shakes getting started, and worse, he'd never faced down with a freckled asshole who wouldn't just get on the fucking floor when he had a gun pointed at him. In thirty seconds, forty, the tremors would be visible. How fucking scary was a gun when the guy holding it couldn't keep it steady?

He let the muzzle drop, M9 along his thigh, steadying his hand against his leg. "Who the fuck are you?"

"Rufus."

Sam came the rest of the way into the apartment, shutting the door behind him and leaning against it. Anything to stay steady, stable, solid. "Why are you in Jake's apartment?"

The cocky smile Rufus had been wearing was gone. Suddenly. Without warning. He stood from the chair, chips cracking under the heel of his Chucks. "How do you know Jake?"

Decision time, Sam thought. He scanned the studio apartment: the unmade bed, the jumble of clothes and shoes in the closet, the spotless kitchen because Jake, like so many enlisted guys, couldn't even boil water. The heat, unnoticed until now, hammered Sam. He could smell Jake, faint and lingering. Smell Rufus too—sweat, sure, also but Dial soap, overpowering in the closed-up, heated room. Something else Sam couldn't put his finger on. Something that tickled his gut, and Sam wasn't sure it was pleasant.

"Jake and I were in the Army together," Sam said. "Now you."

Rufus hadn't broken eye contact. Maybe hadn't even blinked since Sam had said "Jake." "Prove it."

"Do you have a phone?"

Rufus patted his pocket in response.

"Facebook?"

"Facebook is for old people," Rufus said with a short bark of a laugh.

In spite of himself, Sam snorted. "I guess perspective is skewed when your balls haven't dropped yet. You can find a picture of our platoon from basic—search for military yearbook sites. We were at Fort Leonard Wood, 2000, B-5-9, 2nd Platoon."

Rufus tugged his cell free and started typing. He looked up every few seconds, keeping one eye trained on Sam's weapon, before he seemed to have zeroed in on the photo in question. Rufus brought the phone closer, studied the screen, looked Sam over with a critical expression, then said, "You aged like shit."

"Yeah, well, call me when you get pubes and we'll see how you're doing." Before Rufus could respond, Sam added, "Now you tell me how you know Jake."

Rufus gripped the phone tight. His skin had flushed, from the hollow of his neck to the lobes of his ears visible under the beanie. "I know him from work."

"Oh yeah?" Sam's grin was hard, hooking one corner of his mouth. "You a big, butch cop too?"

"*Obviously,*" Rufus said with heavy mockery. "I still know him from work, and I'm not going to tell you anything else." He held up the phone and waved it back and forth. "You were in basic together. Big deal. Maybe Jake hated you. Maybe you're a stalker. I don't even know your name."

"Sam."

"Sam," Rufus repeated. "Ok. It was nice meeting you, Sam. Now you want to move aside so I can go?"

"No," Sam said. "I'm going to level with you, Rufus. I'm going to be really fucking honest with you. I'm tired. I've been on a bus for a day and a half. I hate this fucking city. And you are a real fucking treat yourself. I've been jerked around by Jake's asshole partner; when I ask about forensics, I get answers that ought to make sense, and then it turns out everyone wants to pretend Jake killed himself. And that's bullshit. I knew Jake. He wouldn't have killed himself. Not when he was—" Sam stopped, the contents of that last e-mail burning his lips. He managed to say instead, "Then I get to his apartment and find Lucky fucking Charms eating his chips and willing to tell me fuck-all about why he's in there. So, no, I'm not getting out of the way. We're going to have a long talk. Really long. Until I know everything I want to know."

The color that'd been in Rufus's face—skin marred from maybe embarrassment, maybe annoyance—hell, maybe just the heat—had drained until he was the color of Elmer's glue. Rufus shoved his cell into his pocket. "Jake was—" His voice caught, and he cleared his throat before trying again. "Jake was murdered."

For a moment, the shock was electric, zinging through Sam. "You'd better tell me all of it."

Rufus tugged the black beanie from his head, revealing a shock of red. He ran a shaky hand through the thick hair and said, while staring at the scuffed toes of his Chucks, "I don't know anything."

"You know he was murdered."

"And that's it."

"How do you know that?"

It took another moment before Rufus met Sam's expression. "I found his body," he whispered.

Letting out a ragged breath, Sam knew they had reached a tipping point. Everything had to fall one way or another.

"I'm going to give you three things: Jake and I fucked around together, back in the day; we stayed in touch; he sent me something in an e-mail a few days before he died, something big." Sam blew out another breath, pressing both hands against his thighs, hoping the weakness wouldn't show. "But I need you to give me something too."

Rufus's green eyes stood out in stark contrast to his still pale complexion. His freckles—so many that it'd be impossible to count them all, connect them all—were like tiny craters on the face of the moon. He still looked a little sick. But he also appeared to be processing the imparted truth—trying to square up the Jake of the present that he knew with the Jake of the past that Sam had known. "I'm looking for his phone. Jake asked me for… a favor. And I'm trying to figure out what that was… if it's related to his death."

Sam studied the apartment again, more slowly this time. The evidence of a search, if any, was minimal. If Rufus was telling the truth, he was either a better burglar than Sam expected, or smarter than he seemed—or both.

"You didn't find anything here? Nothing else that might help?"

Rufus waved a hand at the open closet. "Just finished looking when I heard you on the stairs. Nothing's here. Except the chips."

At the mention of food, Sam's stomach rumbled; he thought, although he wasn't sure, that Rufus's stomach did some grumbling too.

"Let's get out of here," Sam said. "We need to talk. Somewhere public, plenty of exits, where I can get something to eat without picking up a case of hepatitis." Then, to himself, "If that's possible in this hellhole."

CHAPTER
FIVE

BlueMoon Diner was a safe spot.

A habitual spot for Rufus, since it was only six blocks uptown from Jake's studio. It was public, of course, had one door that acted as both ingress and egress, which was actually preferable because Rufus was only one man and too many exits became problematic to watch with any sort of long-term success, and they served food. Not great food, but decent food. And he'd yet to pick up an infectious disease from the 24-7 establishment, although the busboys could certainly afford to wipe the damn tables down more than once a week.

So it'd work for Sam, he figured.

Speaking of, Rufus hadn't said a word since Sam—

no last name, which was rude—had followed him out of Jake's apartment building. Rufus had put his sunglasses on, shoved his hands into his jean jacket pockets, and started north. And he didn't have to look over his shoulder to assure himself that Sam was following. He could feel it. Feel the other man's eyes on the back of his head, between his shoulder blades, watching his every movement. Sam's presence was like a punch to the face.

Aggressive.

Relentless.

Powerful—too powerful. Sam was so tightly wound, he gave off the sensation that his own skin could barely contain him.

Rufus had no doubt Sam was ex-Army. Even without the photographic proof, the way he'd entered the apartment, gun at the ready, no fear in his eyes, he'd have suspected Sam had some sort of formal training.

Rufus hated dealing with those sorts.

He'd heard Sam at the studio door, of course. But there'd been no safe escape from the third-story window, leaving him trapped. So Rufus did the only thing he could when cornered: act harmless until a getaway presented itself. It'd been a good decision, too, because even if Sam hadn't had a Beretta trained on Rufus, he wouldn't have had a chance in a one-on-one scuffle. It would have come down to fighting dirty. Very dirty.

Of course, Rufus hadn't expected Sam to have known Jake either. So that'd thrown him for a hell of a spin. The media had lamented the tragic suicide of a decorated officer since Jake's body had been discovered by the landlord at 619 West Thirty-Eighth Street, and this guy—*Sam*—was calling the gospel bullshit. He'd hopped a bus for—what'd he say? A day and a half?—and made a beeline for Jake's place.

Looking for what?

Answers, most likely.

Just like Rufus was.

Because Jake had been *murdered*.

Rufus knew it. He didn't understand why the cops, with all their forensics experts and medical examiners, thought otherwise. He'd been there. He'd seen Jake's body. He'd been shot at, for fuck's sake. But Rufus's life straddled a line—one that blurred sometimes, like he'd had too much cheap gin and never enough food in his gut—and the side of that line where the cops existed? They dealt with him, but they didn't like him. Hell, sometimes they didn't believe him.

Except for Jake.

And Jake deserved justice.

He deserved to be properly mourned.

So if Sam was here to find out what really happened, report it, and get the cops to see their mistake, then ok. Rufus owed it to Jake to sit and talk with this old friend. He owed it to Jake to offer what little information he could bear to part with, to at least put Sam on the right path.

Jake and I fucked around together, back in the day....

Rufus had sensed *that* from Jake. It wasn't horniness, per se. He had had Natalie, a girlfriend who Jake was, in theory, sexually involved with. It had been a certain restlessness in his energy that Rufus picked up on. A glint in his eye. A hunger. Rufus could always sense the closet sorts, though. His ability to pick out the desperate guys was what got him any dick at all, even if most of those fucks left something to be desired. But that came with living in the underbelly of New York City, he supposed. This crowd wasn't much for *gay is ok*. So if Rufus was feeling a need for a deep-dicking, it was either lower his standards or die from the worst case of blue balls in recent history.

Rufus jumped over some dog shit baking on the

sidewalk, snaked around several suited businessmen leaving a bar—probably a late lunch—and sidestepped a vendor unloading his hand truck and passing boxes down to someone inside the cellar of a business storefront. The city ebbed and flowed around him with endless day-to-day activities. Millions of people had no idea his foundation was gone and, once again, Rufus was completely alone.

He stopped outside the door of BlueMoon, briefly closed his eyes, and took a deep breath. Then he grabbed the handle, looked back, and waited a moment until Sam had caught up with him. Rufus yanked the sticker-laden glass door open and stepped inside. BlueMoon was about as typical an American diner as they came. The air smelled of burned coffee and cooking meat. There was a small bar and stools to the left, a register, and a kitchen window where the cook was piling up plates and ringing the bell. The narrow middle aisle of the diner was packed with two-person tables, and booths lined the right side along the big bay windows that overlooked the street.

The diner wasn't terribly busy. The lunch crowd had already made their way back to the offices for the second half of the workday, but a few familiar locals remained at the counter, waiting for the afternoon soaps Maddie always turned on, and a table near the front was shared by a group of tourists who looked to be horribly lost.

Rufus was tempted to tell them that Times Square was back east a few blocks, but he let it go and walked to a booth about halfway into the diner.

"Be right with you, Freckles," Maddie called from the register.

Rufus didn't answer. He reached his usual seat, tugged off his jean jacket, and threw it into the corner of the booth against the wall with energy akin to a low-key tantrum. He sat down on the cracked vinyl seat and scooted sideways until his shoulder rested against the window. He brought one leg up to rest an elbow on his knee, then stared up at Sam.

Sam was eyeing the diner with open displeasure. He glanced at the front door, now to his back, but reluctantly slid into the seat opposite of Rufus.

Rufus removed his sunglasses, hung them from his T-shirt collar, and then yanked his beanie off once again. He absently finger-combed his hair while staring hard at Sam. He had a lot to ask—about Jake, about Sam, about what Sam was going to do regarding Jake—but instead Rufus blurted out the one thing that'd been chafing him since the apartment.

"I *have* pubes."

"I could have gone the rest of my life without walking into a discussion about whether your carpet matches the drapes," Maddie grumbled as she rounded an empty table and slid up to the booth, pen and server book in either hand. She was black and fortysomething as far as Rufus figured, with that critical glint in her eye unique to mothers.

Rufus felt his neck and face start to warm for a second time. "It does," he answered. "And mind your business, Maddie."

"Don't get testy with me." She slapped Rufus's knee with her notepad. "Feet off the damn furniture."

He obediently shifted position, placed both Chucks squarely on the floor, and leaned against the seat with a frown. But Rufus was *not* sulking. It'd been a long day. A long week. A long fucking life. He was hangry too, which was never a good state to be in, and Sam with his perfect manly stubble, staring at him from across the table and probably never having someone question the state of his pubes….

"Just a coffee, Freckles?" Maddie asked without missing a beat.

Rufus nodded. "With cream."

"With cream, I know." She looked at Sam and asked, "What about you, handsome? Coffee? Food?"

Rufus plucked a single-sided plastic menu from where it was wedged between two displays, one dessert and the other the Sunday specials, and smacked it down in front of Sam without a word. He then pushed aside his rolled-up silverware, grabbed a handful of sugar packets from the container on the tabletop, tore the tops off, and started dumping the contents onto his saucer plate.

Sam blinked once at the saucer, slid the menu aside without looking at it, and said, "Eggs over easy, home fries, and—" He looked at Rufus, and Rufus realized the question was directed at him. "Toast or pancakes?"

Rufus's index finger was in his mouth. "*Whut?*"

"You obviously know this place. You picked it for some reason, in spite of the requirements I gave you. So, which is better here: toast or pancakes?"

"I'm on a diet."

"For me, dumbass."

Rufus's ears were burning. He wiped his finger on the leg of his jeans. "Oh. Pancakes."

Sam waited for what felt to Rufus like a full minute before turning to Maddie and saying, "With pancakes. And get him whatever he normally eats. Not sugar packets. No, I'll pay for it; you're giving me cavities just looking at you."

Maddie tucked the pad into her apron pocket and echoed, "Whatever he eats? I'll have to make it up." She patted Rufus's shoulder and left the booth.

After a moment, Rufus licked his finger and stuck it into the sugar again. "I don't need you buying me anything."

Just another of those long pauses before Sam rubbed his face with both hands—that stubble, that goddamn raspy, manly stubble—and snorted.

Rufus shoved the plate to one side, put his elbows on the tabletop, and leaned forward. "I don't know *why* Jake liked you."

"I never said Jake liked me. I said we fucked around." Sam leaned back, stretching, all broad chest and shoulders, miles and miles of him in the booth. "And you haven't seen me naked."

"I wasn't asking to."

"You seem pretty keen to show me your imaginary pubes."

"You're the one who—fuck you. Jake was a decent guy. And I'd have never thought Jake would have *fucked around* with anyone if he didn't at least *like* them." Rufus huffed, sat back, then leaned sideways to rest his head against the window. "Guess he wasn't always on the mark with judging others."

Sam was doing something with his hands—Rufus couldn't see what, but one of them knocked up against the underside of the table—and a moment later, Sam crossed his arms, tucking his hands under them. He closed his eyes; when he started speaking, it sounded so much like Jake that a frisson ran down Rufus's spine. Not like an imitation or a party trick. Not even Jake's voice, not really. But the cadence. It was the way Jake talked.

"I think we're on to something big, something really big. Oh my God, I am so drunk. Natalie thinks I'm working late." For a moment, Sam's voice again: "Then a string of letters like he mashed the keyboard, maybe his head coming down on it as he was blacking out." Then, Jake's cadence: "I met this girl, Juliana, and she said they come in from the north, and the fuckers, we're going to get the fuckers, nobody should do this to anybody, nobody should—" Sam's voice: "More mashed keys." Jake: "I should tell somebody, I know I should tell somebody, but it's not going to change anything, is it? Tell me. Tell me if it's going to change something. And tell me they won't come after me, tell me they won't come after me no matter what I do—" Then, in his own voice: "He hits the keyboard again, and when he comes back, he wants to talk about—" He smirked, just the faintest hint of the expression. "Us. Whatever he was looking into, he thought it was big, and so I'd say, yes: he misjudged somebody, sat on his fucking thumb trying to decide what to do about it, and it got him killed."

Something in an e-mail…. That was a hell of a lot of something, Rufus thought.

"How did you…?" Rufus sat up straight, heart slugging hard in his chest. "No way Jake told you those things. Who are you, really?"

A Fed?

The sudden consideration wormed its way through the fog of hunger and ever-present heartbreak, mixing and churning in Rufus's gut. But no. Undercover agents had that particular aura about them. Auras of half-truths. Auras of misdirection. Auras of something *not quite right*. Sam wasn't a Fed. He was a dick, though. But maybe that's how he handled loss.

Handled Jake.

Rufus's blood sugar was too low and he was getting irritated.

"Your turn," Sam said. "You know him from work? How? Why should I believe you're not the one he misjudged?"

"Do I look like a fucking murderer?" Rufus snapped, briefly losing his sense of place before saying much quieter, "*Jesus Christ*. I can't tell you *how* I know him from work."

Rufus waited for the insistence, the demands. But Sam just sat there, his hands tucked up under his arms, watching him. And then he said, "The murderers I know don't have such dainty wrists."

"You're a dick," Rufus remarked, echoing his prior thought aloud. "I don't have dainty wrists."

"Some guys like dainty wrists." Slowly, Sam worked a pack of cigarettes out from his pocket, tapping one out, fumbling with it—the movement seemed awkward to Rufus, although he couldn't put his finger on why. Sam didn't light it, though; he stuck it between his lips, drawing on it cold and studying Rufus.

"You won't tell me how you worked with Jake," he said, taking the cigarette from between his lips and toying with the filter. "And you're definitely not a cop." Nothing in the tone, but the way his gaze flicked up and down Rufus, the slight crinkle at the corners of his eyes, was enough. "You're not his boyfriend, although I think you wanted to be. You're not one of those tech guys, because why would Jake be texting you to meet him alone. I think you're a snitch," he said before returning the unlit cigarette to his mouth and sucking on it again.

Rufus was flying once more. Defying gravity for that one brief, exhilarating moment before crashing to the linoleum. *Pop. Snap.* Sam was so matter-of-fact. So blunt. His words were like being stabbed, but the knife was so dull that Rufus wouldn't bleed enough to die.

Swallowing the sour taste in the back of his throat, Rufus leaned across the table and snatched the cigarette from between Sam's lips. "Jake had a girlfriend. I don't fuck around with guys who have girlfriends."

Sam's answer was mild: "I just said that's what I thought."

"Yeah? Well, while you're thinking—I'm thirty-three, not fifteen. Talk to me like it."

"I'm sorry."

Rufus leaned back, springs squeaking as he adjusted

his weight in the booth. He glanced at the cigarette and snapped it into two.

Maddie returned to the booth, holding a conversation with someone at the counter across the room while somehow also addressing them at the same time. She slapped down two plates laden with greasy, oily, perfect food. The shine of butter melting atop the stack of pancakes and the hearty aroma of the home fries caused Rufus's stomach to growl like he was housing a monster in a deep, unexplored cavern. Maddie set a canister of cream on the table before filling both mugs with coffee that smelled like it'd been brewed hours ago.

"Everything good?" Maddie asked, looking at Rufus. She hadn't meant the food.

Rufus reluctantly nodded. "It's fine. Thanks, Maddie."

She gave his head a few pats before leaving their booth and resuming the heated conversation with the local at the counter. "I'm *not* playing *General Hospital* again, Stan. It's *Days of Our Lives* today, and if you don't like it, you can scram."

Sam was digging into the potatoes, the over-easy eggs already broken open and soaking the home fries. He spoke in a low voice, his attention seemingly fixed on the food. "I hate this place. The city, I mean. I don't like… people. I don't like being touched. I don't like loud noises. I shouldn't have said what I did."

"A hell of a place to come and investigate, then," Rufus said as he pulled his own plate closer. His meal was a mirror of Sam's. He actually never ate at BlueMoon beyond the occasional fried egg Maddie would slip him if he came in looking particularly pathetic. Rufus's *usual* was coffee and sugar, so this was a hell of a treat. At the realization of his own words, Rufus's hand froze where it hovered over his cast-aside utensils. "That's what you're going to do, isn't it?"

Glancing up, Sam offered a small, bitter smile that seemed turned inward rather than at Rufus. All he said was "Yeah, I guess that's what I'm going to do. Not very easy when Jake's partner tells me he was shot in the forehead and has no gunshot residue on his hands."

"Lampo's a jackass," Rufus muttered over the clatter of utensils being unrolled and falling onto his plate. He picked up the fork and licked butter off the tines.

"You know him? Jesus, maybe you can get a straight answer out of that dickbag."

Rufus stabbed at his home fries. "Doubtful. What did Lampo say to you? Not about Jake's forehead." He stuffed the food in his mouth and talked around chewing. "I know about his forehead. I saw it. I tried to tell him, but Lampo wouldn't listen to me—like *I* don't know a thing or two about death."

"I already told you: no gunshot residue. That's it. Then somebody—his supervisor, I guess—came in. She must have put the fear of God in him because he wrapped things up and got me out of there faster than a twink with a hot douche."

Rufus screwed his expression up, took another bite, and said, "You're all class."

"Have you ever had a hot douche? It's like Satan himself is breathing up your bunghole."

"*Jesus fucking Christ.*" Rufus missed stabbing at a bit of potato, accidentally flicked it off his plate, and watched it land on the floor. He glanced at Sam again. "Lampo really told you there wasn't any residue on Jake's hands?"

"Yes. And he all but told me he thought it was murder too."

"He said that?"

"No, that's why I said he all but told me. He kept saying things weren't typical—where he shot himself, the absence of GSR. 'Pretty damn hard to shoot yourself and not have evidence on your hands' were his exact words. He tried to say the case was open-and-shut, but when I called his bullshit, I think he might have agreed with me. Then his boss showed up, and I was out on the sidewalk with a scorched rectum."

As Sam spoke, Rufus could feel a telltale prickle in the corners of his eyes. He sniffed loudly, blinked rapidly, and stared out the window. "I told Lampo. I *told* him that." Rufus's voice caught like he had a wedge of potato stuck in his throat. "Fucking Jake. *Goddamn it*. There was someone else there when I found him. The guy almost blew my head off. But Lampo—" Rufus made a fist and punched the sagging seat underneath him. The springs protested. "He's never taken anything I've said seriously unless it's filtered through Jake. And Jake's dead, so he couldn't say, 'Lampo, you dumb fuck, of course someone shot me.'"

"What the fuck?" Sam said. "There was someone else there? And you saw him? Why the fuck didn't you say something earlier?"

Rufus hastily wiped one eye and did his best to glare daggers at Sam. "I *did*. I told Jake's partner. Who else is there—*you*? Fuck you."

"Forget me for a minute. Lampo just ignored you? Is he dumber than shit? Lazy? What the fuck? And why were you even there in the first place? Were you supposed to be meeting Jake?"

Rufus stabbed at his home fries again. One bite, two, a third until his mouth was full and his tongue was burned. He washed it down with coffee and then cut a wedge of a pancake with the side of his fork. "Yeah," he confirmed, voice low. "He had a job for me."

"And what was the job?"

Rufus picked up a small container of syrup, the handle

sticky. He drowned the pancake before eating the slice. "A pickup."

"What were you picking up?"

Rufus sucked syrup off his thumb. "If I knew, I wouldn't have been rifling through Jake's underwear drawer earlier."

For a moment, Sam's face was tight. Then he said, "That's why you're looking for his phone."

"Jake has to have record somewhere of what the job was. I tried his personal laptop but that was a deadend. He did most of his business on his phone. I figured finding that was better than letting my bare ass flap in the wind."

"The phone seems like a good place to start," Sam said; it sounded like a concession.

Rufus cut another wedge of pancake. "Sounds like you intend to stick with me after we eat."

Sam's knife and fork hovered over the pancakes. Then, with a casualness that seemed exaggerated, he cut into the mound of fluffy deliciousness. "It would be helpful," he said, the words in time with the slow rocking of the knife, "to have someone else with me. Someone who knew Jake from here, as a cop. Someone who knows the city."

"You think you can buy me one meal and I'll put out?"

This time, Sam's smile was a grin, and it was directed one-hundred percent at Rufus. "A guy can hope. Those dainty wrists and all."

Rufus couldn't recall a single conversation in his adult life that had this much sexual innuendo and didn't immediately end with some guy punching him in the neck for being queer. Even after getting food in his stomach, Rufus wasn't sure what he thought of Sam. Besides the obvious, of course. Sam was gorgeous and probably knew it, confident in his masculinity, and frustrating in conversation. So the dickish personality was probably fairly true to his character and not something Rufus superimposed on Sam merely because he had hunger pains and little patience. Sam was also gay—maybe gay?—*definitely*, Rufus was certain. And that was, on the one hand, sort of nice—the casualness with which Sam embraced his sexuality, the teasing, the possibility of someone to flirt with—but on the other hand, Rufus wasn't any good at that sort of stuff.

Rufus ate some more pancakes. "That next bullet might hit its mark. I don't make it a habit of walking headfirst into danger."

Sam's smile snapped out, and he worked on the food for a while. When he spoke again, his voice had flattened back into its former tone. "Then you could at least tell me what you think might be going on. Where you've looked for his phone. Anything that might help." Then, throwing down the knife and fork, Sam pushed away the plate. "You might not care about Jake enough to risk your life, but I do, and I want to find who did this to him."

Rufus stopped chewing the mound of dough in his mouth and stared at Sam. "I do *too* care."

Sam raised an eyebrow. "Nobody taught you not to talk with your mouth full?" Then, that smirk ghosting across his lips, "Except in certain cases, of course."

Rufus swallowed. "Wow."

"I might have somewhere to start, but I want to know the rest of it. Where else have you looked for his phone? If you had to make a list, right now, of who might have killed him, who are your top five? What don't I know that I need to know?"

"You're serious, aren't you?" Rufus asked with a sort of disbelieving laugh. "Jake was a cop—a good one. Any criminal in this city would want him out of the way. Anyone he's put on Rikers who's got connections on the outside could have done this." But Rufus held up one hand

and began to tick locations off on each finger, starting with his pinky. "I checked his apartment. I checked his car. I checked his secret apartment." He said that and gave Sam the finger. "I checked trash cans, a nearby park—short of going through his desk at the precinct, I've checked everywhere for his stupid phone."

Sam mouthed, *Secret apartment*, shook his head, and ate a few more bites of potatoes. Then, without seeming to realize it, pushed the mostly intact stack of pancakes toward Rufus. "I don't know," Sam said. "If they wanted to scare you off, they might have tossed the phone. Maybe they still have it. We could talk to the girlfriend, see if she's connected to his Find My Phone app or whatever they have. Or… or we try something else, to start."

Rufus inched his fork toward Sam's pancakes as he spoke, stabbed one, and quickly slid it on to his own plate. "Do you know Natalie? I've never met her. I'm not supposed to know about her. But I'm a curious little shit, so said Jake on more than one occasion." He doused the pancake in more syrup and took a huge bite.

Whatever Sam thought about that little revelation, Rufus couldn't tell. Sam watched him again, hands tucked under his arms, the pose now familiar. "No," Sam finally said. "Jake told me about her. Just that she existed, basically. Jake was complicated about that kind of stuff."

Rufus made a sound. "Complicated," he agreed.

"Do you want to cruise the Ramble with me?"

"I'm still on Natalie. She might freak out, you know."

"Oh, she'll definitely be freaked out. But I'd rather have her freak out and give us some answers than us stumble around just so we can leave her illusion of Jake intact." Leaning against the bench, both arms now stretched along the back of the seat, Sam said, "You didn't answer my question about going cruising together."

Rufus's fingertips tingled. He put his fork and knife

down and rubbed his hands on his thighs until the friction against his jeans deadened the sensation. He realized he'd been staring at Sam's broad chest while doing so and quickly averted his gaze to... Sam's biceps that went on for days. Rufus shook himself, looked at Sam's face, and nearly drowned in the other man's deep brown eyes. *Dammit*. "Uh, I don't... at the Ramble... no."

"You don't put out for pancakes," Sam said like a kid doing sums. "You don't go cruising." Then, one plus one equals two, he said, "Oh God. You're a virgin."

"*What*? No, I'm not. Fuck you."

Sam nodded slowly. "Of course not. My mistake."

"I'm *not*. And you know, acting this thirsty to fuck a bona fide redhead is excessive. Just ask nicely."

Nodding again, Sam said, "Ask nicely. I'll remember that." Then, reaching into his pocket, he pulled out a wad of bills and counted out cash. "Will that cover the check?"

Rufus looked down at his mostly eaten meal.

Jake hadn't ever asked Rufus how he was doing on money—Jake had simply done things for him. Little things. Like calling in delivery whenever Rufus broke into his apartment because he was lonely and couldn't stand another night in his shithole studio without someone to talk to. Sometimes Jake would slip a fresh MetroCard in alongside Rufus's CI pay, because Jake knew he jumped the turnstiles and he was trying to deter the petty thief in Rufus. And occasionally Jake would ask Rufus to go buy them both a coffee at a bodega, but he'd give Rufus too much money and Rufus never came back with change and Jake never questioned it.

Sam hadn't offered to buy Rufus a meal. He'd merely done it—in his own aggressive and brutish way, of course—but it'd meant something to Rufus. It meant something when another man could see his fault lines cracking, growing wider, shaking his foundation, and instead of pointing it out for everyone and God to see, they… nudged a plate of pancakes in front of him because Rufus hadn't eaten much in the last few days and it was probably starting to show.

So the least he could do in return was bring Sam to Natalie Miller's apartment. It'd put Sam on the path toward discovering answers, and then he could talk to the cops about whatever he found. They'd believe Sam. He was ex-Army. Jake's friend. He'd see that justice was served. And whoever thought Rufus was a threat would be handled and everything would… go on.

Rufus downed his remaining coffee, collected his jacket, hat, sunglasses, and said with a quick nod, "That's enough." He got out of the booth, put the articles on, and instead of making a show about how he was now, in fact, putting out for Sam, he asked, "Get all those singles from stripping?"

Sam raised an eyebrow as he slid out of the booth. "Ask nicely, and maybe I'll show you." And then he was past Rufus and heading for the door, calling over his shoulder, "Let's go blow another heteronormative world to fuck."

CHAPTER
SIX

While they'd been in the diner, it had been easy for Sam to keep his shit together. Noise—the soap playing on the television mounted in the corner, metal spatula scraping the grill, patrons talking, a balding man laughing on his phone—but a level that Sam could handle, nothing too loud or too abrupt. And smells, too, but for the most part, they'd been good smells: the pancakes, the grease, the coffee, the hint of Rufus's Dial soap that snuck through everything else. In the diner, while Sam could clamp his hands under his arms and pretend everything was fine, he'd been able to work Rufus pretty well, get most of what he wanted without giving away too much.

As soon as they were back on the streets, though, Manhattan invaded. The thrum of a jackhammer; two

51

women shouting at each other from open windows on the fourth floor of a brick building; a screech of brakes as a car swerved to avoid a courier, and the courier swearing as he swerved in turn to avoid a mommy gang pushing strollers. The heat, the stink, the dirt. Sam took deep breaths and jerked his chin at Rufus to take the lead.

It only got worse. Rufus led him down a flight of stairs to a subway station. The rattle of an approaching train filtered through the hub of voices, and Rufus sprinted forward, jumped the turnstile, and glanced back at Sam with something smug all over his face. When Sam hesitated, Rufus shrugged and jogged down another flight of stairs.

Swearing, Sam copied the movement, blushing at the dirty look an older man gave him. Someone shouted after Sam, and he pitched down the stairs, hitting the landing below at a jog. He caught sight of Rufus boarding a car, and Sam sprinted after him, turning sideways to squeeze between the closing doors.

Then they were crammed together. Sardines in a can. Maybe fish in a barrel. The stink of unwashed bodies, of sweat, of spoiled food. And no empty space, no air. Rufus's body was pressed up against Sam's, Sam's sweat-covered back plastered to the door. This close, Sam could feel the wiry muscle running through the redhead, could smell Dial soap and, now, his hair, the wool of his beanie—what a ridiculous piece of fuckery in July—something else, too, something he thought of as just Rufus.

Rufus's thigh was between Sam's legs.

Rufus kept shifting.

There wasn't enough air in the car. There wasn't enough space.

Sam must have made some kind of noise, because Rufus glanced at him. "How you doing? Downtown train at the start of rush hour and all."

"Fine," Sam growled.

The redheaded asshole just kept shifting his weight, his thigh bumping into Sam every damn time.

Sam tried to lean away. He tried to pull back. He tried not to think about the fact that Rufus was actually kind of funny, actually kind of cute, surprisingly sensitive under the veneer, if his reactions were any gauge, and maybe even smart and tough, although some of that remained to be decided. Sam tried really, really hard not to think about freckles, how far they might go down the redhead. Tried not to think about all the jokes that had seemed safe and contained inside the controlled environment of the diner.

Rufus twisted around, his mouth almost at Sam's ear, and said, "We need to get off."

Sam might have groaned. He hoped that the shriek of brakes engaging drowned out the noise, but judging by the way those green eyes widened in amusement, he didn't think so.

Then the doors opened and they spilled out of the car, Rufus catching Sam's shirt—the inside-out tee almost translucent where the white had soaked up sweat—to steady him. A few more minutes, and they were out of the hellhole, emerging into a city that seemed, in comparison, clean and cool and open. Sam hated the city, but he thought he might fucking die if he had go in the subway again.

Rufus led them onto a smaller street. Brownstones ran along both sides, many of them choked by ivy. The trees here were tall, green, shady. After ten steps, Sam wiped his face, dried his hands on his jeans, and felt a little more centered. When Rufus looked at him, though, he just shook his head. He didn't want to talk about it; he definitely didn't want to give the redhead any more of an edge.

"Are we close?" Sam asked.

"We have to walk to Fourteenth and catch the L into

Brooklyn. It's a hell of a trek."

Sam stopped walking. "More trains?"

Rufus paused midstep, looked over his shoulder again, and gave a ridiculous grin. "No. I'm kidding. We're almost there. Near the end of this block."

"Oh," Sam said, hearing the lameness of the response. And then, even worse, but he couldn't seem to stop it: "Good." And he didn't know why he liked that Rufus held that ridiculous grin for another moment before going on.

Rufus stopped at one of the brownstones, distinguishable from the others only by the blue trim on the windows and a flowerbox that had been neglected for a long time.

"She owns this thing?" Sam said. "Christ, is she an heiress or something?"

Rufus removed his sunglasses, hung them from the collar of his T-shirt, and hummed in response. "She owns some startup company. A millennial whose success hinged on mommy and daddy's bank account."

"A millennial," Sam repeated. "Fucking perfect. And you think she'll be home? What are the odds she's going to smile at her boyfriend's old fuck buddy, hand over her phone, and tell us to have fun and be safe?"

Rufus glanced up at Sam. "Aren't you all sunshine and puppies."

"How good are you at—" Sam tried to find the right word, the one that would get Rufus's hackles up and, hopefully, put his ego on the line. "—snooping?"

"I was eating fucking chips when you fumbled your way into Jake's place. How good do you think I am?" Rufus asked, not breaking his eye contact.

"Slightly below average," Sam said with a shrug. "You left crumbs everywhere."

"Are you baiting me?"

"You're cute when you get all suspicious and paranoid. All right. Let's try this. I'll talk to her. You find a way to get out of the conversation and look around." Sam pursed his lips. "Unless that's too difficult for you."

Rufus squared his shoulders, jutted his chin out, and did a very good job at looking well and truly offended. "Natalie carries a purple Michael Kors bag. And I bet—" He paused, patted various pockets, then produced a pack of gum. "I bet *this* that her phone is in the purse. And if this wasn't for Jake, I'd knee you in the nuts for suggesting I'm below average. I'm a fucking *great* snoop."

"Spearmint." Sam made a face. "And I didn't suggest you were below average. I said you were. I guess we're about to find out if I'm right."

Without waiting for an answer, he took the steps up to the brownstone's door and rang the bell. It buzzed deep inside the house, and thirty seconds passed before footsteps moved toward the door. It swung open, and a petite woman with brown hair in a pixie cut and very expensive shoes answered the door.

Natalie Miller made eye contact with Sam's chest, then tilted her head to look at his face. "Um—yes?"

"Sam Auden, ma'am. United States Army Intelligence." He produced his military ID, which he'd smuggled out after everything went bad at Benning, the expiration date still six months away. "This is Mr. Hiscock. May we have a few minutes of your time?"

"Army Intelligence?" Natalie repeated, looking toward the ID, but Sam was already tucking it away. She glanced at Rufus next, who stood a step behind Sam, studied his appearance with a skeptical eyebrow raise, then asked, "What's this in regards to?"

"You were acquainted with Mr. Jacob Brower?"

Her face screwed up into something painful, her eyes bright with wet. "Y-yes," she managed with breath that sounded as if it'd been knocked from her chest.

"If we could just have a few minutes of your time."

Natalie cautiously stepped aside and gestured for them each to enter. She led them into a combination kitchen and living space at the back of the brownstone, obviously a gut-and-update job, lots of expensive-looking appliances and furniture, white subway tile mixed with jute floor coverings, and columns of July sunlight pouring in through the windows. After she motioned to a sofa, Sam and Rufus sat, but Natalie remained standing, wringing her hands once and then adjusting a tiny ceramic bluebird on the console table.

Sam nudged Rufus's knee with his own, waiting for Natalie to make her opening offer, coffee, tea—unless she fell apart first.

"Ms. Miller?" Rufus said, meeting her eyes as she jerked her head up. "May I use your restroom?"

"Oh. Yes, of course. It's the first door down the hall," she said, pointing to the right.

Rufus stood and walked out of the room without making a sound.

Natalie glanced at Sam once the bathroom door had shut. "Would you like something to drink? I don't have coffee. It's not good for you. But some herbal tea, maybe? Or water?"

"Water would be fine," Sam said. Some of what was going to happen next was strategy. And some was intuition. And some was totally predictable. But a big part was conditioning: get her saying yes, answering the little questions, so it all seemed natural. When Natalie came back with a water in a cardboard box like that milk they used to sell in the school cafeteria, Sam struggled not to roll his eyes. The damn thing probably cost more than the lunch he'd just bought Rufus.

"What was the nature of your relationship with Mr.

Brower?" Sam asked, pulling out his phone and pretending to type, as though taking notes.

"Our relationship?" Natalie took a seat in an overstuffed chair directly across from the couch and crossed her legs at the ankles. "I suppose you're asking everyone close to him…. Jake and I are—were dating. A little over a year."

Over her shoulder, Sam spotted Rufus slipping out of the bathroom and heading away from the conversation. Sam focused on giving Natalie a smile, *just business, you know how it is*. It wasn't as easy as he'd thought. *A little over a year*. Images flicked through his head, a carousel of all the precious fucking moments Jake had spent with her: holding hands at the Alice statue in Central Park, gelato in Midtown, kissing at a rooftop bar while the city glowed like flecks of mica on a black beach. Sam could hear himself, hear how casual he'd tried to make it sound to Rufus: *We fucked around*. Then, vividly, punching the breath from his lungs, Natalie on her back and Jake driving into her.

"That's right," Sam heard himself say. "Could you describe your relationship? How were things between you and Jake?"

"Good," she said in a rush. "I mean, you know, it was mostly good. Relationships can be tricky."

Rufus appeared in the hallway again. He held a phone up high and waved it a little, then made a crossing motion with his hands to suggest something was wrong.

That he couldn't get beyond the passcode, Sam suspected.

"Jake worked a lot," Natalie was saying. "He was a detective with the NYPD."

Sam knew that Rufus's semaphores were important. He knew that what Natalie had said was important; she had practically held the door open for him to ask about Jake's work. But what he heard in his head—what he saw, like that sign flashing Dear Evan Hansen when he'd left Port Authority building—was *good.* Things had been good. Good, good, good. And then, he had a hundred questions: did he ever roll over and kiss your shoulder after? Did he ever want to lace your fingers together while you made love? Did he hide things around the apartment, knowing you'd find them—movie tickets, a coupon for fifty percent off a burger, a four by six of the two of you on the Chattahoochee, just sun and skin and water?

It was harder than Sam thought to slam the door on all of it.

"I'm sorry," he managed to say, tapping furiously at his phone. "I should have done this at the beginning. Could you confirm your full name and date of birth for the record?"

"Oh sure," she said quickly, automatically, like she'd been questioned so much in the last week about Jake this was simply more routine. "Natalie Miller. May 23, 1989."

Rufus, still in the hallway, shook his head and made that crossing motion again. He held up five fingers.

Five more attempts to unlock.

Damn it.

"And your Social Security number?"

Natalie looked surprised. "You really need that?"

"I'm sorry," Sam said, frowning. "I thought someone explained all of this to you when they set up the appointment."

"Appointment? I was never—it's been a very hectic week. I must have... missed the call or something." Her cheeks grew red, her brows knitted together, and she clasped a hand over her mouth. She looked ready to take the blame for everything. For Sam's inconvenience. For the failed appointment. For Jake's death.

"Yes, well. I'm very sorry for your loss. The Army

has begun doing these sorts of follow-ups after death by suicide. It's all procedure, you understand. Trying to prevent future tragedies. The records are very thorough. We're doing our best to understand what happened. So"— he offered a soft smile—"your Social?"

Natalie sniffled loudly and wiped her nose on the back of her hand. With her chin practically tucked to her chest, she rattled off a series of numbers.

Rufus had crept closer to the main room in order to overhear their conversation. After Natalie gave her social, he typed, shook his head, typed once more, then met Sam's eyes and held up three fingers.

Three more attempts.

"And when was your anniversary with Mr. Brower?"

Natalie gave a watery chuckle and wiped at her pale cheeks. "Well, it's funny. I always said it was July third. Jake insisted it was July second. But the clock had rolled over. So it was after midnight."

Rufus rolled his eyes like a clock—one of those old flip-number alarms—as he tried the next series of numbers. He immediately held up the phone to show Sam the unlocked homepage before he retreated to the bathroom.

Sam didn't grin, not on the outside. But he had to admit, the look of triumph on the redhead's face had been... cute. Like the caricature of suspicion earlier. So many emotions, all of them worn so close to that very fair skin. It could distract a guy.

"Thank you," Sam said. "You mentioned work. Did Mr. Brower talk about work with you? Was there anything he mentioned that stood out to you, or maybe something small that came up repeatedly?"

"Jake never talked about work with me," Natalie said, finally her words bathed in a tone of negativity. Resentment, perhaps. "It was always confidential."

"Of course," Sam said. "What about his partner? Or other coworkers? Friends? Family? Did he have a good support system? Any recent conflicts? Or long-term strain on those relationships?"

Natalie rolled her little shoulders a few times. "He had *me*. My parents. He hadn't kept in touch with anyone from the Army, but he had more recent friendships with people here in the city."

Sam ran his hand over the cushion, smoothing the tight weave of the upholstery. No old friendships. He never kept in touch with anyone from the Army. *Of course not*, Sam thought. Not when he had a new life, a new job, a new girlfriend. Just those blackout e-mails. Just those invitations to come, for a week or a month, and stay on the couch. But always with a return ticket already booked, always with the exit door propped open. The way it had always been. We fucked around, that way. Which was what Sam had wanted too. Always. Exclusively.

God, Sam thought. *Did a guy ever get used to the taste of his own bullshit?*

"Anything unusual in Mr. Brower's behavior over the last few weeks?"

Natalie considered the question, started to speak, but looked over her shoulder as Rufus made his presence known coming back into the room. "Everything ok?" she asked.

Rufus nodded, smiled, and stood at the couch but didn't sit. "Too much coffee."

She blushed a little. "Coffee is bad for you, Mr. Hiscock." Natalie looked at Sam again. "Maybe it's not unusual, but he'd been working late recently. Like, a lot. Sometimes he wouldn't answer his phone. He always answered, or at least he'd text me and say he'd call back."

"How long had that been going on?"

"The last two weeks. Maybe three."

Sam couldn't help it; three weeks was just the right window of time, and she'd been twisting a knife in him, not even knowing it. Now he wanted to twist back. "Did this happen on your anniversary?"

Her cheeks got red again. But a dark red this time. An angry red. "He wasn't having an affair, if that's what you're suggesting, Mr. Auden."

"Interesting that you should raise that possibility," Sam said. "Did Mr. Brower have any prior incidents of infidelity? Were you concerned about his relationships with other friends or coworkers? Did he give you any reason to believe—"

Rufus leaned over, didn't touch Sam, but swiped the phone from his hands to disrupt the moment. "Mr. Auden, I think we've got the basics," he said a bit too loud. "We really shouldn't keep Ms. Miller all afternoon." He looked at Natalie. "I'm very sorry for your loss, ma'am. Mr. Brower was a respected officer."

Natalie was still staring at Sam, like he was a bug she'd squash with a rolled-up newspaper. Hell, maybe she'd squash Rufus too, simply due to his proximity. "Yes. He was," she clipped out.

Rufus nudged Sam's foot with the toe of his Chuck. "Come on."

Whatever had gotten into Sam's head, it was gone. He drew a deep breath, nodded, and stood. Following Rufus to the door, with Natalie trailing them, Sam said, "Thank you for your time, Ms. Miller. If we have any more questions, we'll be in touch." Then they were at the door, moving out into the July heat, the dense, green smell of the trees mixing with the baking asphalt. After another deep breath, Sam managed to echo Rufus: "We're sorry for your loss."

Natalie didn't respond; she watched them from the doorway as they moved down the steps. Halfway down the block, a spot in the middle of Sam's back was still itching, but he resisted the urge to look. When they turned the corner, though, he risked a glance and saw her still framed by sandstone, her gaze locked on them.

"Well?" Sam asked as they left behind the brownstones and passed a bodega.

"You've got no fucking chill," Rufus answered, finally offering Sam his phone back.

"Don't worry about my fucking chill. What did you find?"

Rufus looked about to answer, but his expression changed and he pulled a vibrating cell from his jeans pocket. He swiped to accept and held it to his ear. "The fuck you calling me for? … Tell it to my mother. No, Jake never…. … Did I stutter? No, I don't have anything. Sure, I'll work on my attitude. Smooches." Rufus hit End while a tinny voice was still talking and shoved the phone in his pocket. He put his sunglasses on and looked back at Sam. "Where were we?"

"Jake never what?"

Rufus raised both eyebrows. "Oh. That was Lampo. He was asking about the pickup that never happened."

"Huh," Sam said. "Well, if you don't need to take any more personal calls, maybe you can tell me what you found inside."

Rufus moved under the awning of the bodega and casually leaned against an outdoor stand. "I found a purple Michael Kors bag," he began with a wicked smile. "And inside was an iPhone worth more than my monthly rent. Also, four different shades of lipstick, a fistful of tampons, some receipts, a hairbrush, one of those little battery-powered fans—"

Sam moved in on the redhead, using his size and build to pin Rufus against a stand of fresh produce: tomatoes, iceberg lettuce, mutant jalapenos the size of carrots. "I know you found her purse. I know you found her phone.

I don't care how many tampons you found and stuffed up your chute. Where. Is. Jake's. Phone."

"If you ratcheted up that testosterone any higher, you'd burst right outta that shirt," Rufus remarked, his smile unyielding. "Phone's pinging from Tompkins Square Park. Or somewhere right nearby."

"His phone is in a park?"

"Near the park," Rufus said again. "There's a handful of bars on the corners. Maybe Jake lost it at one last week? Or it was stolen?"

Sam swore. "Aren't these things supposed to be GPS or something? Can't they be a little more fucking specific?"

"Are you grouchy because you owe me a new pack of spearmint?"

There it was again: the way Rufus grinned, the way his eyes lit up, the way he was just so very fucking alive, and all of it right up at the top, where Sam could reach out and touch it.

"Let's go," Sam said. "And no subways."

"It's a bit of a trek. Hope you don't mind getting sweaty."

CHAPTER
SEVEN

The walk from Seventh Avenue to Avenue A took about twenty-eight minutes for the average pedestrian. Rufus could shave three to five minutes off that commute time when taking into account his long legs, determined pace, and tendency to jaywalk. But it was too hot to speed walk across the island, Rufus thought. Three to five minutes wouldn't make a difference this time.

Jake would still be dead at the finish line.

Besides, Sam couldn't keep up. Oh sure, he had the stamina to walk all over hell and back, it seemed, but he hadn't perfected how to keep pace in an urban jungle. Rufus was liquid. Fluid in his movements, seamless in his ability to adjust to the flow of traffic.

Sam was… a tank.

And they didn't need a body count in their wake.

So Rufus walked at a speed that would deliver them to the East Side in twenty-eight minutes.

This also provided Rufus with three to five additional minutes in which to deconstruct his current predicament, interpret the sudden deterioration of Sam's dialogue with Natalie, and how he himself, a man who had a deeper interpersonal relationship with the cactus he'd rescued from the trash at a bodega in his neighborhood than he did with any actual humans, was going to console Sam.

Rufus stopped at the corner of Twelfth Street and waited as traffic shot down Fifth Avenue. A breeze cooled the sweat on the back of his neck, rustled the branches of trees in the church courtyard to their right, and pride flags, still hung up from June's annual celebrations, flapped and waved from a nearby balcony. Rufus watched the rainbows with a sudden sense of dissociation from the rest of the world pressing down on him.

He'd been seven years old when he met Alvin. Alvin was in college. Studying dance. He wasn't from New York, but he'd moved into the same shitty tenement Rufus lived in while taking courses. Alvin had been nice. Once, he'd given Rufus his carton of leftover lo mein for dinner, because he'd asked why the kid was sitting in the hallway at midnight and Rufus had told him he wasn't allowed inside when his mother had friends over.

Alvin had had a rainbow flag. He'd flown it from his window that one summer they'd been neighbors. Rufus didn't know what it meant, of course. It was just colorful. Pretty. And Alvin had always been *so nice* to the little punk brat no one else seemed to notice. Rufus told his mother he wanted a flag too. To put in his window like Alvin had done.

His mother had slapped him in the mouth until he bled.

Alvin had moved away after that one year.

The city made a sharp reinsertion into Rufus, and the memory was quickly packed away. Rufus led the way across the street. They passed an NYU building, parking garage, overhead scaffolding that briefly blocked out the intense rays of the late-afternoon sun, and then crossed another avenue heavy with rush hour traffic. Rufus slowed his pace momentarily when they came up on the Strand Book Store. Hands snug in his jean jacket pockets so as not to be tempted to abscond with something, Rufus lingered long enough to scan the spines of some of the one-dollar specials lining the sidewalk.

Analysis of Economics in Sub Saharan Africa.

DIY: Artisan Cheese Making.

Photographers Guide to Dry Plate Process.

The Agatha Christie Companion.

Rufus glanced over his shoulder. Sam was studying him, not the books. He moved away from the cheap paperbacks and started walking again, with Sam still in tow. Twelve minutes until they reached the edge of Tompkins Square, Rufus calculated. He took a deep breath of hot, humid air and cracked his neck to either side.

Focus.

First and foremost: Rufus was still involved with *Sam's* investigation. And that was a problem. He'd sworn he'd go as far as Natalie's apartment. He'd owed it to Jake to put Sam on the correct path. But then he'd been coaxed into going inside, showing his face to Natalie, snooping around (which he'd done brilliantly, but that wasn't the point), and now here Rufus was, still tagging along.

Tagging along? Hell. He was quite literally leading the charge.

Which brought Rufus to his second concern: Sam's unhinged line of questioning. Well, that had been obvious enough. Rufus might not have had a romantic relationship before, but his own emotions weren't foreign. They hadn't atrophied. Sam was hurting, more than he'd admitted at the studio or the diner. But Sam also didn't seem the kind of guy who handled grief with tears. He was probably more like the anger, rage, punch-a-hole-through-a-wall sort of guy, if the tampons shoved up Rufus's backside remark was any indication. But Rufus didn't mind letting that one slide. Being face-to-face with Natalie had made the loss of Jake more real to Sam, and Rufus had had front row seats to that show.

The third point, maybe the genesis of all the current shit being flung: How to console Sam. Sam didn't like being touched—his words—so Rufus sure wasn't going to offer to hug it out. A few times already Rufus had noticed the peculiar shake Sam had when the city pressed too close. Rufus had been grateful when Sam hadn't pointed out his obvious downward trajectory at the diner—that he needed food and couldn't pay for it himself—so, likewise, Rufus wasn't going to make Sam even more uncomfortable by pointing out those shakes that he was clearly very fucking aware of. That brief moment in Natalie's living room, though, with Sam naked and exposed and coping with the nastier side of the human condition, it'd made Rufus feel not so alone. And if he were to part now, say *fuck this and good luck*, where would they both be?

Alone.

If he stayed until Tompkins Square and helped Sam find Jake's phone, that'd certainly be enough. Whatever pickup job Rufus had been contacted to handle, the evidence would be on Jake's missing cell. Sam would take it to the police and they'd piece together the clues like on television. And that way Rufus would have done right by Jake. He'd have done right by Sam too. Hell, Sam might even set aside his salty, grouchy attitude for thirty seconds and say something nice that wasn't simultaneously laced with sexual overtones.

That's not entirely fair, Rufus thought. *He thinks you're cute.*

Granted, Sam had also said Rufus was suspicious and paranoid. Still. It'd been nice hearing that. Not many people thought a gangly redhead with a face smattered with just slightly *too many* freckles was cute.

Rufus turned down Avenue A, and a looming canopy of old trees came into view. Tompkins Square Park stood out in stark contrast against the surrounding brick and steel and stone, a reminder that for all the dirt and grime, New York City was still alive. Still breathing and still beating.

Rufus pulled his hands from the jacket pockets and pointed at a hole-in-the-wall joint to their left. The outside of the building was adorned in colorfully painted murals. "This place is Mama's Cafe. And across the street is Queenie's. I think there's two more bars at the end of the block too. Avenue B is more residential—churches, schools, apartment buildings, shit like that. So I'm guessing the phone is on *this side* of the park."

"You're guessing?"

Rufus tilted his head up briefly to stare at Sam through his sunglasses. "Do I look like a mind reader?" He motioned for Sam to follow as he walked toward Queenie's.

"Mind reader?" Sam grumbled. "Wish you could read my fucking mind right now."

Rufus spun suddenly on his heel, causing Sam to stop short of barreling right into him. "By the way—*Hiscock*?"

"I wasn't thinking about your cock. Nice try on the mind reading, though."

"Uh-huh. Is your last name really Auden?"

"It's Auden." It looked for a moment like Sam might say something, maybe ask for Rufus's real last name. Then someone passing by jostled him, and Sam startled, took a deep breath, and looked around. A wild look. Almost a feral look. "Can we—" He made a vague gesture. "Can you just fucking get us off the street, please?"

Rufus pretended not to notice the expression that'd swept across Sam's face. "Grouch." He reached Queenie's, yanked the door open, and stepped inside. Rufus held it long enough for Sam to grab, then drifted into the crowd of grisly patrons.

Queenie's was old as sin. It smelled like cigarettes, despite the smoke-free legislation in the city that required bars to jump through loopholes in order to offer their patrons a Marlboro with their martini. It smelled like cheap booze too, which probably meant they didn't serve martinis. It also smelled like someone had been jacking off in the corner for the last decade and had been leaving their load on the floor. All this, and folks were still crowded inside.

Rufus wove around a few haphazardly placed tables and mingling groups of men at least a decade older than himself before reaching the bar. He didn't touch the countertop. Nope. It looked sticky. But he patiently waited for the bald guy serving beer in glasses with hard-water stains to notice him.

The bartender didn't ask what Rufus wanted. He just threw down a napkin on the sticky bar and raised thinning eyebrows.

"No, thanks. But I'm wondering if you might have seen a friend of mine recently. Tall. Big this way," Rufus said, holding either hand out from his shoulders and giving a vague description of Jake without coming out saying: my friend, the cop. "Blond hair. Butch."

The bartender pulled a grimy towel from his shoulder, flapped it once, and said, "Butch?"

"Yeah. A guy with testosterone to spare," Rufus replied.

"Haven't seen him."

"Anyone report a lost iPhone, then? It's black with a matching butch case."

Those thinning eyebrows wiggled, and the bartender made a face. "Sure, I got it. In a box with all the other butch phones nobody bothered to pick up. Right there with their car keys and their wallets and a few stacks of cash."

"Aren't you charming," Rufus said dryly.

"Buy a drink and I'll be so fucking charming, your little pussy will squirt. Otherwise, get the fuck out."

"Mazel tov." Rufus adjusted his sunglasses with his middle finger, turned, and walked back to the door. "Fuck this place," he said to Sam.

"That went well," Sam said.

Rufus stepped outside and started walking. "Queenie's is the pits."

"The tips of your ears turn pink," Sam said, following. "And the tip of your nose."

"It's a sunburn," Rufus said automatically, tugging his beanie down over his ears.

Sam didn't say anything, but the big dumb fuck was grinning, which was even worse.

Rufus stopped to poke his head into a dry cleaners. A brief conversation with the owner confirmed no one like Jake had been seen in the shop, and no, they didn't have a lost and found beyond unclaimed jackets, one as old as last December. Rufus tried again at a sushi joint, of which there *had* been a lost phone, but the hostess swore she'd chased the owner down the street to return it. More of the same at a Starbucks and even a nail salon. No one had seen anyone matching Jake's description since he'd still been alive, and no one was admitting to having found an unclaimed iPhone.

Rufus was well and truly agitated by the time they

came to a stop at the next watering hole, the late-afternoon light turning the façade gold. Bar. That was the name of this place. It was probably supposed to be funny or ironic or some shit. The door was propped open, and hipsters moved in and out like the tides. At least it appeared night and day in cleanliness compared to Queenie's.

"His phone wasn't moving," Rufus told Sam. He sidestepped a group of college-age kids as he approached the open door of Bar.

"I bet you know how to use your tongue," Sam said. "Conversationally, I mean. Maybe try a little sweet talk this time."

Rufus paused in the threshold, took his sunglasses off, and stared at Sam. "I've been perfectly polite."

"Polite, yes. I said sweet talk."

"Whatever you say, Bruce Banner."

Bar looked like it had been picked up fully intact and moved from Williamsburg to Alphabet City. Tacky, weird art hung on the walls, and loud music played on the speakers by That Band no one's ever heard of. Rufus moved around packs of patrons who probably haunted the front doors of NYU, SVA, and FIT by day, and noted that he sort of looked a lot like them. To an extent, anyway. Lots of skinny kids in preripped jeans. Rufus's wardrobe came about its torn aesthetic through authentic wear and tear.

He slid up to the bar—cleaner, *much cleaner* than Queenie's—and waved a woman over. She was pretty. Brown curls to her shoulders, nose ring, some nice tattoos. Total lesbian, though.

"Hey," she said, voice low and smooth. "Something to drink?"

Sweet talk. Christ. Rufus wouldn't be able to sweet talk a paper bag if his life depended on it. He had two speeds— snark and asshole. It was that redheaded disposition, folks said.

But still, he smiled his best smile and said, "Um, no, not right now. Actually, I'm looking for someone. Maybe you can help. Have you been working the last week? Friday or Saturday?"

Tiny lines at the corners of her mouth were the only hint of a frown. "Yeah. Both nights, actually."

Rufus leaned both elbows on the counter while talking. "He's a big guy. My height, but like three of me across, with blond hair."

"Your boyfriend?" Then she nodded at Sam. "Or his?"

"Huh?" Rufus looked at Sam, then shook his head. "Not—*no*. He's not my boyfriend, the guy I'm looking for. I mean, neither of them are. No one is anyone's boyfriend. That guy's just a friend," Rufus concluded as he jabbed a thumb in Sam's direction before staring at his feet.

One eyebrow went up. She didn't mouth the word *friend*, but it was obvious that she layered plenty of subject onto it. "Nobody like that. You can see what our clientele is like; I'm pretty sure I would have remembered your big, butch friend."

Ok, that time she put a little spin on the word.

"Thanks," Rufus mumbled to the floor. "What about a lost iPhone? Black. Obnoxiously large."

"Actually, yes. Holy shit. I've been holding on to it, hoping somebody would come by." Then she smiled. "Kidding. But we can take a look in the lost and found."

"That was mean," Rufus said.

"Tell my girlfriend. She's always looking for a reason to spank me."

"All you bartenders on A are nuts." Rufus pushed back from the bar.

"Hold on. I said we'd check lost and found, right? Meet me at the end of the bar." She glanced at Sam. "What about big, dark, and brooding? He looks like he needs a drink."

Rufus didn't bother to look at Sam that time. He could place the other man's expression just fine. "Yeah, probably. Something on tap. He'll pay for it. I'm a cheap date."

The girl's nose ring caught the light as she grinned. "So this is a date?"

"*No.*"

She expertly filled a glass, leaving just the right amount of head, and slid it across the bar. "Hey," she called to Sam. "Eight bucks. Freckles here says he's a cheap date and you like draft."

Sam turned a slow, murderous look on Rufus before pulling the wad of bills from his pocket. As Sam paid, Rufus hurried to the end of the bar to wait for the woman. Eight bucks had seemed like a lot, but Rufus hadn't drank at a bar in years, so his sense of cost was a little dated. It was easier to get piss drunk in the comfort of his home on gin toxic enough to scrub a tub clean. And it cost nothing, especially when Rufus was able to lift a bottle from his permanently stoned neighbor.

"Thanks for checking," Rufus said when the bartender joined him a minute later. "Sort of at wits' end trying to find this phone."

She shrugged. "Kind of hope it's in here. But kind of not, you know? I don't even know what to do if it is. Do I give it to you? I mean, I guess I'll have to ask Geoffrey. He's the manager." She lifted a cardboard box onto the bar top, slid it halfway to Rufus, and waved for him to join her in rummaging through the contents.

Rufus poked at a few odds and ends. Someone had lost a shoe. Not a pair of shoes. Just the one. That'd probably been a rough night for Converse size 9. He found a fake ID at the bottom of the box, a pair of fashion glasses—the sort with no prescription—and one condom. Still in the

73

foil, at least.

"I don't see it," he muttered.

"Did you lose that?" Sam said, nudging Rufus and looking at the condom. He had joined them without Rufus hearing him, which seemed impossible for the big lug.

Rufus visibly jumped at Sam's voice and hissed, "*Jesus*." He stared at the condom for a beat before giving Sam side-eye. "No. I did not." He shoved the lost and found back across the bar.

"No joy," the bartender said. "Sorry about that."

Rufus shrugged, waited until the woman left for a new customer, then asked Sam, "That beer worth eight bucks?"

"You're about to find out," Sam said, passing it to Rufus. "I don't drink alone, and I don't drink domestic. Not when I can help it." He queried the bartender about other draft beers, settled on Sapporo, which Rufus couldn't believe they had, and the bartender moved off to get it.

Eyeing Rufus, Sam closed his index finger and thumb around Rufus's wrist. The roughness and heat of his fingers shocked Rufus, especially after Sam's earlier comment about being touched. Sam met Rufus's gaze for a long moment, murmured, "Still dainty," and then called down the bar for an order of loaded nachos. Then, releasing Rufus, he pulled out a stool and sat.

Rufus put his hand to his chest, rubbing his wrist. He could still feel the impressions Sam left behind. Like his touch had seared through flesh and muscle and tendon and branded itself on Rufus's bones. "We're staying?" he asked, hearing how stupid and obvious the question was even as he spoke.

Sam hooked the stool next to him with his heel and touched the tip of Rufus's ear. "They're doing it again."

Rufus plopped down on the barstool. He tugged his beanie off and set it on the counter beside his beer, showing off that, yes, in fact, his ears were pink from a blush. "I'm fair-skinned."

"It's cute."

Cute. There it was again.

"Are you fucking with me? Or should I say thanks?"

Sam just gave him a slow blink. "I like it when guys say thanks." Then, without waiting, "What's your last name? Your real one, I mean."

Rufus looked away. He stared at his reflection in the mirror above the bar, realized what a mess his hair was from the beanie, and vigorously finger-combed it. He grabbed the tall glass next and took a long pull. Rufus lied. He always did. A petty thief turned CI didn't share information that could be traced. That's why he tossed his burner every few weeks. That's why the apartment he'd grown up in wasn't technically in his name. It's why every scumbag he'd helped the NYPD put away over the past few years thought he was a Smith. A Brown. A Baker.

Rufus put the half-empty beer down, looked sideways at Sam, and suddenly it was so difficult to lie. So difficult to spin a whopper to someone who'd dropped their entire life to come here and seek justice for Jake. "O'Callaghan."

"Rufus O'Callaghan," Sam said. The bartender brought him his beer, and Sam took a drink. His hand shook in the middle of it, and beer spilled down his chin, spattering his legs. Swearing, Sam set the glass down hard and grabbed a handful of napkins. He mopped at himself for a minute. Then he shoved the wad of wet paper away. Then he shoved the drink away. He put his hands in his pockets and stared straight ahead.

It was impossible to pretend Rufus hadn't noticed the shakes this time. So he asked, because he was always of the mindset to just rip the Band-Aid off instead of peeling inch by inch. "PTSD?"

Sam laughed, a hard, sharp bark. "No." For a moment,

it seemed like that would be the end of it, but then he added, "It's called essential tremor. It's not a big deal."

Rufus screwed with his hair again. "Do you take anything for it?"

"Not right now."

"Oh."

"So." Sam cleared his throat, and some of the stiffness in his posture eased as he glanced around. "This your scene?"

Rufus snorted. "Hell no. This place is for new-age punk kids who've never heard of CBGB."

Sam actually smiled at that; this time, he managed not to spill any of the beer, although the tremor was still noticeable. When he set the glass down, he leaned on an elbow and turned to face Rufus, his eyes a mile deep and searching. "Tell me about the origins of punk." He shrugged. "Or tell me about anything, really. Tell me a Rufus thing."

Rufus's eyebrows shot up. That seemed a simple enough request: *Tell me something about yourself.* But had he ever been asked that before? "I'm a Gemini. That's what people usually lead with...."

"Gemini is the Twins, right? Christ, are there two of you?" But he said it with a grin.

"No. Thank God. I can't even handle me."

"You've handled yourself pretty well today." Sam slid the wadded napkins back and forth across the bar, exterminating the lingering drops. "The cop you were working with got murdered, someone tried to scare you off, and you kept coming. I think you've been handling yourself really well for a really long time. Hell, you even handled me when I was a total asshole." He shoved the napkins away again. "Sorry about that, earlier."

"You really don't have to bullshit me."

Sam swiveled on the stool, and he caught Rufus's seat and spun him so they faced each other. Sam's body bracketed Rufus's, and Rufus was aware again of the difference in size, of the way Sam sat, of their proximity and the radiant heat of Sam's thighs pincered at his knees. Sam cocked his head as though searching for something, but when he spoke, his voice was neutral.

"I never bullshit about what's important to me. And you still haven't told me a Rufus thing. Not a real one."

Rufus's heart was beating so hard now that he thought it might crack his sternum. Was it because Sam was close—*so close*—touching, even, right fucking there for the taking? Or because he'd suggested Rufus was somehow important and no one but Jake had ever made him feel that way? Fuck. Maybe neither. Maybe it was merely because Sam was waiting for a piece of meaningful trivia to keep the conversation alive, something that would ultimately backfire, fuck Rufus over seven ways to Sunday, all because Sam's thighs were warm and powerful and—he *hadn't stopped staring.*

Rufus could barely hear the music over blood rushing in his ears. He wondered if the flutter in his throat was visible. It had to be. It felt like a panicked bird trying to escape. His entire body was practically vibrating from the pressure and warmth of Sam's touch through jeans and it was a painful reminder of how goddamn starved Rufus was for physical affection. He'd have given his left nut then and there for bare skin, caresses, a kiss.

But Sam didn't like to be touched. So no way was this going any further.

"I'm ticklish," Rufus blurted out suddenly. "The backs of my knees." He smiled and laughed too loudly. "Want to hear a story about that?"

Sam didn't answer, didn't move, didn't even seem to breathe.

"I was having sex with this guy—well, I was about to, anyway. Threw my legs up over his shoulders, but the jackass was wearing some ridiculous polyester shirt he wouldn't take off, and every time he moved, the material scratched my knees and I started laughing. He thought I was laughing at him. He got angry. I tried to tell him what was wrong, but I was laughing so hard, I couldn't breathe."

But Sam wasn't laughing. The bartender brought the loaded nachos, and Sam handed her several bills and slid the food toward Rufus. After another moment, Sam said, "I'll ask you again later. A real Rufus thing. Think about it."

"That's real. I've never told anyone about it."

Sam was still sitting sideways, ignoring—or oblivious to—the shift in posture and conversation. He shrugged and said, "It's a funny story."

Rufus picked up a chip topped with melted cheese and onions and meat, put it into his mouth, licked his finger, and asked around the bite, "What about a Sam thing, then?"

"One for one," Sam said. "I told you about—" He made a gesture to take in the spilled beer. "You still owe me a real thing. Not a story about how you limp-dicked a guy by laughing at him."

Rufus shook his head, grabbed another chip, and ate it. "I don't think so."

Sam smiled suddenly, touching his own ear this time. "Doing it again."

"I *know*. I can't help it. It's an Irish thing."

"It's—" Sam looked like he might say cute again, but instead, he said, "It's new. For me, anyway. You're new. Different. Christ, whatever, I don't know what I'm saying. This whole place has really fucked with my head." Sam riffled his hair, put his head in his hand, and then took a long drink of Sapporo. "Never mind. I'll stop pointing it out."

But Rufus slid forward on the stool, inching his knees a bit further between Sam's thighs. "I'm different in a good way?"

A long, slow exhalation followed. Then, simply: "I think so."

Rufus fiddled with his hair in order to keep his hands busy. He opened his mouth to respond, but whatever he was intending to say was forgotten and he blurted out, "Holy shit." Rufus grabbed Sam's shoulder, jerked back like he'd stuck his hand on a stovetop burner, then shifted on his stool in order to use Sam as a shield.

Sam stiffened, his whole body locking up, and Rufus remembered: *I don't like being touched.* When Sam spoke, his voice was a harsh whisper. "What? What's going on?"

"Behind you—don't look. He's sitting at a table near the back."

Sam didn't quite close his eyes, but they narrowed, and he said, "Yankees cap on backward? Dark T-shirt? About your age?"

"Yes, that's—what the hell?" Rufus met Sam's narrowed gaze. "Do you have eyes in the back of your head?"

Sam just pointed at a mirror.

Cheeks flushed pink, Rufus leaned a little to the right and peered around Sam's shoulder. "Fuck, fuck, fuck."

"Who is he? Why is this such a big deal?" Then Sam's voice changed, suddenly hard with a note Rufus couldn't quite place. "Ex-boyfriend?"

Rufus made a disbelieving sound in the back of his throat and straightened. "He's who I saw. When I found Jake."

Sam glanced down, repeating the words, the tone of his voice making lights go on in Rufus's head: the phone pinging from Tompkins Square Park, and now this guy was here, waiting.

"This is the guy who killed Jake?" Sam asked. "This is the guy who tried to kill you?"

Rufus jerked his head once in a nod.

CHAPTER
EIGHT

The worst part was that Sam couldn't turn around; Rufus had told him not to. Everything else in Bar went on as usual: the clink of glasses, the miasma of hops and industrial nacho cheese, pickled jalapenos sharp over everything else. One part of Sam itched to get a second look at this asshole. But another part of Sam was distracted by how close Rufus was, by the faint smell of his soap, by the way a clump of hair over his ear stuck straight out in a fiery mess. Part of him was distracted by the way it had felt for Rufus to touch his shoulder. Overwhelming, that was the only word for it. The heat of his hand, the rasp of the inside-out cotton tee, the pressure.

"What's he doing now?" Sam asked.

Rufus took another quick glance. "Looks like he's

texting."

Reaching past Rufus, Sam snagged the black beanie. Then he tugged it down on Rufus's head, tucking the red mess up under the wool, hiding a grin at Rufus's expression. He liked the way Rufus's hair felt; it was silky soft, softer than just about any guy's hair that Sam had felt, and he liked how it looked against his fingers.

But all he said was "You're kind of a sore thumb, you know."

Rufus slid his sunglasses on. "Beanie isn't so stupid now, is it?"

"I'd never tell a hipster that his beanie looked dumb. It'd be like pushing a toddler off a trike."

"I'm going to kick your ass later." Rufus took another look toward Yankee. "He's putting the phone away."

"He's going to move soon."

"Yeah. Shit. Like right now—he's getting up."

"When he gets to the door, tell me. I'll go. You count to thirty and follow. If he looks back, I'd rather have him see me; he knows you."

Rufus had nodded automatically, then shook his head and looked at Sam. "What? *No way*. You're not going alone. Not even for thirty seconds."

Sam rolled his shoulders, ready to move when Rufus gave the word. He kept his gaze fixed on the redhead as he said, to get a rise, "I want a weekend, just a solid weekend. By the end of it, you'll know how to sit, stay, speak when spoken to."

Rufus raised a finger and jabbed the air in front of Sam. "Forget kicking your ass—I'm tossing you into oncoming traffic." Rufus quickly shifted in order to free his knees from between Sam's legs. "He's moving."

Sam launched toward the door. He thought he was pretty fast, but Rufus kept up, and they plunged out onto the street together. Night had come down, mantling the city, only it wasn't night, Sam realized. Night wasn't night in Manhattan. Instead of Arkansas nights, Dakota nights, clean air and the dark and the stars, Manhattan night was just a shittier, grimier day, the light smudged like charcoal between the buildings. Yankee guy was already jogging across the street toward Tompkins Square Park. A white Escalade blitzed in front of Sam and Rufus, and then a Corolla with Uber and Lyft stickers on the windshield came the other way. By the time they had an opening, Yankee was past the fence, disappearing into the deeper shadows under the trees.

Sam and Rufus jogged after him. Not a full run, not a sprint, nothing that would make so much noise as to give them away. Sam felt the air change as they passed under the first old oak, the drop in temperature, the relative cool wicking along his skin. He breathed in the lingering smell of sun-warmed mulch and broken leaves, and, still there, Dial soap from Rufus right next to him. Adrenaline heightened everything; the world, always so sharp and intrusive for Sam, took on new edges. He did what he always did: he kept going.

Yankee was a darker shadow up ahead. When he turned, scouting, Sam caught a handful of Rufus's shirt, and they both slowed. A streetlight deeper in the park limned branches, traced the silhouette of the ball cap. Then, a secondary glow lit up Yankee: the phone, the screen held close to his face as he considered something. Another message? Reviewing instructions? No breeze here. On the street, a girl laughed, talking loudly about Pablo's bad behavior when he came over for Sunday dinner. Off to the right, behind the chain-link of a basketball court, a ball bounced hard with a thump that sounded shockingly loud in the park's stillness.

Then Yankee was moving again. Sam's knuckles brushed Rufus's belly beneath the cotton, and he felt the faint tremble there, the careful release of breath. He shook his hand free from Rufus's shirt, his fingers aching, and they followed. Yankee kept to the asphalt walkways, occasionally studying the phone again. When he turned down another path, Rufus stopped Sam, a hand held in front of his chest.

He pointed to the fencing surrounding the walking path, made a shape in the air vaguely resembling a C, then, with a bit of a run to get the momentum, vaulted over the fence to cut across the grass and meet Yankee on the other side. Rufus turned and waved Sam to join him.

Copying the movement, Sam landed easily on the other side of the fence. Then he and Rufus moved into the trees, skirting a line of boxwood, then a nasty blackberry bramble that nobody had uprooted, Sam ignoring Rufus's grin when he hissed at a long line of scratches on his arm. Like Rufus's touch earlier, the scratches were overwhelming; it was only practice and long years that let Sam shuffle them under everything else and keep his head in the game. They kept going until they reached a copse of cherries. When a shadow moved on the other side of the screen of leaves and branches, both men froze.

This time, Yankee came toward them, materializing out of the darkness as he emerged into a small clearing ahead. The ambient light of the city painted him in a chalky glow, the white letters of the cap bright in contrast to everything else. Yankee took a few paces in one direction, then back, then off in a third, then back. Sam felt a moment of frustration; had they followed him this far for nothing? Was Yankee looking for a place to pee? Was this some weird, exhibitionist jerk-off game?

Then a branch cracked off to the left, and Sam grabbed Rufus's arm without thinking about it. Rufus was trembling; not shaking, not fear—or not just fear, anyway—but tremors. Compressed energy. This was personal for him too. Jake had meant something to him too. And Sam found himself adding to the mental list: cute and funny and vulnerable and expressive and clever and resourceful and, now, brave. Oh, top of the list, big bold letters: smartass.

The woman who emerged from the shadows to the left was unremarkable. Mousy brown hair in a ponytail, small head, a pant suit that had probably come off a JCPenney suits and separates rack. Sam recognized her as the woman who had interrupted his conversation with Lampo. The weak light made the rest of her features indistinguishable, but the way Yankee reacted, that was remarkable. He jerked back at her appearance. He touched his pocket like a man with a talisman.

"Where the fuck have you been?" Yankee said in a low voice that carried in the still air of the clearing.

The woman *tsk*ed. Actually *tsk*ed. "Some of us lead busy lives, Marcus. Working fifty-sixty hours a week to put away scumbags."

Rufus shifted. The muscles in his upper arm had tightened under Sam's grip at the sound of her voice.

Sam glanced at him.

Rufus seemed to know her. Enough at least that he mouthed *cop* without pulling his attention away from the scene.

"Hey," Marcus said, "first things first, we gotta get something straight. Five hundred dollars is bullshit—"

The woman shot him. The movement was clean, fluid, and unhesitating. A single shot. With a suppressor, Sam realized. Marcus dropped, flopping on the ground. His breathing had become a wet gurgle. The woman took four steps closer and shot again. Marcus's head jerked once, and then no more gurgling.

For a moment, she considered him, and then she holstered the gun. She produced something from a pocket—disposable gloves, Sam guessed—and crouched next to Marcus. Whatever she did next, the shadows obscured, but Sam had an idea that they weren't going to find Jake's phone tonight.

Except. Except Sam had his Beretta M9. He was still a decent shot; the tremors were bad when he was stressed, but he'd put in a lot of hours at the range, and he just had to hit center mass from—what? Ten yards? Fifteen? But the idea was gone as soon as it came to him. He didn't shoot unsuspecting people. He didn't shoot people at all, if he could help it. And the fact that she was a cop had thrown everything sideways.

Whatever opportunity Sam had, it passed, and the woman rose, studied the scene once more, and then walked into the copse of cherry trees. Sam waited until her steps had faded. Then he counted out sixty seconds, released Rufus's arm, and sprinted for the body.

Marcus was dead; the second shot had been to the head, a small hole—Sam was already thinking about calibers, bullet types—but enough to make sure nobody would ever hear Marcus's story. As Sam patted the body with the backs of his hands, searching for the phone, for anything, Rufus scrambled up beside him, talking in a furious whisper.

"When a cop murders in cold blood, you run the *opposite* way." Rufus motioned for Sam to follow him, to no avail. "*Come on.* That was Bridget Heckler. Jake's sergeant. Oh my God, what the fuck is going on?"

Nothing in the front pockets. Sam rocked the body, checked one back pocket. He rocked him the other way. Pay dirt. Working the wallet loose, he let Marcus's body settle. Then, shaking his head, he said, "Phone's gone."

"It's a trophy piece now," Rufus snapped, his voice so low, it was like the sound of shoe treads on gravel. "*Sam,* we need to go. She gave this fucker a third eye."

Sam nodded, pushing up from the body, and he

motioned for Rufus to lead them out of the park. They took a different route, avoiding the brambles and boxwood, hopping a different section of fence, cutting along the path until they came out of the park near the basketball court. A girl sat on a bench, trimming her weave, while two other girls in matching Knicks jerseys played a fierce one-on-one. Sam felt something unknot in his gut. A cop killing a man in a city park—nothing in him could understand that. But this, this was normal, this was life. He tucked his hands under his arms, hating how they gave him away.

They made it to the end of the block, and then Rufus froze and whispered, "Shit."

Sam followed his gaze and saw Heckler walking the cross street toward them. She seemed to see them at the same time, and the look of shocked recognition on her face would have been comical under other circumstances, a kind of Tom-and-Jerry look when Tom's just had the rug pulled out from under him.

All of this passed through his head in an instant before Rufus grabbed his wrist and pulled him into a run.

CHAPTER
NINE

Rufus didn't let go of Sam.

It didn't matter that Sam could keep pace. It didn't matter that Sam could hold his own, that he was armed. It didn't matter that Sam had tensed up like a stone statue when Rufus had grabbed his shoulder at Bar.

Because for as long as Rufus held on, Sam was right there.

Still breathing.

Heart still beating.

Rufus made a sharp right on Avenue A and cut across St. Marks Place. The street was bustling with evening business—tattoo parlors that'd been inking Black Flag's symbol of rebellion since before he'd been born, as well as a smattering of used record and alternative clothing shops that Rufus knew firsthand welcomed customers of all ages and backgrounds, because any kind of attitude of seniority, in his opinion, went against the very fucking notion of punk. He'd been blacklisted from more than one store within the three-block radius after seeing staff treat young customers who didn't *look the part* like wannabes. He'd regaled the employees with a dissertation on why they weren't punk, told them where they could shove their elitist attitudes, and after being tossed out, had directed the group of kids to better, more accommodating shops.

Nestled between these establishments of youth and anarchy were those desperate to look as if they belonged. A chain burrito restaurant. A chain floral store. A nationwide bank. Bright, clean industrial lights blazed from inside their glass storefronts in stark contrast to the decades of history and grime around them. The irony of corporations bullying their way into prime real estate and trying to suck on the teat of the New York underground was not lost on the locals.

Rufus turned left at the end of the block, raced down First Avenue, and narrowly avoided plowing into a couple exiting an Indian restaurant. The woman tripped backward into her date, who shouted a string of obscenities in Rufus and Sam's wake. But they were fine. They didn't matter. And Sam's hand was still in his, so Rufus kept running.

Rufus shifted his focus to a plane of existence where he thought prey running for their lives also went. One where he could no longer feel the frantic beats of his heart or the searing burning in his lungs. He couldn't hear the racket of the sleepless city around him. He saw nothing but the overhead street signs counting down Seventh—Sixth—Fifth—God, they were almost there.

Almost safe.

Making another sudden right on Fourth Street, Rufus

darted across evening traffic. If tires skidded, brakes squealed, and horns blared, he didn't hear it. They ran over locked cellar doors that bounced ominously under their collective weight, past a row of trash and recycling bins, a bakery shuttered for the night, and then up half a dozen steps to a very unassuming apartment building. Rufus yanked a ring of keys free from his pocket and unlocked the front door. He barreled through the landing, tapped a mailbox mounted to the wall within the cramped vestibule, and led Sam up four flights of stairs without stopping until they reached 4D.

Rufus unlocked that door, put his weight against it, and forced it free from the swollen, crooked frame. Only after the door had been shoved closed, two deadbolts and a security chain engaged, did Rufus finally release the death grip he had on Sam. He took several unsteady breaths while staring through the peephole.

But Heckler never came up the stairs.

Never came creeping down the hall.

Never knocked on the door.

Rufus flipped a light switch on the wall and walked deeper into the studio. An unmade bed was shoved against the far wall underneath two windows that overlooked the street. To the right was what barely qualified as a kitchen: two overhead cupboards, an ancient and discolored fridge, half a countertop with a half-sized sink, and two stovetop burners. The other side of the studio was strewn with what amounted to *stuff* and *things* on the floor, since Rufus had little in the way of furniture. Two piles of clothes—one clean, the other dirty. Besides that, a few dozen books carefully organized into three separate piles, all marked on the spine with New York Public Library. The one door in the apartment was to the immediate right of the front entrance and down a short hall, housing a closet-sized bathroom.

Rufus dropped his jean jacket, beanie, and sunglasses on the floor before his shoulders sagged. Almost like it was too difficult to stand, he got down into a crouched position and hugged his knees. "What the fucking fuck is going on?" Rufus asked, voice barely more than a whisper.

Sam moved to the windows, parting the blinds with a finger, the plastic slats clicking against each other.

"She shot him," Rufus said between breaths.

"Does she know your name? Heckler, is that what you said? Does she know where you live?"

Rufus slowly drew back up to his full height. "I was Jake's CI, but she'd have access to my information, I guess."

"What matters right now is how long it will take for her to find us. She killed Marcus and took the phone; that means she was involved at some level with Jake's death. And that means she already wanted you dead." Sam stepped away from the blinds; they swooshed back against the glass. His gaze roamed the apartment: the books, the clothes, the books, the bathroom, the books, the fridge, the books. "Now we're witnesses to a murder. She has to remove us."

"Heckler doesn't know we saw it, though." Rufus yanked his high-tops off and took a seat on the edge of the mattress.

"Really?" Sam said.

"*Really*," Rufus echoed before glancing sideways. "Wait, what do you mean? Yeah, really. We could have been taking a stroll around the neighborhood."

"Ok. Fine. Let's pretend that's what it was. You're Heckler. You just killed a guy, shot him in cold blood in a public park. And that guy, he just happens to be carrying the cell phone of a dead cop. She grabs the phone, leaves the park, and sees—well, fuck me backward, in the sheerest of fucking coincidences, it's Jake's informant. The one who was supposed to be dead. But, hey, he's probably just out for his evening fucking constitutional."

Rufus's hands were tingling, the blood leaving his extremities and his vision morphing like he was going through a tunnel. God help him if his anxiety actually caused him to pass out in front of Sam.

Tucking his hands under his arms, Sam paced. Tried to pace. The small room made it difficult, and even with black spots whirling in his vision, Rufus felt a moment of—pity? compassion?—watching Sam struggle to control the tremors.

"I can't prove it," Sam said, his voice locked down again. "I'm telling you I saw her face, and that woman knew who you were and was surprised to see you walking around."

"I might vomit."

Sam glanced around the apartment, grabbed a popcorn bucket off the counter—purchased on one of Rufus's rare mother-son outings, vintage plastic, circa 1999—and pressed it into Rufus's hands.

Rufus held on to the bucket for a moment, gripping the plastic hard enough that his fingertips squeaked against it. But he didn't have anything to clean it out with if he upchucked, and then the smell would permeate the plastic and it'd be one more moment in his life when everything turned to dogshit. Rufus carefully set the bucket on the floor beside the bed, planted his hands on his knees, put his head down, and took a few breaths. Strangled breaths at first, but then he thought of the yoga book on the floor in the return pile. Not that Rufus had been interested in taking up the practice, before or after reading the text, but there'd been a segment on the art of breathing in chapter two.

He walked himself through those paragraphs from memory. *Notice you are breathing. Be aware of it. Is your breath fast? Slow it down. Deeply now, from your toes, through your core, then release.* The topic had gotten more complex after that. Something about classic pranayama techniques, alternate nostril breathing, (which, aside from when he had a cold, Rufus had no idea how to do), but the principal remained.

Be aware.

He felt a little better after a minute or two.

"I don't know what to do," Sam said, and somehow the tank managed to perch on the edge of the mattress like a bird on a birdbath. "Can you tell me what you need?"

"I'm ok," Rufus insisted, slowly raising his head to look at Sam.

"You need to disappear for a few days. Maybe a week, tops. Do you have somewhere you can go? Somewhere no one will find you?"

"What about you?" Rufus asked.

"What about me?"

"She saw you too."

Sam just shrugged.

Rufus tugged at his hair with one hand. "So what does that shrug mean? I run away and you go stomping around New York, throwing your dick around?"

"You stay safe," Sam said. "You did your part, getting us this far."

Keeping his hand stuck in his hair, Rufus said, "You have no idea the level of depravity you'd be walking into. You don't know anyone, what some of these people are capable—"

Sam kissed him. Then, pulling back, he screwed up his face almost like he wasn't sure what he'd done. He must have figured it out pretty fast because he leaned in for another kiss. This one was better, in Rufus's limited experience: softer, slower, more assured. Not tender. Not even close to tender. More on the demanding end of the spectrum. But, like everything with the tank, it was a confusing mix.

Sam's hand found Rufus's waist as he kissed him again, rolling him onto his back, chasing him with kisses. That hand played with the hem of Rufus's T-shirt, inching it up, the fingers tracing what felt like a sunrise across Rufus's belly, an arc of heat and light that made Rufus want to squeeze his eyes shut. Sam rucked up the shirt higher, splaying one hand across Rufus's chest, the calluses sending Rufus's brain into overdrive, and he remembered reading *A Brief Guide to the Ancient World*, and the index, *pumice, erotic uses of*, and then Sam was pulling back.

Rufus was flying. And not the brief suspension before the lurch, the fall, the *pop* and *snap*, but like he was a projectile from a slingshot. Falling up into the stars, rocketing through the troposphere, the stratosphere, still going—still flying.

Grinning, Sam drew his touch back to fingertips, tracing something on Rufus's chest. "Freckles," he whispered, leaning down for another kiss. His lips touched Rufus's.

Freckles.

Maddie's voice cut through the static in Rufus's brain, echoing that nickname over and over. Then it was like someone had switched the knob on an old television and the black-and-white snow was replaced with images of his surreal day. Eating at BlueMoon with Sam watching him from across the table. Rummaging through Natalie's bedroom. Tromping through Alphabet City. Sam working that beanie back over Rufus's hair. Yankee's gurgling last breaths. Heckler pocketing Jake's missing phone.

"Stop," Rufus said, crashing back to earth breathless and panicked. "Hang on."

Sam stopped, but he had that little furrow again, the one that had made Rufus think about crossword puzzles in bed. The *cute* one, although Rufus shoved the thought away as soon as it came.

"What?" Sam asked.

"Jake's dead. And his killer had his own brains blown out. I can't do this right now."

Stretching back, Sam worked his shoulders. Rufus was suddenly reminded of how big Sam was, towering over him like that. "Ok," Sam said slowly. "But it's just a fuck."

There it is, Rufus thought. Like every guy before Sam he'd dropped trou for. "Yeah. Just a fuck." Rufus shimmied out from underneath and got to his feet. That nervous sense of hope that'd been growing like a balloon in his chest popped like a needle had pricked it.

Riffling his hair, Sam stared at him. "What's going on with you? We're both feeling shitty. I'm horny. You desperately need to get boned. I don't get what the big deal is." Then Sam rolled one huge shoulder. "Besides, you're so damn cute, the way you get protective and go on and on."

Rufus had turned to stare at Sam as he spoke, a line working its way between his brows as he frowned. "No, thanks," he said simply.

"Fine."

"Good."

"It's just sex, Rufus. It's supposed to be fun. A way to blow off some steam. Feel alive."

"I know how dopamine works—don't talk to me like I'm stupid."

Something had changed in the room.

Sam slid off the bed. "Yeah," he said. "Sorry."

"Forget it." Rufus walked toward the bathroom. "You can stay," he called over his shoulder. "But no sex." Then he closed the door, locked it, and sat on the toilet lid.

Heavy steps moved in the other room, and then Sam's voice filtered through the closed door. "Probably better if I find somewhere else tonight."

Rufus wiped his nose on the back of his hand and said, "There's a... a YMCA on the West Side. Cheap hostel rooms."

"Yeah, thanks." The silence that followed was its own kind of thunder, and then Sam said, "Are you ok? Like, can I get you something? Do something?"

"I'm fine," Rufus told the door. "But promise you won't go running off half-cocked tomorrow without at least saying something to me first."

The doorknob jittered, as though Sam might have tested it—or maybe just bumped it. When Sam spoke, it was that same locked-down voice that gave nothing away. "I think it might be better if we go our own ways. I don't want to drag you into something. You should lie low for a few days. Take a trip or something. And...." More of that tremendous silence. "Thanks."

Then the steps moved away, and the apartment's front door opened and closed, and the old boards in the hallway creaked away from the room.

Rufus stared at his hands until they'd gotten so blurry, he couldn't see more than something abstract—like the hands Pablo Picasso would paint. And it pissed him off that Sam walking out that door could make Rufus cry like Alice had during her adventures in Wonderland.

CHAPTER
TEN

Sam walked west—he figured west was the best way to get to the West Side, although, fuck, in this city, who the hell even knew—five blocks before he remembered that he'd left his ruck checked with Greyhound. For thirty seconds he stared at an orange Don't Walk, considering leaving it until tomorrow. Then he thought of what it would be like. Bad enough to sleep on cheap linens, smelling like cheap detergent, only to wake up and wear the same clothes with his sweat and the day's dirt on them. Sam had a lot of tricks, by this point in his life, for dealing with how his senses betrayed him, but that combination sounded like too much.

He trekked back to Port Authority Bus Terminal. The grayscale darkness shrank in places, pushed back by marquee bulbs or flashing neon signs, and in other places it pressed down like a layer of smoke. On one corner, two guys were passing a joint, laughing loud enough to chase off a trio of women who looked like they were doing their own self-guided *Sex and the City* tour. Two blocks later, a white girl with locs was packing up her guitar while she argued with another girl over whose turn it was to pay the electric bill. He passed a diner that looked a lot cleaner— almost impersonally antiseptic—than the BlueMoon. And he saw himself in the glass, a ghost, and had the idea of going back, buzzing up to Rufus's apartment, having a fuck-all fight, really going at it, even though he wasn't sure what they'd fight about.

He got his bag. He walked the blocks back to the YMCA that Rufus had mentioned. He got a private room, telling himself he'd be good, but he didn't pay for the private room with the private bathroom, because, fuck, maybe he was going to change his mind about being good.

In the room, he unpacked: the dopp kit, everything organized; a clean white tee, already inside out; a fresh pair of jeans; socks, already inside out. More: travel pods of All Free and Clear; a nub, in its plastic travel case, of Dr. Bronner's Pure Castile Soap, Baby Unscented; sensitive-skin lube; a condom; his towel with the loose threads on one seam. He stripped, wrapped the towel around his waist, and headed to the bathroom.

A door stood open; inside, two guys lounged on bunk beds. They had to be young, in their twenties, and they had light brown skin. One had a nice beard. The other had a mole on his jaw. The one with the beard was on the bottom bunk, wearing nothing but red CK briefs. Sam couldn't tell what the one with the mole was wearing—he was on the top bunk—but the guy didn't have a shirt, and he leaned over the rail to watch Sam.

Sam paused in the doorway. He looked at one. He looked at the other. He waited until the guys looked at each other, and the one with the mole laughed.

No need to smile or nod or raise an eyebrow; Sam just unwrapped the towel, slung it over his shoulder, and kept going down the hall. The bathroom was empty at this hour. He found the handicap-accessible shower with a no-barrier entry and a curtain instead of a door, turned the water to hot, and stepped under the spray.

Two minutes later, the curtain rattled on its rings, and the guy with the mole stepped inside. Naked. Hard. His eyes roving all over Sam. "Hey. I wanted to tell you something. If I rated you from one to ten, you'd be a nine because I'm the one you're missing."

It wasn't really worth answering. Sam tilted his head, inviting the guy under the spray of water.

"Where you from, big guy?" Mole asked, sliding close.

"No talking," Sam said.

Mole splayed his hands across Sam's chest and moved them down to his hips. "Why not? You've got a sexy voice."

Planting a hand in the guy's chest, Sam gave a shove. Not too hard, but hard enough. "No talking. Or leave."

Mole gave Sam a pout—was that supposed to be cute? But when it clearly didn't have the desired reaction, he simply turned and pressed back against Sam.

After that, Sam knew how things were supposed to go. He'd done this a lot. A lot of guys. A lot of places. A lot of quiet that filled up with the slap of flesh and a few strangled groans. When he'd finished, he pushed Mole toward the curtain and turned his face into the spray.

Getting out of the shower, Mole wiped wet hair away from his face and tried one more, if not the worst, pick-up line Sam had ever heard. "So, I lost my phone number. Can I have yours?"

Sam kept his face in the spray, holding his breath, hot

water needling him, until he heard the curtain rings jingle again and he knew he was alone.

After the shower, back in his room, he lay on top of the sheets. The air was too warm even with the AC chugging; he was sweating. He closed his eyes. He tried to run through the train timetables that he'd passed twenty minutes on the bus memorizing, but he kept mixing up the 6 and the 6 Express, and it made him so mad, he had to count down from a thousand by primes. Then he tried constellations: Orion, the Big Dipper, Cassiopeia, Taurus, Gemini. But Gemini got him riled up all over again—*Christ, are there two of you?*—and Sam started thinking about the maze of freckles he had glimpsed under that System of a Down shirt, the intense effort it had taken not to get lost in them, finding new patterns, constellations that he could kiss across the delicate sculpture of Rufus's chest.

Sam was panting—huge, angry breaths—as he tried to shove the thoughts away. Rufus pushing on his shoulder. Rufus saying stop. Rufus saying, *No, thanks*. Rufus's voice from behind the locked bathroom door. The hurt in it, audible no matter how Rufus tried to conceal it.

The knock at the door startled Sam up off the mattress. For a dizzy moment, he thought it was Rufus, that somehow Rufus had come here, found him, wanted to— apologize? Fuck? And then his head cleared and he knew how stupid that was. When he cracked the door, he saw the other guy, the one with the beard and red briefs. He still had the beard, but he'd lost his underwear somewhere along the way.

The fuck was quick and brutal. Sam grabbed the back of Beard's neck, wanting to grab Rufus like that, wanting to plow into Rufus until the little shit—what? Begged? Christ, why was it so hard to know what he wanted when it came to the redhead?

When he came, he saw red: wispy, mussed red, like it

had been under a beanie all day.

He kicked Beard out and slept the rest of the night without dreams.

In the morning, he woke to July sunlight and the hum of traffic. He showered again—needed more soap—and pulled on the tee and jeans and socks, laced up his boots, and repacked his ruck. Sam had a plan, and it didn't involve getting dragged down to a subway by a redheaded prick who didn't know when a good thing was happening to him. Sam still had all of Jake's e-mails, still had the lead he'd started with: a sex worker in the Ramble, someone named Juliana, someone who had tipped Jake off about whatever this big case was. So the next step was to find Juliana, gain her trust, and find out what she had told Jake.

In a small store downstairs, Sam ignored the morning waves from Beard and Mole, who stood in line holding granola and yogurt and bananas. They didn't seem upset; if anything, they seemed to find the whole thing hilarious, elbowing each other and laughing and talking to each other in what sounded like Urdu. Beard was doing a lot of explaining with the banana he held in one hand, and Sam figured everybody else in the store had gotten a pretty good accounting of last night's activities, Urdu or no Urdu. He grabbed a bottle of two-percent milk, found a protein bar, and stood in line. He tried to plan out the day while a banana did stand-in duty for him.

The problem was getting Juliana's trust. Somehow, Sam needed to convince her to talk to him. A big guy like Sam, showing up unannounced, trying to get Juliana alone? Maybe, if he offered to pay. But then, when he wanted answers, what was she going to do? Freak out? Run? Would she believe him? Sam had no idea. He had relatively little experience with sex workers, aside from occasionally dragging an enlisted guy out of a crib or a flophouse. What he needed was someone who knew the city, who knew Jake, who knew how to talk to someone like Juliana and win her over.

What he needed was Rufus.

Sam groaned as he stepped up to pay for his food. He glanced over. Beard was eyeing him, making suggestions with the banana, and Sam nodded. Beard was totally right.

Sam was fucked.

CHAPTER
ELEVEN

Rufus had measured the length of time that'd passed, sitting on the flipped-down toilet lid until his bony ass fell asleep, by the sounds of life that punctuated the silence of the old tenement. 4B across the hall came home, unlocked her door, and slammed it shut hard enough to rattle the thin walls. She was a waitress at some swanky, is-this-food-or-garnish restaurant rated one of New York City's Top Ten Must-Eats of the Summer. So it was 10:00 p.m.

Pauly Paul, the permanently stoned neighbor who'd moved into Alvin's apartment—and even after twenty years, Rufus still thought of 4C as Alvin's—came home by 10:30 p.m., after the music studio he rented space in to play drums with his band closed for the night.

Rufus heard the echo of Mr. Gonzalez directly below

him in 3D. Gonzalez had been the landlord his entire life. Since the time the East Village had been like standing on a different planet, when college girls were being dismembered in bathtubs and grandfathers were shot and robbed for ten bucks and a portable radio. Since Rufus's mother used to pace the studio floor, smoking her slim 'n sassy Misty Lights into the late hours. Since the day Rufus had been brought home from the hospital by a teen mom who had fuck-all concept of how to care for a newborn child. Gonzalez was in his seventies now, and his hearing was starting to go, so that television downstairs was cranked high enough that Rufus could pick up muffled commercials for toothpaste and reruns of *Jeopardy!* through the floor.

Rufus would often watch the Game Show Network in the evenings with Gonzalez, when he didn't want to be alone and had nowhere to go, which was always. It was a way to pass the time, and he enjoyed his landlord's gruff company. Plus, it tended to be a better decision than drinking his toxic gin alone and waking up the next day with a hangover that made him want to fucking die.

Jeopardy! reruns now put the time just after 11:00 p.m.

Rufus unlocked the bathroom and padded out. The studio was empty of course. He'd listened to Sam leave, shut the door behind himself, and Rufus had counted his steps until they faded from earshot between the fourth and third floors.

He listened to the murmur of the television downstairs for another moment, even took a step in the general direction of the door, but—

It's just a fuck.

That one throwaway statement had made Rufus so goddamn angry. Sam wasn't wrong, though. Of course it was just a fuck. They hardly knew each other and there was no emotion involved. That was on par with what Rufus's sex life consisted of—hookups where he could get it, with men he hardly knew. So why had those words cut so deep that the marrow of his bones felt disturbed?

Sam Auden.

Because Rufus had learned his name, perhaps. And because he'd not lied to Sam.

"What's your last name? Your real one, I mean."

"O'Callaghan."

In retrospect, that moment of naked honesty had already fucked Rufus over.

Jake's death was like a candle had been snuffed out and Rufus was left in the dark. He was blindly stumbling around a city that had no time or place for him, frantic for attention, affection, and for a moment—*a single moment*—Sam had hit the spark wheel on a lighter and Rufus could see again.

He wanted to be something to someone. Something more than just a fuck. And Sam thought he was cute. Sam had bought him lunch. Sam had trusted Rufus, if only briefly.

The utter desperation Rufus felt, to think anyone— Sam—would give a petty thief like himself even a second glance was so humiliating that he couldn't bear the thought of sitting with Gonzalez. His landlord would read something in his expression and just confirm what Rufus already knew: he wasn't worth loving.

And *that* thought....

"Jesus fucking Christ Almighty." Rufus grabbed the bottle of gin from atop the fridge and sat down on the bed. He unscrewed the top, let it fall to the floor, and took a swig directly from the bottle.

Audience applause echoed through the floorboards.

Sunlight found its way through the one broken blind and stabbed Rufus directly in the left eye. He winced and grabbed his head as a headache akin to a pickax driving into his brain greeted him good morning. Rufus rolled onto his side and slowly sat up. The empty gin bottle lay on the floor.

So he'd gotten smashed last night. That explained why he felt like death warmed over.

What had happened that warranted the impromptu sobfest into a bottle—?

Rufus's head shot up and his stomach lurched at the sudden motion. Yankee. Heckler. *Sam.* His stomach kept protesting as the seconds passed while he recalled the shitshow that was yesterday, and Rufus realized the queasiness was now going to be a full-on puke. He stumbled out of bed, the sheets tangled around his feet. He half ran, half fell into the bathroom and had just enough time to lift the toilet lid before he was sick. Nachos and hard liquor. Rufus ralphed again and didn't move from the floor until his stomach spasms were nothing more than dry heaves.

Rufus flushed, brushed his teeth, and managed a quick shower that helped a bit but left his head spinning. He massaged his left eye while walking naked through the studio. He crouched beside the pile of clean clothes, pawed through the threadbare options, then settled on a pair of skinny jeans tattered at the knees and a black T-shirt with a severely faded skull and crossbones on the chest. It took another minute of rummaging to find socks and underwear, but by the time Rufus had dressed himself, he vaguely resembled a living, breathing human being.

He decided to take a walk. A long walk. All the way to Hell's Kitchen, where maybe Maddie would feel bad enough for him that she could score Rufus a fried egg under the table. That seemed like a sensible decision. He'd walk off the last of the gin, and get some food and plenty of fresh air in the process. At least, as fresh as air could be on trash-collection day in the middle of July in an urban jungle. And Rufus could decide what the hell he was going to do about… everything. Because despite the hangover, he hadn't forgotten what Sam said, about needing to disappear for a few days—a week, tops.

Yeah, right. With what money?

Rufus drunk-stumbled as he yanked his Chucks on. Did he still have a job as a confidential informant? Jake was his connection, after all. He'd always made sure Rufus got paid for putting his ass on the line. Who would do that now—*Lampo*? Fuck's sake, Rufus might as well draft himself a résumé and start applying for nine-to-five jobs.

Hand on the security chain, ready to unlock the door and step out, Rufus paused as he listened to unfamiliar footsteps coming up the stairs and down the short hallway. He knew the steps of all his neighbors, their habits around the building, and the frequent guests who dropped by. Not because Rufus was intentionally a nosy shit, but because it was his one useful skill and he honest to God couldn't help himself most of the time.

Shifting his weight from one foot to the other, Rufus held his breath and looked through the peephole. On the other side was a distorted, fishbowl image of Bridget Heckler. Still petite, but now wearing a different, shapeless suit in charcoal gray. She stopped directly outside of 4D and glanced over one shoulder at 4B, who at this hour was still asleep, then at Pauly's door, who could have been sleeping, stoned, or dead. Rufus took several steps backward when she knocked on his door.

He needed a weapon.

Rufus didn't have one, though. He was better at blending in, disappearing, running away, or shoving himself into some nook or cranny until the danger passed versus trying to fight it head-on. And if he was in a real pickle, where he had no choice but to defend himself, Rufus never fought fair. He wasn't above clawing at the face or kicking a guy in the nuts if it meant escaping with his life.

"Rufus," Heckler called, her voice calm, professional, so wicked that it was like ice water in his veins. "Rufus, it's Sergeant Heckler. I worked with Detective Brower. It's important I speak with you."

"What about?" he called, already halfway across the studio.

"What you saw last night."

"Oh yeah? What'd I see?"

"I'm not going to shout through the door. Open up and let's talk about this like adults. This is a very sensitive situation—you have no idea the shit you've stepped in."

Rufus swallowed a panicked flutter in his throat and flexed his tingling fingers a few times. "I'm not opening the door," he replied, pulling his phone from his pocket. He needed to call for help—and it wouldn't be to the police. Rufus tapped the passcode, opened his scant number of text messages, and realized he'd never gotten Sam's number. Never mind that even if he *had*, what the fuck could Sam do from the West Side? He pocketed the phone again.

Heckler hammered on the door. "Rufus, open the door."

"Get bent," Rufus called back. He hurled himself across the bed, opened one of the windows, and scrambled onto the fire escape. He heard Heckler pound on the door, but he didn't stop moving. Rufus climbed down the ladder, ran across the rickety metal grating, and moved down the next set of stairs until he had to drop the last several feet onto the sidewalk below, startling the hell out of a dog-walker.

"Sorry," Rufus said breathlessly, holding his hands up when the poor girl visibly jumped and nearly lost control of the excited pack in her care.

"Rufus!"

His head snapped toward the door of the tenement. Heckler stood in the open threshold, hand hesitating at her coat. Her service weapon. Would she go for it in broad daylight? Shoot him in the forehead like she'd done with Marcus?

Rufus bolted. He ran like New York was the Labyrinth, Heckler the Minotaur, and his only chance at escaping with his life was a single thread—one tendril of hope—and it led to Sam.

Heckler was shouting for him to stop, identifying herself as police, but Rufus didn't slow. He dodged one burly civilian who thought to help the nice lady cop, and kept running west. If Sam had even gone to the Y like Rufus suggested—no, he didn't even let himself consider the alternative. Sam *had*. Rufus trusted his gut and could swear he felt the tug between them pull him along.

He slid down the handrail of the Broadway-Lafayette subway station, shoved through the morning crowds, and jumped the turnstile as an Uptown B was pulling in. He walked the platform to the far end in order to board the last car, but before he made it, even over the rumble of 85,000 pounds of train and screeching brakes, Rufus heard Heckler's voice telling him to *stop at once*.

The train doors opened and the mass exodus began. Rufus pushed through the passengers getting off and started running through the crowded, cramped car. He passed the middle door and caught sight of Heckler bullying her way inside. Unable to get off at the last door, Rufus opened the door between cars and moved ahead to the next one. All the seats and most of the standing room was taken. Passengers swore at Rufus as he slammed into them, tripped over bags, and knocked coffees out of hands.

"Stand clear of the closing doors, please," said the automated voice, and then the B was rolling out of the station.

Rufus heard the emergency exit open behind him, the sound of wind and steel briefly filling the car as Heckler determinedly followed. Rufus didn't stop moving. He reached the third car, then the fourth by the time the B came to a stop at West Fourth.

He looked over his shoulder and watched Heckler. She shouted *NYPD* again, and the sardines in the can managed to make room for her to come at Rufus. He waited one second, *another*, made like he was going to jump between cars again, but as soon as the safety recording told passengers to mind the doors, Rufus lunged out them and fell onto the platform. He rolled over, looked up, and watched Heckler bang on the closed door with her fist before pointing at him—finger aimed like a gun. Then the train vanished into the tunnel, stirring up hot air and loose newspaper pages in its wake.

"You ok?" a businessman asked from where he sat on one of the few available seats against the wall.

Rufus got to his feet and brushed himself off. "Morning commutes are a killer."

By the time Rufus caught the next Uptown B, disembarked at Columbus Circle, walked to West Sixty-Third Street, and saw the overhead flag of the YMCA flapping in the morning breeze, he'd already run through the full gamut of human reactions to danger.

Anger.

Fear.

Exhaustion.

And now, finally, *relief.*

Rufus pulled open the door and walked through the lobby of the Y. There was some kind of shop behind him and to the left, judging by the *ping* of a register, two elevators along the far wall, and the cool air had the faint tang of chlorine, likely wafting through the AC system from the pool on the premises.

He went to the front desk, and while yanking his jean jacket off, asked, "Do you have a Sam Auden staying as a guest?" Rufus knew he probably looked half-insane to the nice-looking blonde woman on the other side of this conversation. His face was flushed from all the running, adrenaline, and unrelenting heat, and Rufus was sweating everywhere. He'd just showered too, dammit.

"I'm sorry, we can't give out information on our guests," the clerk replied.

"It's important."

"I understand—"

"No, you don't," Rufus interrupted. "You don't need to tell me his room number, just call it yourself and say there's a redhead here to see him. He'll know what that means."

Her eyebrows, by this point, had reached her hairline. "Sir, I can't do that."

"I'm not leaving until I talk to him."

"Please don't be difficult." She picked up the receiver but said, "I'll have to call my manager."

"Lady, you don't want to see me at 'difficult.'"

"Rufus?"

Rufus spun, nearly overextending himself. There was Sam, standing in the open doorway of the shop.

"What's going on?" Sam asked. "Are you ok?"

Rufus pushed off the counter and moved like he was ready to fling himself into Sam's arms. Because he'd had—*pressure and heat on bare skin*—the shit scared out of him—*tracing freckles across his stomach*—and Sam would know what to do about Heckler. Rufus stopped short of touching Sam, yanked his beanie off, and wiped his forehead. "I've had better mornings."

As though Sam didn't realize what he was doing, his hand came up. To straighten Rufus's hair? Rufus had no idea, but he watched as Sam realized what was happening and pulled his hand back. Sam said, "I didn't expect to see you. I thought you were going to take a few days and get out of the city."

Rufus smoothed down his hair himself. "How exactly would I pay for that impromptu vacation? I mean, what should I do? Raise a pant leg, show some skin, and hope someone picks me up on the parkway? I about got killed getting here—I could do with a bit of sympathy."

Sam frowned, holding out a protein bar to Rufus, and said, "Heckler?"

Rufus snatched the bar. He tore the package open and crammed the entire thing in his mouth. "Fuggin' 'itch," he grumbled around peanut butter and nuts and oats.

For maybe fifteen seconds, Sam seemed to be somewhere else, thinking. Then he looked at Rufus dead-on. "You're hungover."

Rufus swallowed and stuck a finger in his mouth to pick at a bit of protein bar stuck in a molar. "Aren't you so sweet in the mornings."

One dark eyebrow went up, and in that irritatingly mild Sam voice, he said, "I just meant, I'm going to pick up a bottle of water and some ibuprofen from the store. Then we're going to sit down, and you're going to tell me what happened." He turned to go and added, over his shoulder, "For the record, I'm very sweet in the morning.

And I don't even need a guy to pull up his pant leg for me. Even if I do think twinkie twig legs are cute."

Rufus frowned and rubbed hard at his left eye until he was seeing spots. It felt good in the way that dull pain could. He blinked away the stars and watched as Sam grabbed a bottle from a cooler before approaching the register. Rufus noticed two younger guys seated nearby. They were watching him watching Sam. Then one smirked, looked pointedly at Sam, and swallowed down the length of his peeled banana.

Sam came back with a small foil-wrapped packet of ibuprofen, which he held out, and a bottle of water. "Drink all of it."

Rufus snatched both without saying anything in the way of thanks. He tore open the foil, swallowed the pills dry, then cracked the seal on the water. After downing half the bottle, he motioned it at the two men with their sex fruit while staring at Sam. "Thank God you found someone to give you a hand last night. Or two. Or ass. Whatever it was they offered."

After a quiet moment, Sam nodded. "Ok. Get it all out of your system?"

"I've got piss and vinegar for days."

"If that's what you want to call it."

Rufus screwed the cap back on. "Do you still have a room?"

One of Sam's hands wrapped around Rufus's, clutching the bottle. His other hand removed the cap. "I said drink all of it."

Rufus narrowed his eyes. "I can't if you don't let go of me."

Sam released him, but then he stood there, a big dumb fuck of a tank, waiting.

Rufus briefly considered how satisfying it'd be to pour

the water on the floor. He was trying so hard to rile Sam up because—*fuck*, he didn't even really know why. He just was. And Rufus wasn't getting the reaction he wanted. But he ultimately opted to finish the water, not because Sam told him to, but because Rufus had done a lot of running in July heat and was thirsty.

"Come on," Sam said. "I've got the room until eleven thirty."

CHAPTER
TWELVE

Sam led Rufus past the elevators and toward the service stairs. He needed the time to pull himself together, and the thought of being in a metal box, inches away from Rufus, threatened to push him over the edge. They climbed the cement steps in silence, the only noise the soft *whick* of their shoes.

Part of Sam tried to focus on Heckler. His guess had been right; Heckler not only had thought Rufus was dead, but now she needed him dead. She had taken another risk today—a major risk—by showing up at Rufus's apartment and chasing him through the city. She had tipped her hand. And she had shown how far she was willing to go to bury anything that might reveal the truth about what had happened to Jake.

But another part of Sam kept going back to Rufus: the flush in his cheeks when Sam had seen him in the lobby; the way the thin T-shirt clung to him, damp with sweat; the firestorm of hair. The night before, in thrall to two separate rage fucks, Sam could pretend he had gotten Rufus out of his head. Seeing him again, though.... Well. Damn. So much for that.

And the way Rufus had said, *Thank God you found someone to give you a hand last night.* The note in his voice. The way he had pressed on it, not letting it go. He'd heard the same thing in his own voice, the time or two he'd tried to talk to Jake. The thing about relationships, Sam thought—shocked to hear the word in his head, shoving it away before he could acknowledge it—was that nobody ever had new lines. You just played the same parts with the same script a hundred different ways.

Oh Christ. He needed to get laid. Again. And get far away from redheaded trouble.

In the small room, though, there wasn't anywhere to get away. There was Rufus, right there, filling up the space: the smell of clean sweat, Dial soap, his hair. Sam took a spot on the far wall, hands under his arms, putting as much distance as he could between them.

"So?" he said.

Rufus tossed his jacket and beanie on the bed, walked to the window AC unit, and cranked the knob to High. He hiked his shirt up and leaned over the vent. "Heckler came to my apartment," Rufus began, staring at the city below. "All she said was it was important we *talk*."

"But you ran."

"I went out my window and down the fire escape. I ran to the subway and she followed, but I lost her at West Fourth." Rufus cocked his head and stared at Sam. "Do you want a Rufus thing?"

Sam did, but Rufus was too close. He moved to the

other end of the room and dropped onto the foot of the bed. Then he nodded.

Still holding his shirt up, Rufus turned so he could cool the sweat on his back. "I've got a record. I was arrested for pickpocketing when I was a punk kid. Two years ago I ended up in some hot water—Jake was the detective involved. But when he learned who I'd stolen from and the information I had... he convinced me to testify in exchange for no jail time, and that criminal is serving a life sentence now. Jake made an arrangement with me afterward. In exchange for having my juvie record scrubbed, my details under lock and key, and the occasional paycheck, I inform."

The window unit chugged; the hiss of cold air was like a stream of static through Sam's head. This, Rufus telling him this, was more than just facts; it was a Rufus thing. A small one, yes. But a peace offering.

"Thank you," Sam said. "For telling me."

Rufus shrugged.

"So you know what she really wanted when she came to your place."

Rufus put a finger to his head and imitated a gun. "She showed me what she wanted."

"You worked as a police informant. Maybe the best thing for you to do now is go to a stationhouse, tell them everything. You know cops, right? Tell them what you saw, everything you've figured out about what happened to Jake. If you can't leave town, maybe that's the next best thing."

Rufus yanked his T-shirt down. "I'm sorry, I'm still a little hungover. Did you say go to the police and snitch on a cop? A *sergeant*? She's a decorated officer and I'm a petty thief. Who do you think they're going to believe?"

"I meant one of the cops you know. One that you trust."

"Without Jake here," Rufus said, voice dropping like a sinking stone, "all my hopes and dreams rest on Lampo." He tugged his phone out and stared at the screen like he needed a moment to swallow his pride. "Lucky me," Rufus finally concluded. He tapped in his passcode, pecked in a number, then set the call to speakerphone as it rang.

"Lampo."

"Dickhead, it's me. You alone?" Rufus said.

"Jesus Christ. What, Red?"

"Is Mommy dipping into confiscated coke or something?"

Lampo groaned. "This is why my sciatica acts up. This. You. I'm hobbling around like Gandalf the Elf over here because Red fucking Skelton won't leave me the fuck alone. What are you talking about?"

Rufus was glaring at a spot on the wall over Sam's shoulder. "Heckler."

"What about her?"

"She's elbow-deep in some serious shit," Rufus answered. "Come on, man, are you kidding? You have no idea what I'm talking about? She tried to shoot me this morning."

A long, groaning "Oh, Christ" followed, accompanied by the squeak of a chair. Lampo huffed into the phone, and then something sounded like a door closing. "Now, Red, that's a very serious thing to say. Just what the fuck are you talking about, what the fuck are you getting me into, and how the fuck am I supposed to walk when you're giving me the fucking sciatica this bad?"

Rufus's grip on his phone tightened to the point that Sam could see his knuckles whitening. "Do I need to spell it out for you with alphabet blocks, Dickhead? Last night, I saw your sergeant cap a dude—the same guy who killed Jake, and the same guy you thought I *imagined* because there was no evidence. So again I ask, what the fuck is going on with the boys in blue?"

Lampo's labored breathing rasped across the call. Then he said, "You got any proof?"

"P-proof?" Rufus stuttered. "Are you literally shitting me right now?"

"Yeah, proof. It's this crazy new thing. The courts go nutso for it."

"My own two eyes, Lampo," Rufus retorted. "That's my proof. Since when have I ever lied to you or Jake?"

"I'm not saying you're lying, Red. But you're talking about a decorated sergeant. My sergeant." Lampo's breath hitched, the sound of someone who'd moved funny, and he said, "Listen, I'll look into it. You say this other guy, the one you said you saw before, he's dead?"

"As a doornail."

"You got a name?"

Rufus made eye contact with Sam, who'd taken the wallet the night before, and repeated his whispered answer at regular volume: "Marcus Borroff."

"All right," Lampo said. "Next time, we're doing this face-to-face so I'm not sitting on a stack of toilet paper, bent over halfway to giving myself a zinger. I'll call you when I've got something."

"You fucking better." Rufus hit End.

"I still think you should lie low for a few days. How much do you need to get out of the city? A hundred? Two hundred?"

"I'm not going anywhere," Rufus snapped at Sam before that now-familiar blush colored his neck and face. "I'm not running away from this," he answered, a bit calmer. "So shut up about that."

The next part was hard to say. "I know what I want to try next, but I need some help."

Rufus arched a brow and cracked a smile. "Rub one off on your own."

"Not to be crass, and not to brag, but so you know: it never comes to that. I'm talking about something else. In a few of his e-mails, Jake mentioned someone named Juliana. She's a sex worker; she's in the Ramble a lot. I told you part of one e-mail, where he mentioned her saying something about coming from the north. He refers to her in several others, but obliquely, always part of a story he knew he wasn't supposed to tell me but kept leaking out. I want to talk to her. I want to know what she told Jake." Sam fought to keep a grimace off his face. "I don't know if she'll talk to me."

Rufus took a few steps across the room before seating himself beside Sam on the bed. He spread his legs a bit, leaned forward, and settled his elbows on his knees. "You afraid the Incredible Hulk thing you got going on will intimidate her?"

"Sure."

"And you think I'm more, what, *approachable*?"

It was too much. The heat of Rufus against him, the friction of his thigh against Sam's, the way their elbows nearly bumped. Sam lurched off the bed and moved to the window unit, face turned down into the hiss of cold air.

"Yeah. Yes. I don't know. I thought—" Sam wasn't sure what he thought; the walls were closing in. "I don't know," he said again in a tight voice, eyes shut, and then he started counting down from twenty-nine in his head.

"I know I ran, but I don't stink that bad."

When the countdown ran out, Sam forced himself to stand up straight and look back at Rufus. "It's not that. It's—look, will you help me? Please? I'm sorry about last night. I'm sorry I—I offended you or upset you or hurt you. Whatever I did. I'm sorry. I get it; you're not interested. I won't make that mistake again, I promise."

Rufus rubbed the very light bristle on his chin. "I didn't say I wasn't interested."

"Very funny."

"It's just a fuck," Rufus said, parroting Sam's words. "But I don't want to be *just a fuck*. I trust you. I've told you things no one but Jake knew. And—" Rufus cast his gaze down at his high-tops. "—it mattered to me that you said I was cute."

A hundred things tried to escape from Sam's mouth, a hundred different stories and explanations: his first time, with Chad Obralt, just hand stuff in the backseat of his dad's Oldsmobile, and then Chad laughing it off when Sam came around again and again, finally cornering him behind the Save-A-Lot to tell him it was just a one-off, to quit making such a big fucking deal about it; Ovejuna, in the barrack showers, biting his arm as Sam plowed into him and then, in the mess hall, picking up his chow and moving tables when Sam sat down next to him; Jake, twining his fingers through Sam's that weekend they'd floated the Chattahoochee, the sand in Jake's hair like ribbons of gold, and then the e-mails after his move to New York, the new girlfriend, *it was fun, let's not pretend it was anything else*. All the nights of his life a series of one-offs, no big fucking deal.

But it all got jammed, and Sam didn't even know where to start, how to tell it so it made sense. So he shrugged and said, "Ok. I'm sorry."

Rufus looked up again, and after a long silent moment, he nodded. "All right. And I know we aren't married or anything, but keep the boy toys to a minimum and I'll help you with Juliana." He grabbed his beanie and got to his feet.

The suggestions enclosed in Rufus's words, that he was interested, and interested in more than just casual sex, came too close to a line Sam had drawn for himself in the sand. Here, and no further. He needed them both to back down while he tried not to freak the fuck out; hell, he needed—for himself, anyway—a cold shower.

But instead, even though touch was so difficult for him to handle, even though it threatened to overwhelm him, Sam didn't back down. In a few steps, he crossed the distance between them. He plucked the beanie out of Rufus's hand, and then he slowly worked it over the silky red tangles. He used his thumbs to tuck the last of the hair out of sight.

"We need somewhere we can stay," he said, taking the sunglasses and settling them on Rufus's face. "Somewhere we can hide until tonight."

Rufus hadn't moved an inch. Hell, he might not have even breathed until Sam spoke. "Jake's apartment," he said in a sudden rush. "Don't give me that look. I mean his other place."

"Right," Sam said after a moment, "the secret apartment. The one only you know about."

"*Am* I the only one?" Rufus asked, tone teasing as he thoughtfully tapped his chin with one long finger.

"Have I ever mentioned you are one sneaky fuck?"

Rufus smiled widely. "Thank you."

CHAPTER
THIRTEEN

Jake had never told Rufus about the second studio he rented on the Upper West Side, but snooping was the name of the game and Rufus was the reigning champ. He was a sponge for information, regardless of the consequences. Curiosity killed the cat and all that—except his cat always seemed to land on its feet and came running back for more. The teeny-tiny studio was far enough away from Jake's precinct and girlfriend that it had struck Rufus as odd at the time of learning about it, but after meeting Sam—well, it made sense. Jake had a thing for guys and he hadn't wanted *anyone* to know.

With Sam's buff body shielding his actions from any curious passersby on the street, Rufus used the lock tools he carried in his jacket to unlock the building's front door. He stepped into the vestibule, rapped his knuckles against the mailbox marked J. Brower 9F, bypassed the elevator that he knew had a security camera inside, and led the way up the winding stairs. After picking the lock on 9F, he opened the door enough for them both to slip inside, then shut it. There was a loft directly above their heads with a ladder near the couch at the opposite wall. The ceiling wasn't terribly tall, which could make for an uncomfortable situation for anyone flirting with six feet— which both of them were. The studio was impersonal and sparsely furnished. A small desk and chair, a micro kitchen, and bathroom, all in a 20x20 box.

Rufus threw the deadbolt. "We should be fine here. Only Jake had a key to this place."

"The unit's in his name; I saw the mailbox."

"So?" Rufus asked, making for the kitchen. He opened a cupboard and rummaged through the contents.

"Heckler could find it."

"Do you know how much paperwork she'd have to do before finding this place?" Rufus opened a box of crackers, removed a sleeve, and stuffed a few in his mouth. "Pretty sure this was Jake's hookup pad, if you catch my drift."

Maybe Sam did, because his eyebrows went up once, but all he said was "I'm going to rack out for a few hours. That's the only bed?"

"Nah, there's a foldout under the sink. I'll take that one, Prince Charming."

Sam honestly looked like he didn't know what to say to that. Point, Rufus. After another of those annoyingly ambiguous shrugs, Sam lumbered into the living room, dropped onto the sofa, and was snoring lightly in thirty seconds.

Rufus finished the sleeve of crackers, returned the box to the cupboard, and spent a few minutes poking through the contents of the desk and bathroom cabinet. He didn't find anything of interest, though, and after giving Sam a brief look, Rufus climbed the loft ladder and passed out on the bed.

There were a few different directions Rufus considered in order to reach the Ramble inside Central Park. Some easier, some more direct. But when evening came and Rufus hadn't felt like a microwaved burrito upon stepping foot outside, he opted for the long way. The long route included passing through Cherry Hill and walking across Bow Bridge as the sun set over the horizon of The City That Never Sleeps.

It was, of course, absolutely not romantic. Not one bit.

Rufus hung his sunglasses from the collar of his T-shirt. "Once we reach the other side, it's not very far," he explained to Sam, motioning toward the opposite side of the bridge.

Looking back, Sam said, "Did we walk around the park to get here?"

"The scenic route," Rufus corrected. He looked sideways at Sam. "Why?"

"Trying to get my bearings."

"Oh. Over there is Strawberry Fields," Rufus said, motioning with one hand. "And that way is the Alice statue. Ahead is the Ramble." He made a quick step to the right, brushing against Sam, in order to avoid a couple who'd stopped short to take a selfie.

Sam seemed to move away automatically, his gaze sweeping across the bridge, then the water, away from Rufus. "Do you come here a lot? Good spot to hook up, I mean."

Rufus sighed audibly. "No, I don't."

"Too bad."

Which could have meant just about anything.

"If you say so." Rufus quickened his pace, took the lead, and reached the other side of Bow Bridge first. He turned, his hands in his jacket pockets, waiting for Sam.

"This is the Ramble?" Sam asked, joining him.

"It gets more foresty a bit farther in," Rufus explained. "And there are lots of different paths. It's not as overwhelming in winter, of course, but the rest of the year? There's a reason it's been such a good working spot for so long."

"Will it be hard to find Juliana?"

Rufus flashed Sam a cocky smirk. "Nah. My Juliana GPS pings whenever I'm within five hundred feet of her."

"Sounds useful."

"It's no fun if you don't play."

"Dork," Sam said as he passed Rufus and headed along the path.

"Weak comeback. We'll work on it." Rufus hurried past Sam and took the lead again. He spun and walked backward, saying, "I have a pretty good idea of where she'll be. Don't ask me why I know—I just do, ok? It's not because I cruise."

"Of course not."

"I'm serious, you prick."

"We'll work on that," Sam said. Then, before Rufus could respond: "Snake!"

Rufus's response to the threat of a wild animal—though a snake wasn't anything like a bear—involved yelping about three octaves higher than usual, while tripping *forward* as he'd been walking *backward*. His arms flailed for purchase as he simultaneously looked down for the snake. He mistook his shoelace for danger and fell into Sam's arms while trying to escape.

"You sonofabitch!" Rufus shouted. "You scared the shit out of me."

Sam was holding him, keeping him from falling, and the big man's body was trembling; it took Rufus a moment to realize it was suppressed laughter. This time, Sam wasn't quite as quick to separate, although he did disentangle himself faster than Rufus might have liked. When they were both standing again, Sam had a hand over his mouth, looking surprisingly boyish as he very carefully studied something off in the middle distance.

Rufus adjusted his jacket and T-shirt with what little dignity he could salvage before pointing a finger at Sam. "If you tell anyone I made that noise, I'm going to shove you off Bow Bridge."

Hand over his mouth, Sam arched his eyebrows. After a moment when he seemed to be struggling to control another burst of laughter, he managed to ask in a relatively normal voice, "What noise?"

Rufus growled, spun on one heel, and took the first right they came upon, the woods of the Ramble swallowing them whole. He didn't say anything for a while, just trekked deeper through the maze of walking, running, and biking trails that made the steel-and-concrete part of the city feel so very far away. At length, Rufus asked, "Do you know how you can gain your bearings if you're lost in the park?"

"Walk in a straight line?"

"*No*." Rufus slowed to fall in beside Sam. "The streetlamps are numbered. The first two numbers indicate the closest street, the others—even or odd—mean you're on the east or west side."

As they passed the next streetlamp, Sam glanced at it, then at Rufus. "Cool." They made it another yard before Sam asked, "How'd you know that?"

"The streetlamp thing is practical, I guess. But I like to

read. Passes the time."

Another yard of the soft *whick* of their shoes on the pavement. "What's a good book I should read?"

Rufus exhaled what might have been a very soft laugh. "What do you enjoy?"

"When we walked past that bookstore, the one with the books out on the sidewalk, you stopped to look. Were you looking for something in particular?"

Rufus jutted his thumb toward a left path as they came to a juncture. "Something I don't know anything about."

"Where'd you go to college? What'd you study? Something hard, I bet."

Rufus looked at Sam that time. "I dropped out of high school when I was sixteen." He shrugged, tried to roll the bitterness off. "What about you? Did you go to college?"

"Not right out of high school. I enlisted in the Army. Got one of those Bachelor's of Whatever-the-Fuck you can get by taking enough gen ed classes at the local college. I couldn't get into OCS until I had one, so I did it, although it took plenty of time. Christ, I sound ungrateful, I guess. It wasn't really my thing." His hand came up; he scratched the stubble on his cheek. "So, you're just really, really smart, huh?"

Rufus stopped walking. He asked, with an obvious note of wariness, "Why would you say that?"

"Those books in your apartment—" A ghost of a smile flitted across Sam's face. "—I saw some of the titles. I don't even know what half the words mean. And you knew about the streetlamps. And the way you talk. The way you look at things, people, problems. When we were trying to find Jake's phone, for example. And I know you said you were just looking at those books, the ones we walked by, but I saw your face. You were... I don't know, hungry. We had a guy in our platoon like that. Loved books. Disappeared into them. So damn smart, I never knew what he was talking about most of the time."

Rufus stared at Sam. It wasn't a mean stare—more like disbelief. His entire life, no one had called him smart. Sure as hell not his mother. His teachers had all but given up on the redheaded punk in grade school. And as an adult, the wrong sort of people thought Rufus was clever—cunning, even—with a smart-mouth attitude in spades. But they never equated him with anything more. And then he'd met Jake. Jake had teased him relentlessly about the trips to the library—*Plutarch's* Essays? *Do you even know who Plutarch is?*—but always in the end he'd say to Rufus, "I know you're smart."

And now, to hear that from Sam?

Rufus started to speak, but the words were tangled around a lump, so he cleared his throat. "You're still not bullshitting me, right?"

Sam shook his head slowly. "This is what me bullshitting you sounds like: 'Gee, Rufus, you're so big and muscley.'"

Rufus laughed and felt some of the tension ease. "Why, thank you."

"Those shoulders. Those arms. Those gams."

"Don't get carried away." Rufus started to speak again, swallowed down a few words that didn't taste right, then said simply, "Thanks."

"Sure," Sam said. "Now flex for me."

Rufus rolled his eyes and began walking again. "Come on. We're almost there—this has been a hotspot for business since the '90s."

"Not that you'd know personally, of course."

"Nope."

"Uh-huh."

Rufus ignored the jab and led Sam around a bend before cutting off the main path and following an unofficial trail that took a sudden dip down a hill. The path was overgrown on either side, and the old forest created a thick green canopy overhead. *Sycamore, oaks, and hackberry*, Rufus told himself. A sweat broke out under his arms, on the back of his neck, and his gut churned uncomfortably as Rufus walked deeper into his memories. He shook himself of that nervous, flip-flop feeling and focused. Yellowwood and Black Cherry were aggressive and required constant upkeep from the Department of Parks and Recreation. Plant lists from the 1800s suggested that while native species had outnumbered the invasive by over seventy percent, most of those trees were found to have been long dead and rotted by the time another survey was conducted in 2006. The invasive trees now outnumbered native, and it was a whole *thing* with arborists.

A cigarette lighter briefly illuminated a man's face just ahead, and a woman's laugh echoed from somewhere deeper in the trees. Her voice bounced off a nearby rock face and filled the forest with a haunted chuckle.

Stopping a few feet short to give distance to the stranger, Rufus called, "Hey, is Juliana around?"

Branches trembled—*yellowwood*, Rufus thought again—and a figure emerged out of the shadows, light catching him at the waist: painfully thin, bare skin stretched tight over ribs showing under a pinstripe vest, track marks running up the inside of his arm. His face was lost in the darkness, but his voice had a saccharine layer as he cooed, "Juliana? Fuck Juliana, baby. You don't need that old cooz. Come here. Let me get a closer look at you."

Rufus held a hand out toward Sam. "I need money," he murmured.

Sam pulled out of his stack of bills, peeled off some, and held them out with a raised eyebrow.

Rufus snatched the offering, tucked them into his front pocket, and moved toward the skinny guy. "I'm not interested, no offense. Have you seen Juliana?"

"What'd you got in there?" This close, Rufus could smell something like overheated electronics, or burning plastic—the smell of somebody tweaked out of his mind. "You playing pocket pool for Boy George?"

"Ten bucks if you tell me where she is."

"Ten bucks? I wouldn't spit on your dick for ten bucks. Big boy, over there, on the other hand...."

"Pass," Sam said in a dry voice.

Boy George, or whoever the hell he was, rocked on his heels. "Why do you want to find that bitch so bad?"

Rufus cracked his neck to one side and huffed. "Twenty bucks, George. I'm not asking what you'll do with Andrew Jackson, so don't butt into my business with Juliana."

"Come here. I seen you around here before?"

"Probably not," Rufus answered.

Sam made a very asshole-ish noise in his throat.

"You're kinda pretty. You sure?" Then George held out his hand and laughed. "Oh shit, your face. I'm just messing with you; Boy George is very discreet. Lemme see Andrew."

Rufus pulled his hand from his pocket, the bills still clutched tight. He tugged free a twenty and waved it.

"You got plenty there," Boy George said. "Your big fuck boyfriend gave you plenty. Gimme a hundred, and I'll tell you where Juliana tricks."

"George, I know how these games work. Twenty is enough for the information I'm after. And if this is how you talk to clients, you'd better be more careful."

"Who the fuck are you, coming around here, talking to me like that? I ought to tell you to fuck right off." Only Boy George stayed right where he was, one hand massaging the inside of his elbow. "You're a fucking asshole, that's what you are."

"Forget him," Sam said. "He wants to dick us around. We'll find someone else."

Rufus nodded, but to George, he said, "Tell me where Juliana is—for twenty bucks and a thank-you from Daisy."

George's hand froze on his elbow. He leaned in, sending another cloud of that burned-plastic smell swirling past Rufus, and for a moment, hints of his face were visible: too-tight skin across the skull, around the eyes, the sweat-slick hair lank over a high forehead. "Daisy, huh? Haven't heard that name in a while. Come here again."

Rufus took a reluctant step forward. He held up the folded bill again. "How about it?"

"Well, shit, Red. Isn't that fucking something?" Then, before Rufus could react, George grabbed the bill and squirreled it away. "She works on the other side of the rock. Up this path." He pointed vaguely to his left. "At the little gazebo."

"How far is it?" Rufus asked.

"Few minutes."

Rufus thanked George and motioned Sam to follow as he rounded the rock face and started up the path as directed.

"What was that all about?" Sam asked.

"He thinks Andrew Jackson is hot."

"No, the part about Daisy."

"Boy George must like flowers."

They walked another pace before Sam said, "Uh-huh."

Rufus followed the man-made shortcut—grass stomped down and worn away from the constant use of sex workers in this area of the Ramble. Bits of leaves and twigs scraped underfoot, but those were the only whispers between him and Sam. At the top of the hill around the rock face was an official pathway, and partially concealed by the summer greenery, a wooden gazebo about a hundred feet away. Inside the gazebo was the shadow of a person—sort of. It was a decidedly odd shape, someone sitting on one of the benches, with a sort of hump in front of them.

Rufus halted when his brain finished deconstructing the shape as actually being two people—one sitting, yes, and the other on their knees between open legs. He held his arm out to stop Sam. "We'll have to wait."

"What—uh. Oh." Sam cocked his head. "Guess grass is easier on your knees than asphalt. Or bathroom tile."

Rufus rubbed at the light bristle along his jaw. "I've never given a blow job in the grass."

"You have to be careful you don't get stains." Sam gestured at his knees. "They're a bitch to get out."

Rufus had to work his mouth to keep from grinning outright. "Yeah? I'll remember that. Next time I'm in the grass, about to get sexy—take my pants off."

Nothing really changed on Sam's face, nothing Rufus could point a finger at, but suddenly his whole expression was different. Intense. Focused. And Sam made a soft noise that could have meant anything.

Rufus stared at him for another second, two, three—hell, maybe an entire minute. He would have been happy to stare at Sam for the rest of the night while trying to imprint all of those unique, minute details of Sam's face into his own long-term memory. The mask of nothing absolutely meant *something*, and Rufus thought, if he could study Sam a bit longer, he'd be able to decipher it.

Then a small smile broke Sam's expression. "You're teasing me."

Rufus blinked. "I am?"

The look that followed wasn't what Rufus expected: trouble broke the stillness of Sam's expression like a ripple on smooth waters, there and then gone. He turned to look ahead, into darkness.

Rufus tucked away that mental snapshot of Sam, tamped down the unyielding need to grab the other man and kiss him until both were gasping for air, and turned to study the two shadows now standing in the gazebo. "Looks like they're done."

No reply from Sam. The big man had his hands tucked under his arms again, and his face was a blank wall.

Rufus started walking as the customer left the gazebo, moved onto the path, and vanished into the dark. "Juliana?" he called. "Boy George said I could find you here. Can I talk to you?"

The voice that came back was husky, and although that could have been dismissed as the result of the most recent transaction, other clues told the rest of the story as the woman moved into the light: the shoulders, the hands, the hips. "Who's asking?"

"My name's Rufus. I'm a friend of Jake's."

Juliana froze. Slowly, one of her hands moved to press against her leg, fingers trembling at the hem of the short skirt.

Sam didn't actually do anything so crass as lean forward and whisper, *She's got a knife*, but the way the big man started rumbling and rustling, it was pretty close.

"Who's Jake?" Juliana said.

Rufus held his hands up in an act of submission. "The cops ask for my help now and then. I keep an eye on the nasty fuckers in the city, and Jake kept an eye on me in return." Rufus's voice caught a little and he had to clear his throat. "Something terrible has happened to Jake."

Juliana had to be past forty, but she moved on kitten heels without a hint of a wobble as she scurried toward the path. "Look, I'm sorry about your friend, but I don't know a Jake. You guys should... you should clear out of here."

Rufus took a shot in the dark and called out, "What about Sergeant Heckler?"

"She's going to run," Sam said quietly.

Juliana's face blanched, and she managed two long strides before one of the heels snapped and she tumbled sideways. She came down hard on her knee, swearing, "Shit, shit, shit." And then she scrambled up, covering her leg where road rash from the asphalt peeled it open, and faced them, limping back and away. "Stay there, ok? I don't know Jake. I don't know Heckler. I don't know anybody, ok?"

Rufus still hadn't moved, still hadn't lowered his hands. "Jake mentioned your name, Juliana. Now he's dead and Heckler tried to take me out too. What's going on? Whatever it is, we'll help you, I promise."

"Tell her about bringing them in from the north," Sam said, bending to speak the words low into Rufus's ear.

Rufus nodded and quickly said, "He told my friend 'they were brought in from the north.' What does that mean?"

Indecision twisted Juliana's face, but she stopped moving. "You can't—you can't just make me disappear. People know me. My girlfriend's coming right now to check on me, so you just—just stay right there."

Her fear was palpable, so viciously relatable, that Rufus felt a very physical pang in his heart. "I'm not going to allow anyone to make you disappear. But I have to know what you've seen and heard."

"I don't know you. I don't want to know you. You say you helped Jake?" Juliana scoffed. "Look how he ended up. You want that? I don't. I shouldn't have told him, shouldn't have opened my mouth. Let this go, walk away. Christ knows I'm going to."

Rufus tugged his beanie off. "Juliana," he tried once more, voice thick. "Hang on, please. Daisy didn't say anything and look what happened to her."

At some level Rufus expected what happened next: the chain reaction of confusion, recognition, disbelief, sorrow, and then all of it burning out like a magnesium strip. "Oh, child," Juliana said, which was a silly way to talk to a man in his thirties, but still hit Rufus hard, harder than he would have liked. Struggle worked its way across Juliana's features once more, and then she nodded. "Ok. But let's sit down. My leg is killing me, and don't get me started about my knees."

Rufus took a few steps backward and pointed in the direction of a wooden bench along the edge of the path and nestled up against the tree line. He took a seat first, on the far right, allowing Juliana plenty of space.

She perched on the end of the bench, crossing her legs at the ankle and massaging the edges of the scraped flesh. Between hisses of pain, she looked at Rufus, dark eyes buried under a mountain of foundation. "I haven't thought about Daisy in a long time," she said, her massage slowing. "I don't mean anything bad, but life moves on, you know? How'd you get caught up in this mess?" Then, nodding at Sam, "And who's this big brutal bite of a man?"

Rufus leaned forward to put his elbows on his knees. He eyed Sam briefly before smiling and saying to Juliana, "He's pretty cute, right? He got an e-mail from Jake, who mentioned meeting you, and now here we both are, trying to figure out who would have wanted Jake dead."

"He didn't say much," Sam added, "but he told us you gave him information. They were bringing them in from the north. What does that mean?"

"You don't even know? You're swimming with the sharks, boys, and you think you're still in the kiddie pool." Juliana stretched, cracking her back, and said, "You said

Heckler tried to kill you?"

Rufus nodded. "What the fuck is going on in Major Cases?"

"A cop tried to kill you, and you're still scooting around the city? Jesus Christ, boy, get your butt on a bus. Take strong, dark, and beautiful with you. You're walking around with a death sentence on your head."

"No. I'm not running without understanding why."

"He's just as dumb as he looks, isn't he?" Juliana said, glancing up at Sam.

Rufus didn't look back, couldn't see the smile, but he heard it in Sam's voice when he said, "He has his moments. But he's right about this: we're not leaving until we know why they killed Jake and how high this goes."

"Men: obstinate, ornery, and impossible, the whole lot of you." Juliana resumed the slow massage of her leg as she spoke quietly, "Jake told you about bringing them in from the north? Those poor kids. They don't have any idea what they've gotten themselves into. And then they're here, and it's too late. I... I wouldn't have said anything if I hadn't seen it myself. The look on their faces as they started to figure it out. That's hell, pure and simple. I wouldn't have said a single word if I hadn't seen it myself; you can't shake something like that."

Rufus shifted, angled himself more toward Juliana as she spoke. "Sex work, then? Girls? Boys? Both? How old were they?"

"Both. Teens, mostly, although a few that might be in their twenties. Can't understand a word they're saying. Most of them are Asian, don't know what countries, can't tell the languages apart, but one time I heard Spanish and I can recognize that."

Rufus asked, while his brain sped to catalogue every word, every detail, "Would you be able to describe who was overseeing them? Or know how Heckler ties into this?"

"I saw her once, and it was... it was after what happened to Jake. I think something must have gone wrong, because she was shouting, raising hell, handing everybody their asses. They've got a place out in Queens, this brick duplex, and that's where they keep the kids. Upstairs, I think, so it's harder for them to escape. I know I shouldn't call them kids, but that's what they look like—poor things." She shook her head. "I just happened to be walking the block. It was late, really late, and there was the van, Maine license plates, kids coming out of it like it was a clown car. You could tell they had no idea where they were. One of the boys had a big bruise on the side of his face—I could see it from a distance, even with just the porch light. This many years walking the street, I know when something's hinky, and that stuff, those kids getting out of the van, it was hinky as shit."

"*Jesus Christ*," Rufus swore. He ran both hands through his hair, making it stick up. "Where in Queens?"

"Flushing? I wrote it down for Jake. The address, I mean."

"Have you talked to anyone else about this?" Rufus continued. "I mean, fucking *anyone*. Your girlfriend? The mailman? Pet cat?"

"I haven't told anyone else." Her hand moved to the waistband of her skirt, her fingers playing with the elastic. "But a guy's been asking around about me. He got pretty close, actually. I was zipping Mr. Hoover up when I saw him waiting for me, and... and I freaked. He tried to talk me down, but—" She flashed them a smile. "I guess he wasn't as charming as my little redheaded prince."

"Charming," Sam said. "Exactly the word I would have chosen."

Rufus ignored Sam's interjection. Those crackers he'd eaten at Jake's had been hours ago, and the combination of renewed hunger and growing fear was churning stomach acid and creating a nauseating flip-flop feeling in his gut. "Did you get this guy's name?"

"Detective Lampo," Juliana said. "Jake's partner, the one who needs to invest in a hair piece."

"You know Lampo?" Sam asked.

Rufus glanced up at Sam, still standing all the while. "It makes sense. They were working together on whatever this shit is."

"Baby boy, I don't want any deeper in this than I already am." Her fingers twisted in the elastic again, and this time, she produced a business card from behind the waistband. "You tell him to stop bothering me. I hurt for what happened to Jake. Broke me up pretty bad. But I've got my own pert ass to worry about." She seemed to hesitate, and then she worked a stub of pencil out of somewhere. She scribbled something on the card and held it out. "That's the address I gave Jake. And don't you come around anymore either. Daisy was a long time ago."

Rufus's reach for the card fell short. Yes, Daisy had been a long time ago. But Daisy was also yesterday. And today. Daisy would be tomorrow too. And that stuck to him like a burr. Rufus didn't say anything more to Juliana as he took the card and got to his feet. He offered it to Sam without reading the details.

On the *click-wobble-click* of the broken kitten heels, Juliana moved away from them. Off in the distance, someone was singing Kylie Minogue in falsetto, and the night air moved thickly in the oaks and sycamores and hackberry. Mixed with the lingering smell of mulch and grass and honeysuckle came a chemical cloud of mango— Juliana hitting that vape as she hobbled away.

Sam didn't take a step, but he leaned in, the heat of his body flickering against Rufus. "What's wrong?"

"Hmm?" Rufus put his beanie on and looked up.

"Nothing's wrong."

"Right," Sam said. "Nothing's wrong. That's great. You get all quiet, you won't even look at her, but nothing's wrong. Who's Daisy?"

After a long minute, Rufus shrugged and said simply, "She's a Rufus thing."

CHAPTER
FOURTEEN

In the dark coils of the Ramble, Sam processed what Juliana had just said: *Jake's partner*. Had Lampo come to Juliana for the same reason Sam and Rufus had? To find out what had happened to Jake?

Footsteps moved somewhere close to them, and then a low exchange of voices. Sam came back to himself with a start. He packed up the revelation, caught Rufus's eye, and nodded the way they had come. "Is there a shorter way back? Or are we taking the scenic route again?"

Rufus pointed in a different direction, opened his mouth, but his stomach let out an audible growl before he spoke. He snapped his jaw shut and rubbed sheepishly at his belly.

"Really?" Sam asked.

"Sorry. If we follow this path, we'll get to Central Park West quicker than going back over Bow Bridge."

"Romantic Bow Bridge," Sam said, not even sure why he fucking said it. Then, hurrying on, "And when I said, 'Really,' I meant, 'Really, you're hungry again?'"

"My metabolism is a wild animal."

Making a gesture up the path, Sam tried not to smile; he thought he did a decent job. "Food, then. And then back to Jake's so we can figure out what the fuck is going on. Let's go, fearless leader."

Rufus led them out of Central Park, and he'd been telling the truth: they had taken the long way to get to the Ramble, and, yes, it had been a much nicer view of the park. Not that this second route was bad, it just wasn't....

Romantic? Sam heard in his head.

He told that little voice to fuck off. It'd been cute, the way Rufus had said, *The scenic route*, as though he could squelch the little blush that had come into his cheeks. Sam liked that little blush. He liked the way Rufus's eyes got wide and outraged at half the things Sam said that seemed, to him anyway, perfectly common sense. He liked the way Rufus's ears got pink when Sam said things that Rufus liked but was embarrassed about. He liked that Rufus wore his heart on his sleeve in a million ways, hurt and happiness and excitement and amusement all right there for Sam to see, even though Sam knew that the real Rufus, all the real Rufus things, were locked away. Maybe hadn't been shared with anyone. Ever.

The branches of a massive oak creaked overhead as a gust of warm, humid air swirled past them, winnowing the grass clippings along the curb and fanning them across the asphalt. A shadowed pair stumbled into an intersection of paths ahead of them, pausing, leaning against each other, whispered consultations that erupted into giggles and then a long, sloppy kiss before the pair staggered off again. Sam's heartbeat climbed into his ears, drowning out this noisy, impossible-to-escape city for a moment.

He knew he should be thinking about Jake, Marcus, Heckler, Juliana. About kids dragged here from around the world, trapped, used. He knew there was so much on the line—more than he had thought possible when he'd come to learn the truth about Jake.

But Rufus was three inches to his right, close enough that Sam could reach out, if he wanted to. How the hell was he supposed to think about anything else when the universe had just gotten so very fucking small?

I didn't say I wasn't interested.

The memory of Rufus's words made Sam stumble, and when Rufus glanced over, Sam felt his face heat, and he was grateful for the thick shadows.

When they reached the edge of the park, Rufus led them onto Central Park West. Green-tinged darkness dropped away, replaced by the granular nightlight of the city: like the ugly version of a summer rainstorm, particles of light suspended in a haze of exhaust and heat-warped darkness instead of in raindrops. At Seventy-Seventh Street, they cut west; the Museum of Natural History had shadows petaled around it. At the end of the block, Rufus jogged across Columbus, ignoring the single, frantic blat of a taxi. The redhead barely seemed to notice; he was in that Rufus place, dealing with Rufus things, alone.

Alone wasn't new for Sam; he'd always had a part of himself that he kept separate, isolated. The part that wanted more than a one-off. The part that thought about stupid things like the future. But Rufus took alone to a new level. Sam had been with him for almost twenty-four hours now, and he hadn't seen any sign that Rufus had anyone in his life. Jake, maybe. But Jake was dead now. Who did Rufus call when he needed help moving that enormous stack of books in his apartment? Who did Rufus meet for lunch? Did people "do lunch" in a place like this? Or was that just a thing on TV? Who did Rufus hang out with, go to the movies with, shoot the shit with? In a city of almost nine million people, it seemed impossible that the answer was no one.

Sam followed him another block, watching Rufus more carefully now. But Rufus stopped at the next street, Amsterdam, and glanced back at Sam. The intersection was a mix of old and modern: red brick and stone stood alongside hulking modern designs of glass and steel. A girl jogged past them, not even glancing at them as she got in her 5K of sidewalk running or whatever the hell people did in a city for exercise.

"How about that?" Sam said, pointing to a Halal food truck twenty yards down the block.

Rufus turned in the direction Sam motioned to, then looked back with wide eyes and a growing smile. "Really? Yeah, that stuff's the best." He headed toward the cart against the curb with a new determination in his step. Rufus was already ordering by the time Sam reached him. He pointed at the picture menu to the side of the service window and then motioned with his hands for something the size of his head.

When it was Sam's turn, he tried to decipher the four-color-process print on the side of the cart, but the images had been sun-bleached into ghosts of lettuce and french fries and who knew what else. After twenty seconds, he gave up. "Whatever he's having."

He paid, and a few minutes later, the man was handing them their food in disposable Styrofoam carry-out containers. Rufus snatched his before Sam could touch it, and Sam bit the corner of his mouth to keep from grinning.

"Should that guy count his fingers?" Sam muttered.

Rufus was holding the container to his face and

smelling the food through the tiny flap that held it shut. "Don't be an ass."

About a hundred yards down Amsterdam, Sam spotted a twenty-four-hour convenience store. Passing his container of lamb and chicken to Rufus, Sam said, "Hold this. And don't eat it." He let some of a smile slip out on the last part, and then he jogged down to the store. He picked up what he wanted, paid, and jogged back. "Did you eat it?"

"I spit in it," Rufus replied without missing a beat. "What'd you need at CVS?"

"Stuff. Jake's is back that way, right?"

Rufus looked mildly interested, but the expression didn't linger. "Yeah." He took the lead again, and they returned to a tall, slender building between avenues— Jake's Home Away From His Other Home. Rufus reluctantly passed the food to Sam in order to help himself to the doors of the building, and after a tap on the mailbox and nine flights of stairs, they were safely behind a set of shiny, modern deadbolts.

In the small kitchen, Sam pulled out drawers, asking over his shoulder, "Do you need a fork too, or do you just inhale it?"

"I'm not a vacuum cleaner." Rufus tossed his jacket and beanie on the desk in the corner, sat down on the floor in front of the couch, crossed his legs, and popped open his dinner container.

Sam waited until he had found the forks, was standing over Rufus, leaning down to hand him a utensil, waited until Rufus was taking his first bite before asking, his voice purposefully low and rough, "Oh, really? So you don't suck?"

Rufus choked. He tried to swat at Sam's leg, but the other man moved back a step. "Stop that, perv."

It was time to stop fighting the smiles; fighting them

was taking up all of Sam's energy. He stood at the counter, his body and Rufus's and the bed in the loft making a triangle. He ate, still smiling when he saw the scowl on Rufus's face. But after a few minutes, with the food congealing in a delicious mass of grease in his belly, Sam decided there were more important things they needed to talk about.

"So," Sam said, "what the fuck is going on?"

"Well," Rufus said thoughtfully, in between big bites of lettuce and lamb. "Sounds like Heckler sold her soul to a sex trafficking ring."

"That sounds right. And Juliana spotted it, told Jake, and Jake was stupid enough to get himself killed." Sam frowned. "What about Lampo? Where does he fit into this?"

Rufus pointed at Sam with his fork. "I think Lampo's lucky he hasn't eaten a bullet. I mean, if he'd been at the pickup meeting, maybe he'd be dead too. But Jake always met with me alone because Dickhead's a sugar-free Trident-chewing ass who's always gone out of his way to annoy me." Rufus scraped the container with the side of his fork and shoveled another bite into his mouth. "I assume Jake wasn't generous with his intel, even with his own partner."

"That's an understatement," Sam said, "if Lampo is poking around, trying to follow Jake's bread crumbs. Like us, I'd like to point out."

"So Jake must have known about Heckler," Rufus concluded. "*Right*? And he... avoided putting facts into writing? Didn't know who to ask for help? Either way, he didn't make the right choice."

"He waffled. Jake was a notorious waffler. I'm going to do this. I'm going to do that. I'm going to suck a few cocks. I'm going to get a girlfriend. I'm going to go career, full twenty in the Army. Never mind, I'm going to be a cop in New York City. Fucking exhausting."

Rufus stared at Sam as he spoke, then shrugged. "Should have just stuck to sucking a few cocks."

"You're not kidding." Sam drummed his fingers on the counter. "From what I can tell, you were supposed to be in that tub right next to Jake. Ok, we've got to make some decisions. You, for some reason, refuse to cover your ass and go somewhere safe. So what do we do next? We've got the address for the house in Queens; we can check that out, see if it's as bad as Juliana made it sound. We can try to track Heckler for a few days, although how the fuck that's going to happen when she has a car and we're digging down to Satan's anus to ride the subway, I have no idea." Sam blew out a breath. "Or do your usual Rufus thing and tell me the smart option I didn't think of."

Rufus offered an awkward smile. "Do you know how to hotwire cars?"

"If it's old enough," Sam said. "Newer models are bullshit ever since they put computer chips in them."

Rufus made a "what can you do?" motion with his hands. "If Natalie hasn't had it towed or impounded or whatever, I know where Jake's car is."

"Yeah? Well, Jake talked really big about all the fast, expensive cars he was going to buy once he was out of the Army. Hell, even when he was in the Army, he blew paychecks on shit like that. You're telling me now he's got a junker piece of shit we're going to boost?"

"He rents two apartments in New York City. He's lucky he's got enough left over for a junker."

"We get the car and what? Go look for this house in Queens?"

Rufus lifted one shoulder in a shrug. "Sure. Since you're so sensitive about the subway."

The rational part of Sam's mind recognized the teasing

for what it was, but the rest of him reacted with animal fear at being exposed. He was tired. He was exhausted—not necessarily physically, but from the city's incessant assault on him. He was tired of trying to hold his shit together, and for some reason, the jab worked its way under the armor Sam had pieced together over the years.

"Who the fuck are you calling sensitive?"

Rufus's light-colored brows rose. "The jolly giant across the room."

"Sorry. I guess it's strange I don't like getting dragged underground through piss and shit and then being crammed into a car with a million other people. I guess that's really fucking sensitive." He pushed off from the counter, abandoning the half-eaten meal, and headed for the bathroom. On his way, he grabbed his ruck. "I'm calling it; that's a night. I'll see you in the morning."

Rufus didn't move from his spot on the floor. "You going to sleep in the bathroom?"

Sam answered by slamming the bathroom door. Childish. Stupid. But it felt really good. For the first minute, he braced his hands on the sink, trying to keep his body from betraying him. But the shakes got worse with adrenaline, with cortisol, with rage. So then, because he knew trying to stop the tremors was a big joke, he stripped, found his soap and shampoo, and showered.

Jake's shower. Jake's bathroom. Jake's second apartment. Jake's city. Hot water needled Sam's back. Was this what Jake had meant, all those times he'd invited Sam to stop in Manhattan? Stay here, at my second apartment, where nobody will even know about you. Fuck, that was worse than having to sleep on the couch and smile and go to brunch with the girlfriend and pretend they were just Army buddies. It made him hate Jake, and he hated hating him, hated that, for a moment, with steam billowing up, he was glad Jake was dead.

Sam slammed the shower's handle until the water stopped, and then he dried himself off, didn't bother with dressing. With any luck, Rufus would already be in the loft; if not, the redheaded prick—Sam's rational part pointed out that Rufus really hadn't done anything wrong—would have to be satisfied with Sam wrapping a towel around his waist. He opened the door and stepped out.

A brief assessment of the studio did tell Sam that Rufus was now in the loft. His black T-shirt was hung over the back of the chair at the desk, wet and dripping from one corner. Rufus must have washed it in the kitchen sink to rewear tomorrow. Quiet movement overhead indicated he wasn't asleep yet.

"Hey." Rufus's head hung upside down from the loft. "Come up here."

At the sofa, Sam fluffed—ok, punched, vigorously—the cushions.

"There's only enough room for one punk in this relationship," Rufus commented wryly, "and I long ago claimed that title."

Sam crossed the room and hit the lights, plunging the loft into the soft gray surf that rolled in from the street. He said fuck-all to modesty, dropped the towel, and stretched out on the sofa.

Rufus's sigh broke the stillness. "All right, Hercules, I'm impressed. But come sleep in the bed so you don't get a kink in your neck."

Sam rolled onto his side, face buried in the cushions, smelling dusty upholstery, maybe the faint trace of Jake's cologne. Imagination? Who the fuck knew anymore? Now that the first surge of anger was pulling back, Sam could think more clearly. He knew Rufus had been teasing him. Knew Rufus hadn't meant anything by it. In fact, Sam had the sneaking suspicion that if he told Rufus everything, explained it, Rufus might actually understand.

I didn't say I wasn't interested.

Sam tried to squirm deeper into a sofa that was approximately two-thirds his size. Rufus was interested. Sam was interested too. Even the way Rufus riled him up got him interested, made him feel alive and engaged and in contact with another human being in a way Sam hadn't felt in a long time. Right then, Sam was interested in a very pointy way that was leaving an impression on Jake's poor sofa cushions. But Rufus didn't want to just be a fuck, either. And that made things complicated, because keeping everything at just-a-fuck level was safe. It was easy. It was fun.

Better?

Well, Sam wasn't sure about that. But if you kept things simmering at just a fuck, guys didn't walk away in the mess hall, guys didn't drop their eyes, guys didn't veer off when they saw you coming. Guys didn't lie to you. Didn't spend a weekend on the river, sun and water and beer and nights under the stars, and say stupid, impossibly stupid lies to you. And you wouldn't believe them.

On the walk back to Jake's, Sam had thought about Rufus being lonely, and now he had to face facts, boner-in-pillow facts, that maybe he was just as fucking lonely. Maybe he was lonelier.

His voice was rough when he called up to the loft, "Come down here."

There was a shuffle of footsteps, and then Rufus was hanging over the edge again. "Why should I? You're being a grump."

Rolling off the sofa, Sam moved toward the bathroom. He fished through his ruck and found the bag from the CVS, his hands trembling and the plastic crinkling as he riffled it. He closed his hand around something and carried it toward the loft, set his foot on the bottom rung, stepped up until his face and Rufus's were level—although

Rufus was upside down, which pretty much summed up everything about the redhead.

Sam held up the pack of spearmint gum.

Rufus stared at the gum for what was maybe only a second, and then a smile broke out across his face. He took it with a sense of uncertainty, closing his fist around the pack.

Sam held out his hand, palm up, waiting.

Rufus made a sound under his breath that was definitely amusement. He carefully peeled the package open and offered Sam a stick.

Fingers trembling, Sam unwrapped the gum and tossed the stick aside. And then he did a silly, high-school thing. Something he'd wanted to do for a long time. He folded the silver wrapper into a flower.

"I'd like to kiss you," he said, his voice so rough and low, he barely recognized it, and he held out the flower.

The haze of city lights painted Rufus's face in shades of dirty orange-gray and lit up the wet of his green eyes. He accepted the foil flower and whispered a choked, "Ok."

Sam kissed him, one hand behind Rufus's head. It was the first upside-down kiss of Sam's life, but it was pretty fucking awesome, to quote his high school self. Something hot and bright and wild woke in Sam's chest, and he kept climbing, still kissing, scooping up Rufus and carrying him into the loft with his momentum. The space was tight, a queen bed squeezed under a low ceiling, but Sam wasn't worried. He wasn't planning on doing a lot of standing.

Together, they tumbled backward onto the bed. And credit where credit's due, Rufus was an unbelievable kisser. The first few kisses were great. Then, as they found their rhythm, the right match of demanding and giving, taking and resisting, the kisses got even better. Too many guys had to be in charge one-hundred percent—if they wanted to kiss at all. This, with Rufus, this back and forth, this was so much better. Sam's hand splayed low on Rufus's belly, relishing the charged heat of his skin, drifting up, across his ribs. Sam wanted to do this in the sunlight, where he could count every freckle, kiss every one of them. Although, doing it in the gray haze of the city was fine in Sam's book. Hell, he'd have been perfectly happy in pitch dark, just the two of them.

Rufus brought his hands up and clasped the back of Sam's neck. He combed his fingers through the short hair at his nape with one hand, while the other kneaded and dug into Sam's muscles. Rufus shifted underneath and brought a jean-clad leg up, rubbing and pressing against Sam's thigh.

It was too much. It was all too much. Sam started shivering, and the shivers turned into all-over shakes. He had to pull away, breaking the kiss, muttering, "Shit, shit, shit." He had to cover his eyes with one hand and take deep breaths.

"What?" Rufus asked—well, more like panted. He propped himself up on his elbows. "What's wrong?"

Starting at seven, Sam counted himself down. Then, no more wiggle room, no more pussyfooting. But he kept his hand over his eyes. "You know, uh, you know how the backs of your knees are ticklish?"

Rufus drew both legs up instinctively. "Are you going to tickle me? Don't be a buzzkill."

The smile broke across Sam's face in spite of his best efforts; he dropped his hand and met Rufus's eyes. "No. But… that's the best way I can explain it. I told you I don't like touching, right? Well, not because it hurts. It's—I don't know—overwhelming. Sounds too. A lot of the time. And smells, sometimes. My brain doesn't know how to handle all of it. But touch." He shivered again. "Fuck. Which is why I wear my T-shirts inside out like I never finished third fucking grade. Which is why I go commando. Which is why my socks are inside out, and sometimes upside down because of the stitching over the toe. Lots of stupid, stupid, stupid shit." Another residual shiver worked through him. "Shit, I messed everything up. I'm sorry."

Rufus scooted until he was sitting upright. "It's all right. Would you prefer I not kiss you? Would that help?"

"You should definitely kiss me. And, uh, keep doing that thing, um. With your leg. But—fuck, why do I feel fourteen fucking years old right now? Just, if I freak out, or seem like I'm freaking out, uh, it's because I really like it but don't know how to handle everything going on, ok?" Sam leveled a finger at Rufus, trying to regain some semblance of self-respect. "For the record, this is why I fuck guys and send them on their way, without all the touchy-feely stuff. Not because I'm an asshole. Well. Not exclusively because of that."

Rufus cracked a smile. "Touchy-feely, huh?"

Grinning, Sam crooked a finger. "I'll show you."

Rufus shifted and knee-walked across the mattress.

Hooking an arm around Rufus, Sam tugged him closer, his fingers worming under the waistband of Rufus's jeans, sliding under the elastic of the briefs, and then he tugged again, until Rufus was almost pressed up against him. He bent and kissed a line from Rufus's shoulder to his neck.

"Like that," Sam whispered, pulling back to look at Rufus, running his free hand through the red chaos of hair. "Or that." He kissed Rufus once, and then he moved forward, his weight bearing Rufus down into the mattress again. Sam shifted until they lay side by side; he traced Rufus's cheekbone. "Or that."

Rufus's smile was bright now, encompassing his entire face. He mirrored Sam's motions—slipping fingers through Sam's hair before rubbing stubble along his strong jawline with the pad of his thumb. Rufus leaned close and kissed Sam's neck. Sam shuddered again, but didn't tell Rufus to stop—so he didn't. "I've always wanted a touchy-feely kind of guy," he whispered before kissing Sam's mouth once.

A smart response was probably expected. Rufus probably liked guys like that, guys who were clever in bed, who had their shit together. Sam, on the other hand, had his eyes half-closed, his breath a whirlwind in his chest. "Uhh." Well, that was some kind of response, right? And, all things considered, with Sam's brain overloaded and frying, with his dick so hard that he was afraid he was going to shoot from Rufus touching him like this, it seemed like a pretty good response.

Rufus sat up. He put his hand on Sam's shoulder, encouraged him onto his back, then swung a leg over to straddle his hips. "This not too much?" he asked, leaning over to kiss and gently bite Sam's neck some more.

Rocking up into Rufus, trying to get contact, stimulation, anything that would push him over the edge and end this, Sam just groaned again, shaking his head in an attempt to answer. His hands were trembling, and he locked on to Rufus's thighs, running his hands up and down, the denim rasping.

"Do I have to rip these off?" he managed to say.

"I'd rather you didn't," Rufus said against his throat before sitting up. He lifted up, unbuttoned the jeans, then took a moment to wiggle out of them. "I don't have enough clothes for you to be tearing them apart every time you want to get laid."

"Shit clothes," Sam said on a thin breath, because most of his attention was on Rufus in nothing but a pair of gray briefs. Hooking his thumbs in the elastic leg openings, dimpling Rufus's pale thighs, he added, "These too." Then he ran his hand between Rufus's legs, felt him hard, and said, "Please."

Rufus laughed, and it sounded wonderfully carefree. "Since you asked so nicely." He yanked the underwear off, straddled Sam again, and firmly pressed his knees into the man's sides. Rufus's breath hitched a little as their naked flesh came into full contact. He rocked against Sam, held his face, peppered his mouth with hungrier, more insistent kisses.

It wasn't so much that Sam lost track of time. It was that he lost a measurement for time. His mind, always tuned so precisely to the persistent presence of the world, now seemed unmoored. He had to settle for new anchors. New ways of measuring time. Heartbeats, of course, although they stopped being useful as his heart accelerated. And then the rhythm and meter of Rufus's kisses. The grit of skin against skin. The explosions of breath when everything became too much, and Rufus would ask quietly, "Ok?"

Sam would answer something, anything, because this was more than ok. This was better than any shower fuck or midnight blow job, better than the frantic need to get off and get out, better than all the one-offs of Sam's life stacked together. So no matter how intense it got, no matter how overwhelming, until Sam didn't know where his body ended, he said yes. When Rufus asked, he said yes. And yes. And yes.

CHAPTER
FIFTEEN

Rufus watched soap suds swirl around his toes on their way down the drain. He'd been lingering in the hot shower, one-tenth for the sheer enjoyment of not being the one stuck with the gas and water bills at the end of the month, nine-tenths because he'd had sex with Sam last night and had been on the cusp of losing his mind since the minute he'd woken up to a still-dark city.

Sam's confession in bed, about fucking guys and sending them on their way—Rufus had understood that. And while he was typically the one in the *sent-away* position, he nonetheless comprehended Sam's situation and how different last night had been for both of them. They'd touched and caressed, and Rufus's starved body soaked in the attention and affection that Sam provided, even when it threatened to undo him. And they'd kissed. *God*. Sam's kisses were like whispers from Heaven across Rufus's lips.

He touched his mouth at the memory. The sensation, pressure, warmth, and rasp of stubble still lingered, as if Sam had just assaulted his mouth seconds ago and not the night before.

Last night had been incredible and a little terrifying.

Because now Rufus had to look Sam in the eye this morning without any idea as to what their situation was. Was he supposed to acknowledge the earth-shattering sex, or pretend it never happened? Was he supposed to say the stupid, embarrassing sweet nothings that spun around in his head like the soap suds at his feet, or swallow them down and let them simmer in stomach acid? Rufus wished he'd checked out more books from the library about relationships or communication or *something* like that, because he was starting to panic a little and it was mixing with his already questionable humor:

Title: *Help! I Had Sex with a Man While Investigating a Murder.*

Subtitle: *I Like Him as More Than a Friend but I've Never Been in a Relationship, So What's Next? A Rufus O'Callaghan Story.*

Rufus turned the shower handle. He grabbed a towel—Jake's, he tried not to think about that—and dried himself. He shook his head like a dog, sending a spray of water across the small room, then pulled on yesterday's jeans, which he'd had to grope around the loft floor to find, and wasn't that a particular sort of embarrassment. Looking for one's pants.

Hand on the doorknob, Rufus spared Sam's ruck a glance. Had it belonged to anyone else, he'd have gone through it. Not to steal anything—it was just that itch for details Rufus had never been able to shake. The desire to understand the inner workings of another human. And maybe also the thrill of being somewhere he shouldn't. But Rufus left the room without touching the ruck. It felt wrong, taking a *Sam thing* without asking.

In the kitchen, Rufus stared at the Keurig on the counter, opened a cupboard, and rummaged through the contents for the coffee pods. He found a half-empty box labeled Decaf and shook his head. "Whoever you were banging, Jake, I sure hope he gave good head." Rufus tossed the box into the cupboard again, found a supply of hazelnut a moment later, which was better than nothing, then went about filling the Keurig and cleaning out a mug. He tapped the icon for a medium-size brew and turned to lean back against the counter, still sans shirt.

Rufus ruminated on his shower thoughts. *I've never been in a relationship.* While true, where had that bubbled up from? And why? Did he want to be in a relationship with Sam?

Yes.

He didn't know much about the guy, but didn't every relationship start out that way? People learned about each other as they went along. At least, Rufus thought that's how it worked. Maybe some folks broke the ice playing Twenty Questions or Truth or Dare, or maybe that was why speed dating appealed to others.

All Rufus knew was that Sam had bought him gum after losing to a fair-and-square bet. He'd asked permission for a kiss. Asked permission for more. He'd made Rufus feel loved and beautiful last night. But even if that *did* mean a relationship was on their horizon, what about the fact that Sam didn't live in New York? He'd only come to the city because of Jake's suspicious death. When this shitshow was behind them, Sam would want to leave. He hated the city. Would he expect Rufus to go with him, back to… wherever home was? Rufus had never left the city.

He couldn't imagine living elsewhere. And considering he was a dropout with an—albeit scrubbed—record, what the fuck could he do for a living that wasn't CI work?

Wasn't this just fucking *grand*?

Rufus took a few steps forward, grabbed the mostly dry T-shirt from the desk chair, tugged it over his head, then sank into a crouched position. He held his head in both hands while trying to focus on the gurgle and sputter of coffee. Keeping that sound in the forefront of his mind kept Rufus in the here and now. It kept the panic at bay, only barely. He could feel his fingers starting to tingle and that weird, high-pitch buzz in one ear. It was the kind of panic that stole his breath and sent him to rooftops. He squeezed his eyes shut and briefly considered whether he needed to vomit, but the physical sensation was practically scared out of him when a voice broke the stillness.

"Morning," Sam said, moving over to the Keurig, then padding around the apartment naked, as though completely oblivious to the fact that Rufus was *right there*. Sam picked up things. Put things down. Examined the towel he'd dropped on the floor as though he'd never seen a towel in his whole life. After what felt like two hours of consideration, he swung it over his shoulder and continued his naked inspection.

Rufus stood and waited for Sam to say something, like "Why were you on the floor?" "Why're you as white as a ghost?" "Are you going to puke?" But none of that came. Was this like what he'd done before Sam explained his tremors—pretend you didn't see anything?

Rufus cleared his throat and pointed a slightly shaking hand at the Keurig. "There's coffee, but it's hazelnut."

After sweeping his gaze around the apartment again, Sam seemed to realize, oh, hey, Rufus still exists, and came across the room. He cupped Rufus's face, brushed his lips across Rufus's, and then moved back to the kitchen counter.

"You smell nice," he said as he rummaged for a second mug.

Rufus scrunched his face up while thinking. He'd spent the last thirty minutes quietly losing his mind, and after all that… he got a good-morning kiss? So had he overthought the situation, or not panicked *enough*? "I showered. Not that I usually don't."

"Huh."

"What's that mean?"

Peering into the mug, Sam worried the ceramic with a thumbnail. He glanced up. "What? Oh. Nothing."

Wasn't this an epic clusterfuck in the making….

Rufus silently joined Sam at the counter, picked up his mug, and took a sip of coffee. He was staring at Sam as he lowered the cup.

"Are you ok?" Sam asked as he fiddled with the coffee maker. "You're hungry. I guess normally I'm supposed to make you breakfast or something, but—" His gesture took in Jake's loft. "So I should… go out and pick up some food?"

Rufus furrowed his brows. "Make me breakfast?" he echoed. "Why would you do that?"

"Are you mad at me? What's going on?"

"I'm not mad. I don't understand why you'd make me breakfast."

The blush was barely there, just a hint, but Sam rolled those massive shoulders and played with the towel. "Yeah, that was stupid. I don't know what to do. I kind of thought that's what I was supposed to do, you know, when someone stays over." Yanking the towel down from his shoulder, he took off for the bathroom. "I should get dressed."

Rufus put his mug down with a clatter. He spilled coffee across the countertop, the floor, and his hand. He hissed and shook his fingers while following after Sam. "Hang on. That wasn't stupid to say." Rufus stopped in the middle of the room, watching the bathroom as he raised his red hand and sucked the skin.

Dragging the ruck into the living area, Sam opened the bag and pulled out a white tee, a fresh pair of jeans, and socks. He froze, stared at the towel, and then he dug around in the bag until he came up with soap and deodorant. Hands full, he headed into the bathroom.

"Thanks," he called over the white-noise rush of the shower starting. "But you don't have to be nice. It's fucking embarrassing that I'm thirty-seven fucking years old, and I have no fucking idea what to do when a guy I like is actually still in bed with me in the morning."

A rattle and then a clash punctuated the sound of running water, and Rufus imagined the shower doors being manhandled by an overanimated Sam. Then Sam's voice came back through the din: "Give me ten minutes and we can pretend I didn't act like an asshole out of a romantic comedy."

Rufus slowly crept into the bathroom and sat down on the toilet lid. "You didn't act like an asshole. It caught me off guard, is all. I have no idea what to do either. I've never...." He sighed and put his face into his hands, muttering around them, "Fuck me."

The shower door rattled back an inch, and Sam poked his wet, shaggy head out, a small grin on his mouth. "I knew it. You *were* a virgin."

Rufus shot him a glare between parted fingers. "I was not."

Sam disappeared back behind the clouded glass, but the shower door stayed open an inch. "So this is new for you too, huh?"

"Yeah," Rufus said as he lowered his hands into his lap. "I have no idea what the process is for interacting with a guy I came on last night."

The shower door rattled again; Sam stuck his head out, short dark hair heavy with water and spiking across his forehead. "I think the only polite thing to do is come on them again."

Then he was gone, vanishing into the steam. But the door clattered open a few more inches.

"You're getting the floor wet, you know."

"Then you'd better decide. In or out?"

Rufus hesitantly stood. "I already showered." But he yanked his T-shirt off and made quick work of his jeans before slipping into the shower behind Sam. "I'm going to get pruney."

Sam closed on him, drops slicking his chest, steam wicking up from his shoulders, a grin on his face as he spun Rufus into the spray and kissed him. Then, pulling back, he said with an even bigger grin, "Trust me: I know how to do things fast in the shower."

Sam hadn't lied. It'd been fast and hot and a little rough, also Rufus's first time screwing around with a guy in the shower, which turned out to be more pleasant than he'd expected. After getting dressed for a second time, his thick, fiery hair dripping water onto the shoulders of his T-shirt, Rufus stood just outside the bathroom, studying his fingertips.

Taking his hand, Sam examined the wrinkled fingers and kissed them. Then he said, "Rufus, I need to tell you something. It's, uh. It's kind of serious. It's probably going to feel really sudden. It's going to change this whole thing between us, and I don't know if you're ready, but I have to say it. I need to say it."

"The hell are you talking about?" Rufus asked, tugging

his hands from Sam's hold and having to consciously stop himself from taking a step backward.

"For the first time since meeting you, I think I might be hungrier than you are."

Rufus's shoulders dropped and he let out a huge held breath. "*Jesus Christ.* You nearly made me shit myself." He walked into the main room, picked up his Chucks, and hopped from foot-to-foot as he yanked them on. "You're paying."

In the bathroom doorway, Sam stretched, huge biceps flexing behind his head as he lolled against the jamb. He shrugged. "I'm always paying."

"That's because my skinny ass is always broke." Rufus tugged his beanie down over his wet hair, slid his arms through the jean jacket sleeves, and walked to the front door. "But you wanted to make me breakfast, right?"

"Yeah," Sam said with a smile so transparently happy that it came close to breaking Rufus's heart. "I did."

CHAPTER
SIXTEEN

At breakfast, while Sam watched Rufus devour a platter of eggs, pancakes, bacon, and potatoes—and, to be fair, while Sam devoured his own platter of food— they decided to check out the address Juliana had given them in Queens. Rufus led them to a long-term spot in a parking garage where Jake had stashed his car. *Cool* and *sporty* weren't exactly the words Sam would have used to describe it; the 1992 Impala was only slightly bigger than a Matchbox car, with an underbelly of rust that flaked when Rufus planted both hands on the trunk and rocked the vehicle on its suspension, as though concluding some sort of sales pitch.

"See?"

"Nobody likes a know-it-all."

It wasn't exactly easy to boost the car, but it wasn't exactly difficult either. The not-difficult part included smashing in the back passenger window, reaching his arm through, and unlocking the door. The not-easy part consisted of squeezing his torso into the driver's footwell, fumbling with panels and wires. Rufus skipped along the cement, seemingly with the sole intent of seeing how loud he could make his Chucks squeak while belting out show tunes. He seemed to know most of *Chicago* by heart.

But after some time lying in the mulch of old leaves and gum wrappers in the footwell, Sam got the right wires, and the Impala choked and wheezed to life, and a few minutes later, they were on the road, the Impala's tiny engine purring like a kitten in a noose, until they were driving through Manhattan in the stop-and-go traffic that seemed endemic to a city this size.

"All the way east," Rufus said. "You need to get on the FDR. We'll take the tunnel into Queens." He popped open the glove compartment like he knew what he was hunting for. "Three bucks," he mumbled, grabbing the single bills from the stash of junk people often collected in their glove compartments. "Oh, and fifty cents." He turned to Sam. "I need another five bucks. For the toll, not me," he added with a grin.

Queens wasn't exactly what Sam had expected. In his mind, it had existed as an extension of Manhattan, more glass and steel, everything crowded together until it shot up like saplings desperate for sunlight. A spillover, more or less. The same thing, just on the other side of the East River. But in reality, Queens wasn't just more of Manhattan. Sam knew he was missing lots of little things, the nuances that someone more sophisticated and urban savvy like Rufus would immediately intuit. But he could still point out some of the differences.

Queens still felt like a city to him, but more the kind of city he was accustomed to: apartment buildings and dense commercial corridors, but also strip malls and parking lots, single-family residences, churches with lawns that needed mowing. Instead of the snake scale of brick and stone undulating through Manhattan, here clapboard, vinyl, and even old asbestos shingles sided framed buildings. Some of the signs were in multiple languages—English and Korean predominated, although up one street Sam spotted the gleaming white thumb of a minaret, and Arabic script on the front of the mosque burned where sun touched the brass.

The address from Juliana took them to a quiet residential street—well, quiet was relative now, Sam realized. On one side, two brick apartment buildings shouldered against each other. A woman in a hijab was jogging with a stroller, phone pressed to her ear. On the other side, single-family homes in weathered siding lined the block. Sam eased Jake's car down the block, nodding at the house they were interested in: it had probably once been robin's-egg blue, and it had bleached to a color that a yuppy home designer would probably call slate or river-stone or something like that. Two stories, a narrow driveway with an aluminum carport sticking out like a broken wing. In all of the windows, blackout curtains were drawn.

"It'd be nice if they could put bars on the windows and concertina wire around the place," Sam said. "Just so I didn't feel so fucking freaked out by it."

"You're thinking of Sing Sing," Rufus replied, staring out the passenger window at the home. "For a place housing a dozen kids, at least, it seems kind of quiet. I mean, for a nine-to-fiver, it's normal, but this home shouldn't feel like all the others." He turned to Sam. "Right?"

"Definitely. No van in the driveway either." He turned

at the end of the block; catty-corner at the intersection stood a bodega with a frayed banner announcing it Park's No. 3 Flushing, and Sam marked it on the mental map he was making. He drove around the block—more houses, more apartments, an Assembly of God church slanting hard like it had had a little too much to drink. All of it went on the mental map. "Park on the same street as the house? Or should we ditch the car before we get there?"

"Ditch it. If someone *is* there, if they maybe knew Jake, they might know this piece of shit as well," Rufus said, tapping the dashboard.

Sam found a spot on the cross street, jiggled the wires, and let the Impala shudder and die.

"Maybe we'll get lucky," Sam said, staring at the broken window. "Maybe somebody'll steal it before we get back."

Rufus opened the passenger door and said while climbing out, "You won't like the 7, so don't jinx us." He looked at Sam over the rooftop. "Although, lots of trains in Queens are above ground. If that helps."

"The only thing that's going to help is that this time, I wouldn't mind having a certain redhead grind up on me on purpose and pretend it was all the train's fault."

Rufus's cheeks got red and blotchy, causing his freckles to stand out in contrast. "It *was* the train's fault."

Unable to help the little scoff in his throat—or, for that matter, the little grin—Sam took off on the sidewalk. He noted the buildings around him, trying to catch a feel for this place the way Rufus had. One of the apartment buildings had a small playground, the old-fashioned kind with everything made out of steel that got screaming hot on a July day like this. A couple of kids, both under five, sat unattended on the gravel fill, both of them seemingly content, looking around seriously. But otherwise, the street was empty for the moment. As Rufus had said, it was a work day, and people had to work. It made sense; it just didn't make Sam feel any better.

"Shit," Sam said, his heartbeat rising, pressing his hands against his jeans. They had maybe twenty yards of sidewalk before they reached the house. Curtains drawn. No van. Nothing, in fact, that made it seem like anybody was actually in there. "Shit, do you really think it's empty?"

Rufus removed two small lock-picking tools from his inner jacket pocket. "Only one way to find out."

"Ok," Sam said. "Go for the carport. Heckler's the only one who's seen me so far; nobody else knows me from Jesus. I'll knock on the front door. If anybody answers, you get your ass out of there. Got a clipboard? I'm going to play the Jesus card."

"I called you God last night—you don't need a clipboard," Rufus said, dead serious and without missing a beat. He kept moving forward and vanished into the carport.

Even if Sam had known how to respond, he didn't have a chance. He kept going until he got to the walk that led to the front porch, and then he took it at a brisk pace, shoulders squared. What did people who went to church talk about? What did they want? What did they wear? Probably not white tees, inside out, bought extra-large to cover a holstered Beretta. Well, fuck, he'd seen the Assembly of God building, and he was going for it.

When he got to the door, he knocked. Then he counted down by threes from ninety-nine. Then he knocked again, harder, the door rattling in the frame. He started his count again, this time by fours from a hundred and twenty. As he raised his hand to knock a third time, though, the door swung open.

Rufus grinned up at him and waggled his eyebrows. "Whatcha sellin', hunk?"

Something snarky flitted through Sam's head, but then

he smiled as he walked past him into the house. "That's a good look on you, so you know."

"What is?" Rufus asked, his voice just above a whisper. He gently shut the door and turned to Sam.

"When you're really proud of yourself like that and trying to hide it, but you're such a punk, you can't keep it all inside." Sam tried to keep a straight face, pretending to study the empty entry hall as he added, offhand, "It's cute."

Rufus bit his lower lip. "Ah, well, thanks. Anyway, I think the house is empty."

"It looks empty. There's a difference." Sam unholstered the Beretta from under the tee and held it low, pointed at the ground. "Please don't tell me you want to split up."

"Against the odds, I've made it to thirty-three."

Sam hemmed. "So, if I tell you, just hypothetically, that you and your freckled ass are staying behind me until I'm one-hundred percent satisfied that the house is clear, because I'm not very useful but I do have a small skillset that might apply in this situation, let me guess.... You'd tell me to... fuck off?"

"Hypothetically speaking? There is a distinct possibility of that, yes."

"Did you at least bring a gun?"

Rufus held both hands up. "I don't own a gun."

"How about this, then? You at least try not to step right in my way when I'm shooting. Deal?"

Rufus saluted Sam. "*Oui, mon capitaine.*"

"If I die with a smartass," Sam said as he moved toward the archway on the left, "do I have to spend eternity with a smartass?" Without looking back, he added, "Don't answer that."

They moved through the main floor room by room. Without furniture or rugs to muffle any of the sound, the wood floors made every movement louder, and no matter how hard Sam tried, he couldn't keep their progress through the house completely silent. Ancient joists creaked and groaned. Hinges protested. In the kitchen, Sam's foot caught a plastic bowl that was the exact same color as the tile underfoot, and it clattered away explosively, the noise making Sam's breath hitch. Rufus smirked about it for two more rooms until the redhead started hissing and batting at the air and stumbled into a French door.

"Jesus Christ," Sam growled. "We might as well have brought your whole fucking tap-dance studio with us."

Rufus at least had the decency to look chagrined as he whispered, "It was a big spider."

They found nothing on the main floor that corroborated Juliana's story. As they completed the circuit, Sam caught Rufus's eye and pointed a finger up, then down.

A visible shiver shook Rufus's body. He worked the material of his beanie with one hand, like he wanted to yank it off and tug at his hair in a nervous method. He eventually pointed up.

The stairs, which didn't look structurally sound, creaked under their weight. Carpet strips, probably intended to prevent slips and falls, had been glued on at some point, but many had been ripped away, leaving only trails of resin or, in a few cases, a few patches of carpet fiber. At least one of the risers was missing, and Sam pointed it out so Rufus wouldn't accidentally put a foot through the empty space. Halfway up, Sam caught a whiff of something foul, and he pulled his tee up over his nose. It wasn't rot, not exactly. But it made him think of death, and cold sweat broke out on his back, his shoulders, his forehead.

The first two rooms upstairs were just like the downstairs: completely empty. But the bathroom was another story. Someone had ripped out one side of the shower curtain rod, and it now hung across the tub at an angle. *Another wounded wing*, Sam thought, picturing the aluminum slant of the carport. Whatever had caused it had happened recently; plaster dust lay fresh on top of the toilet tank. As Sam got closer, he could see the rust-colored stains on the shower curtain, and more of the stains on the aging grout. Balancing himself, Sam leaned over the fallen curtain rod for a closer look and grunted. A tiny web of cracks worked through the ceramic. Something had hit the tile hard.

Stepping back, he glanced at Rufus and jerked a thumb at the destruction, eyebrows raised in a question.

Rufus first inspected the side of the bathroom door. He ran his knuckles lightly against wood around the locks, freshly splintered. He slipped around Sam next to study the tub stains and then the tiny window that'd been left open a sliver. It was like watching a man take apart the world around him, piece by piece, Sam thought. Rufus deconstructed a situation, studied each portion of the whole, then put it together again to see how it functioned as a singular moment. The problem with that: Sam was becoming more certain that Rufus's understanding of these studies in brutality came from a place of practical experience.

And that was shattering.

"Someone was hiding in here," Rufus said, voice still low. "Put up a fight, but couldn't make it out the window in time."

With a nod, Sam motioned out of the bathroom. They followed a hallway toward the back of the house; like the floors below, this one creaked, and so Sam kept his steps close to the wall, where he was least likely to put stress on the protesting boards and joists. He glanced back and saw that Rufus was already doing the same.

Two doors waited at the end of the hall. Sam opened

one and found only darkness and the smell of mold. It was a linen closet, empty except for green-black speckles that marred the ancient cabbage-rose wallpaper that had been laid down on the shelves. Shutting the door, Sam moved to the next room.

At some point, this had probably been intended as the master bedroom, although the house had obviously been built long before anyone had started doing en suite bathrooms with Jacuzzi tubs and whatever the hell else suburban wives dreamed of. It was bigger than the other bedrooms, though, with a closet that, not quite walk-in, might be described as shuffle-in. Two mismatched windows, one large and one small, looked out the back, their glass thin and old.

What held Sam's attention, though, were the unmistakable smells of piss and shit, of something else he could only describe as fear. It was a miasma, polluting the room. Pushing the door open as far as he could, he rucked up his shirt again to cover his nose and mouth, and then he paced the perimeter of the room. On the wall with the door, he found what he was looking for, beckoned to Rufus, and pointed.

The work had obviously been done quickly, without any care for the damage to the walls, and some effort had been made to remove the most incriminating pieces. All that remained was a series of thick bolts anchored in the studs. Plaster crumbs flecked the floorboards, and although someone must have swept, the effort had been sloppy— maybe, Sam thought, even hurried. Not even enough time to remove the bolts, which told the most important part of the story.

Rufus tilted his head to the side as he studied the wall. He put his wrist against the bolts, frowned, then moved into a crouch—which was where his body needed to be for everything to line up.

"These kids were chained," he said, but the statement inflected upward into a question, almost like Rufus needed confirmation because it was too fucking gross to believe on his own.

Nodding, Sam held out a hand. "Some of them, at least. Stand up; it's bad enough knowing without having to see it too."

Rufus grabbed Sam's hand and got to his feet. "Disgusting…."

"Have you seen anything that might tell us where they went? They left in a hurry, I think." Rufus hadn't let go of Sam's hand, and Sam didn't let go either. Walking through a nightmare like this was bad, really bad, and having Rufus helped. "Maybe because of Jake? He got too close? Christ, I don't know."

"That's a distinct possibility." Rufus moved to the doorway, tugging Sam with him. "I want to check the fridge." He shot a look over his shoulder and clarified with "To see if anything is spoiled. It'll give us a timetable, at least."

"And then we have to check the basement."

Rufus grunted. He went back down the hall, slow and careful steps all the way to the death-trap staircase, then to the first floor. He let go of Sam's hand once they entered the kitchen, walking more confidently across the room to the fridge. Rufus leaned in to examine the sparse contents, grabbed a gallon jug of whole milk, popped the top, and took a sniff.

"Not spoiled," he said before putting it back. He shut the door and studied a dated toaster surrounded by crumbs on the countertop. His gaze roamed over dirty dishes in the sink, and then he began to open the lower cupboards before finding a garbage bin. Rufus crouched and dug through the trash—almost exclusively fast food wrappers. "There's dozens of burger wrappers in here." He looked at Sam. "No Happy Meals, but I don't think I need that kind of evidence to conclude they were feeding a lot of people—*kids*—the cheapest shit they could buy."

"When you're hungry enough, you'll eat anything," Sam said. "And it's one more mechanism to ensure good behavior."

Rufus frowned and shoved the bin back under the cupboard. He rose to his feet and pointed at a closed door on the other side of the fridge. "Basement, I'm guessing."

"If you want," Sam said, "you can check the main floor and upstairs once more. Make sure we didn't miss anything."

"I'm not afraid of basements," Rufus protested, squaring his shoulders. He stepped over the bowl from earlier and opened the door. He reached into the dark and felt around the wall before finding a light and switching it on. It was barely bright enough to illuminate the staircase. "Just spiders," he concluded.

Sam hooked a finger in one of Rufus's belt loops, hoisting him up an inch with an improvised wedgie, and said, "This is one of those times when I'm going to gently remind you that I prefer you stay behind me until you have your own gun."

Rufus squirmed out of Sam's hold and tugged at his underwear through his jeans. "That was *not* gentle."

Raising an eyebrow, Sam slipped past him and started down the stairs, adding quietly over his shoulder, "Later, I'll kiss it and make it better."

The stairs were wood, open on both sides, with a single wobbly rail that probably was supposed to offer some kind of support. Sam took his hand off it after the second step; it was loose in the wall, and the tremors in his hand made the handrail rattle.

The basement was dark and smelled like cold cement; only as Sam's eyes adjusted could he make out the papered-over windows. He took out his phone, turned on the flashlight, and swept the light in an arc.

The basement was 'finished' in that half-hearted way of so many older homes: exposed support beams spray painted black, a few metal columns, the cement floor painted and sealed, and from what Sam could see, the sealant yellowed with age. No effort had been made to divide up the space into rooms. He spotted a washer-and-dryer combo straight out of the '70s, one of the big plastic water barrels people used to collect rain, and a behemoth of an oil furnace. The weak glow from the flashlight didn't reach all the way across the basement, so Sam's first move was to walk the perimeter again, playing the light in wide arcs, making sure he got an initial look at every inch of the room.

By the time he got back to the stairs, Rufus had his head in the washing machine, his bony butt in the air. Sam sighed and moved to check the furnace. It wasn't like a wood-burning stove, though, so he didn't find any doors that opened where someone might have burned incriminating evidence. Unfortunately. He moved back over to join Rufus and saw that the redhead was picking through the plastic barrel.

"Shit," Sam said, "what reeks? That smells like gasoline."

Pinching cloth between two fingers, Rufus held something up from the barrel.

"A blanket?" Sam said.

Rufus nodded and dropped it back in before warily plucking at the rest of the contents. "Bedding. Old sheets, nasty blankets." He wiped his hand on his jeans. "Guess they planned on burning it all."

"In a plastic barrel?"

Rufus shrugged and rubbed his jaw. "Human traffickers are monsters—no one said anything about being evil geniuses."

"Jesus Christ. We're dealing with morons. All we have to do is keep following them, and the dumbfucks will back themselves into a corner. They're probably too stupid to have any sort of exit strategy."

The sound of the front door opening ran through the house, and steps moved above them. At the same time, Sam and Rufus both looked at the stairs, which were the only way out of the basement, and then at each other.

"You were saying?" Rufus said.

CHAPTER
SEVENTEEN

Rufus crept toward the rickety staircase and looked up at the partially open door. He listened to the sounds overhead—steps, weight, and tread distinctly two individuals—cautiously moving from the home's entrance to the empty room on the left. Rufus pictured the strangers making a circuit like he and Sam had done, poking their heads into what might have been a sitting room and eventually ending their search in the maybe-dining room with the... *French doors.*

Rufus climbed the rickety steps without a word, quieter than Sam had managed on the descent. In the threshold he poked his head into the kitchen, confirmed it was still empty, and turned to Sam, who was starting to come up behind him. Rufus held his hand out, motioned for Sam to stop, then vanished into the kitchen and around the corner. Hugging the wall, Rufus drew closer to the doors he'd previously smacked into after flailing around with the spider. He grabbed the handle to one of the doors and not-so-gently slammed it shut, the glass rattling in the frame and bouncing off the empty walls and wood floor.

Rufus fled to the kitchen as the intruders returned to the home's foyer and continued onward to inspect the commotion in the dining room. Sam stepped out of the basement, and Rufus grabbed the sleeve of his T-shirt while running by. He led the way into the empty sitting room in order to dart out the front door while the strangers had their backs turned.

During the whole search of the house, Sam had kept the gun at his side, barrel pointed down. Now it came up, and although Rufus could still see the tremors in Sam's hand, he could also see something drop over Sam's face like an iron curtain. The guy who liked to tease, who liked to say, *it's cute*, who had folded a foil gum wrapper into an origami rose—that guy was gone, buried under the iron. As they moved into the next room, Rufus spotted the newcomers, and Sam was already shouting, "Put your hands up, motherfuckers."

Two men turned in unison, only one raising his gun in time to be pointing the weapon at Sam. He had cropped blond hair and those nerdy glasses that reminded Rufus of NASA engineers à la Apollo moon landings. The second man was a few steps deeper in the room, gun at an awkward midpoint that did nothing for him. Both wore dark clothes and had gloves on, which in July heat made it painfully clear they had no intention of leaving fingerprints in their wake.

"Who the fuck are you?" the blond asked. He had the slightest hint of an accent, but it was bastardized from living in New York for so long that Rufus couldn't place it.

"Drop those fucking guns," Sam shouted. "Drop them!"

"However you got in here," the blond continued, his aim rock-steady, "just go right back out the same way. We're not looking to have to dump a couple of bodies."

Rufus's brain fired on all cylinders. He memorized the strangers' faces, clothes, noted the illegal suppressors on their pistols, repeated NASA guy's words over and over, perfecting that slight lilt in his voice in case it was all he had by way of identification for the police. Then a single thought wormed its way through the haze of adrenaline, fear, and details being catalogued, and that was: *two to one.*

Sam had to defend them both because Rufus was skittish of guns and never wanted to touch one, let alone own one. And now, barrels raised and fingers on triggers, he stood there like a complete fucking useless lump with nothing to fight with except his bare fists. But Sam was ex-Army. He could handle this, right? If he hadn't been trained for this sort of situation, then what the fuck were Rufus's nonexistent taxes even paying for?

Two to one.

Rufus was pretty sure he heard the unaccounted footfall first. Maybe because he wasn't laser-focused on a target. His eyes flicked toward the front door left open several inches. He thought at first a breeze and rusting door hinges must have been the source of the noise. But no. There was no breeze. It was hotter than the subway platform of West Fourth Street. Then the door opened wider—enough for a woman to poke her head in, startle, swear, and grab for the holstered gun on her belt.

"Put your weapons down," she ordered, still struggling to free her own.

"For fuck's sake," Sam muttered, but he didn't shift, the gun still pointed at the Bobbsey twins. "A little help?"

he said to Rufus.

"What am I supposed to do?" Rufus hissed through clenched teeth, watching the front door.

The woman had a black shingle bob like Louise Brooks. *Ophelia Hayes*, Rufus belatedly recognized. A beat cop nowhere *near* her regular stomping grounds. Hell, she wasn't even in the right borough.

"Just about anything would be fucking fantastic," Sam growled. "For fuck's sake, I'll take the fucking cha-cha at this point."

NASA swore—*Russian*, Rufus acknowledged, and he could have smacked himself—and turned toward the door. He shot and missed, splintering wood.

Ophelia fell out of sight. She called from outside, "NYPD!"

At the same time that NASA's gun swung toward Ophelia, Sam shouldered into Rufus, forcing him away from the firefight and bringing up his own gun. He squeezed off two shots, and NASA's buddy dropped. Blood misted the wall behind him.

Ophelia's arm came into view through the doorway, now holding a service weapon, probably her off-duty one, considering she wore street clothes. She squeezed the trigger, caught NASA in the throat, and he dropped like a boat anchor. Blood pumped from the wound, pooled around him on the floor, and he made a few sick gurgles before his body and breathing stilled.

Ophelia slowly eased into view, the gun shaking in her hold. She glanced to her left and then pointed the weapon at Sam. "Drop it!"

Sam had his gun trained on her. "Point that thing somewhere else," he said. "Right fucking now."

Ophelia looked from Sam to Rufus, who winced and awkwardly held his hands up in submission. "Unless you've got a badge too, put the weapon *down*."

"Badge," Sam said; the tremors in his hands worse now. "Slowly."

Ophelia reached into the back pocket of her jeans, yanked a black wallet free, and with one hand, she raised the badge high enough for Sam to see.

"Well?" Sam said, shooting the question toward Rufus.

"Hi, Ophelia," Rufus said in response to Sam, but he kept his eyes trained on Ophelia.

From outside came shrieks of laughter, kids running past the front of the house, and then the grumble of a diesel engine.

Sam lowered the gun.

Ophelia was tall. Not Rufus or Sam tall, but still taller than most women, with a light complexion, sharp nose, and thin eyebrows that complemented the bob hairstyle. She stepped into the study, keeping her weapon at low-ready. "What the *hell* is going on here?"

"What does it look like?" Sam said. "These assholes tried to kill us."

Rufus lowered his hands and moved around Sam. "We were considering buying the place," he explained, pointing at the floor, "but I've never been a fan of blond wood flooring."

Ophelia raised an eyebrow. "You fucking joking?"

"A little."

"Great. Glad two guys blown to fucking chunks are such a laugh. Get down on the ground. You too, big boy. Slide the gun over here."

Sam just looked at Rufus.

"Whoa, Ophelia, come on," Rufus protested. "It's *me*. Look the other way and I'll scram out the back door, ok?"

"Down. Right now. And I wasn't joking about that

gun."

"The fuck," Rufus said, a bit more astonished. "You'd be dead if we didn't intervene."

"So would you. Listen, I saw what I saw. Those guys shot first. But I watched your buddy put a bullet in that guy. Old times are old times, Rufus, but you're in some deep shit right now. This is the last time I'm going to say it: down. Right fucking now."

"Rufus?" Sam asked.

"Hang on," Rufus countered. "Make a call first to Detective Anthony Lampo. Tell him I'm here and he'll know what to do. I'll even give you his card if your happy little trigger finger will let me get my wallet."

Ophelia's mouth thinned, and her eyes moved to the dead men. Then she said, "Sure, you get your wallet, and let's see what the fuck I walked into. And your big-ass action figure can put his gun right back in that fucking holster and keep his hands where I can see them."

"Better put your G.I. Joe gun away," Rufus whispered in Sam's direction while he took the wallet from his back pocket. He kept the money flap closed and carefully thumbed through where a regular person would have stored credit cards. Rufus instead kept a library card, an ID with his photograph but not his name, a card for a free pizza slice he'd won last month and hadn't yet claimed, and both Jake and Lampo's business cards. Rufus tugged the last one free and offered it.

Ophelia took the card and fixed Sam with a gaze. Only after Sam had holstered his piece did Ophelia place the call, holding the phone to her ear as she watched them.

"Officer Ophelia Hayes," she said before rattling off a badge number. She listened. "Yes. Yes. I understand, sir, but I've got an unusual situation here." She frowned. "Yes, that's right, he goes by Rufus. How did you—"

"Of course he knew it was you," Sam muttered.

"I understand," Ophelia said, "but I've got two dead men, and this is an officer-involved shooting. I can't just—" This time when she cut off, she glared at Rufus like he was responsible for the whole thing. "Yes. Yes, I understand. Just a minute. You two. Bozos. Up against the wall. Spread 'em."

"For fuck's sake," Rufus grumbled as he turned and put his hands on the nearest wall. "If Lampo's so curious, tell him I dress to the left."

Once Sam was in position, Ophelia moved behind them. She patted Rufus down in quick, efficient movements, turning up his wallet, his phone, and the pack of gum. When she repeated the process with Sam, she produced his phone, folded cash, an ID, and the gun. She held on to the gun when she backed away.

"That's mine," Sam growled.

"No, sir," Ophelia said into the phone. "Nothing but the weapon."

Rufus turned around. "The weapon that saved you," he added, loud enough that Lampo might have heard his voice in the background.

Ophelia ignored him. She was still talking into the phone—well, doing more listening than talking. "If you say so, sir. Yes, sir." Then, once more, biting the words off savagely, "Yes, sir." She disconnected and shoved the phone in a pocket. "You two dumb fucks have the first get-out-of-jail-free card I've ever seen actually work."

Grinning triumphantly, Rufus raised his hands and clapped them together. "Lampo smacked your butt, didn't he?"

With a grimace, Ophelia passed the pistol back to Sam. "Both of you are supposed to clear out. Right now." She hesitated, and then she said, "Are you here about the kids too? Lampo said you were doing something for him and that I shouldn't jam you up."

Rufus's smile waned, and he glanced at Sam before asking, "How do you know about that?"

"CI," Ophelia said. "I think you might know her. She seemed to have some second thoughts about sending 'such a sweet little boy' into the jaws of hell."

Sam snorted.

"Juliana's a CI?" Rufus asked, surprised. "*Fuck*. All right…. Lampo's coming, then? We'll bail." He turned to Sam and pointed toward the carport.

Nodding, Ophelia said, "Rufus, this isn't stealing Pop Rocks out of a bodega, ok? Juliana said—well, there's bad people on the other end of this. Dangerous people. Whatever you think you're helping with, you might want to lie low for a while." She held out a business card. "If you think you've got something, get in touch. Otherwise, let us clean house."

Rufus hesitated a beat but then took Ophelia's card. He gave Sam's T-shirt sleeve another tug and led the way to the side door he'd previously broken in through. Rufus quietly shut it behind them and glanced at Sam. "Let's get the fuck out of here before someone else pulls a gun."

Sam just nodded and let Rufus drag him to the sidewalk. When they were clear of the house, he asked, "What was that about?"

Rufus put his sunglasses on and shot Sam a sideways glance. "What, Ophelia? She caught me stealing a package of pomegranate seeds from a bodega years ago. The owner didn't catch me, but I guess she thought I was cute and was watching me." He smirked and waggled his eyebrows above the rims of his sunglasses.

"It's the air," Sam said.

"*I* think I'm cute," Rufus continued.

"No, it's the air in this fucking city. Car exhaust. Pollution. Too many rats and not enough trees. Nobody's getting enough oxygen. That's why you're all fucking batshit." Sam pointed a finger. "I'm talking about the pat down in there. What was that about?"

Rufus shrugged and stuffed his hands into his jacket pockets. "Well, Rambo... you were armed and she's a cop."

"Yeah, but she did it because Lampo asked her something. That was part of her little report back before she let us go."

Rufus considered Sam's comment as he jumped over a few cracks—not that his mother was in danger of breaking her back. "I don't know why Lampo would ask her to pat me, and you by proxy, down."

"I don't either," Sam said. "But I don't like it."

Stopping abruptly, Rufus cut Sam off and turned to face him. "You think Lampo wants the pickup Jake meant for me?"

With a frown, Sam shrugged. "It makes sense, right? Jake contacts you for a pickup. Jake gets killed. You're supposed to get killed, but you Rufus things up and get away. If I were Lampo and my partner had just gotten murdered, half the cops wanting to pretend it was a suicide, then yeah, I'd want to know what you were supposed to pick up."

Rufus thumbed his bottom lip thoughtfully. "Except I was given jack-all and it's like he doesn't believe me. I wasn't in the room very long with... Jake... but I didn't see anything. I mean, nothing that'd make me think it was a tangible object for me, at least." He began ticking points off on his fingers. "Marcus stole Jake's phone. It was clearly hot. Heckler took Marcus out. Heckler stole Jake's phone." Rufus looked at Sam again. "Maybe we should scope out Marcus a bit more. I mean, I know he's dead, but he lived somewhere, yeah? Who knows what sort of shit he was involved with?"

"That makes sense," Sam said. "If Jake had the pickup with him, Marcus must have grabbed it. Maybe he stashed it as some kind of insurance, which did fuck-all for him because Heckler blew his brains out anyway."

Rufus was already nodding as he spun on one heel and continued walking.

"Good thing you've got me with you," Sam said, a tiny smirk tugging at one corner of his mouth. "Maybe this time you'll find something better than a bag of chips."

"Jake's place was clean. The chips were about all there was to find."

"I watched that place for half an hour after you went in there. It took you half an hour to find a bag of chips?"

Rufus turned to walk backward. "I had no reason to rush," he said with a touch of defensiveness. "In fact, let's bet again—who finds the pickup first."

"I'm going to feel bad taking your money."

"What? No. You can't just—you're not going to find it before me. Ten bucks."

"I barely got out of gum debt." Sam hemmed. "Let's go big: loser buys dinner."

"If you win, then your dinner is going to be coffee and sugar packets." Rufus licked his finger and motioned dabbing with it. "Gotta use your finger too."

"Why do I get punished if you lose?"

"Life sucks."

"Snake," Sam said.

"Don't you dare. Come on. You still have Marcus's ID, don't you?"

Sam tapped one pocket.

Of course, they were nowhere near where Marcus

called home, and Rufus had to provide directions to get them back into the city—115th and Second Avenue, to be precise.

Rufus passed some of the time stuck in midday traffic fiddling with the car radio. Finding nothing but the latest Top 20 pop songs and an endless stream of local, cringeworthy commercials, he tapped the power button and leaned back in the passenger seat. He glanced at Sam's profile. "You know something? You're pretty cute."

"It's my moisturizer."

"It is not." Rufus shifted uncomfortably in the seat. It wouldn't go back farther and his knees were practically knocking the dash. "Do you use moisturizer? I didn't look in your ruck, cross my heart."

"No, not usually. Do you usually look in other people's bags?"

"What do you think?"

"So I'm cute? I feel too old to be cute."

"How old are you again?" Rufus asked. "Thirty-five?"

"Thirty-seven."

Rufus made a so-so motion with both hands. "All right, so maybe you're not *cute*."

Sam leveled a look at him.

Rufus started laughing. "*What*? Christ, I was going to say you were hot. But if you're going to give me fuckin' stink eye...."

"You're lucky I'm driving."

Rufus was still laughing under his breath as he turned to study the building numbers out the side window. He pointed suddenly. "That blue building, I think."

"Later," Sam said.

Rufus was patting his jacket pockets to confirm his tools were still tucked inside. "What's later?"

"Later, you're going to tell me I'm hot. And you're going to be very convincing."

Rufus raised his eyes to the roof, hummed dramatically, and in general, made a show of contemplating Sam's words. When Sam pulled to the side of the road, Rufus said to himself, "Maybe you don't deserve the compliment now."

Yanking the parking brake, Sam turned to look at Rufus again. Then his hand slid to Rufus's thigh. Then his hand slid up. And Sam's eyes were dark and alight all at the same time, his expression closed. "Rufus, baby?"

Rufus suddenly couldn't swallow, his mouth parched. "Y-yeah?"

Sam kissed him, hard and quick, and whispered, "I'm really, really sorry." Then he kicked open the door and got out of the car. "Now move your ass so you can buy me a saucer of sugar or whatever the hell you were talking about."

Rufus opened his door, started to get out, and was choked by his seat belt. He swore loudly, hit the release, and stumbled out. "I want a fancy dinner," he called, slamming the passenger door and catching up to Sam, who was already approaching the old apartment complex. "For when you lose. Something with tablecloths and candles and shit."

With a grunt, Sam jerked his head at Marcus's building. "This is a lot of fucking foreplay just so you can lose a bet."

Rufus slipped in front of Sam, drew dangerously close, and tit-for-tat, whispered huskily in Sam's ear, "You haven't had foreplay until me, hunk." He smirked at Sam's expression and then went to the front door.

Rufus looked through the grimy glass window, confirmed the vestibule was empty, then made quick work of the dated lock on the door. A handful of seconds and they were inside, studying the mailboxes lining the wall. Rufus knuckled 2B—Marcus Borroff—and headed up the stairs that had been painted a dozen times over in landlord high-gloss black. He paused at the staircase landing long enough to take in all the sounds of the building, but it was afternoon and no one—on that floor, at least—sounded as if they were home. Rufus moved to the first door on the left, broke in with such speed and dexterity that he could have made it an Olympic sport, and motioned Sam inside with a sweeping gesture.

"Wow, what a dump," Rufus said after closing the door. His nose wrinkled a little. "All right, so I know it's conjecture, but what do you think we're even looking for?"

"Let's make some educated guesses. Educated guess number one: Jake had something tying Heckler to those trafficked kids. We know Juliana pointed him at the kids, and we know Heckler's dirty. That doesn't seem like too much of a leap. Educated guess number two: whatever Jake had was solid enough that Heckler was worried—otherwise, she would have let Jake flail. Educated guess number three: Jake waffled because he's Jake, classic fucking waffler—otherwise, he would have sent the evidence to the FBI or the state attorney general or somebody instead of standing around with his dick in his hand."

Rufus was frowning as he moved into the garbage-littered living space. He listened to Sam while watching a roach scurry out from under a pizza box—the damn pest was big enough to wield a knife. "Incriminating evidence against a badge," Rufus began. "If Jake trusted a petty thief more than anyone else." Taking his sunglasses off, Rufus turned and added, "More than one of the 'good guys.' So a tangible item, yeah? Like a notebook? Tablet? Something used to keep track of the comings and goings of the business?"

"Photographs," Sam said. "Videos. Shit, what if he

was going to tell you a name?" He shook his head. "Never mind, that's a dead end, so let's not even think about that. Something physical. Something you could carry. Let's start there. Did Jake ever have you do other pickups? Did he ever give you anything—I mean, anything, ever?"

"Yeah. A few in the past. He'd text me a meetup address—always different—have me hang on to something or do a drop-off. Then I'd ditch the burner." Rufus was thoughtful for another moment, and then he smiled at a recollection. "Jake bought me dinner sometimes. As a job well done, I guess. He bought me a book at the Strand too."

"Well, I don't think he gave Marcus a book." Sam glanced around the apartment. Then he looked back at Rufus. "What book?"

Rufus felt his cheeks warm but he shrugged. "I don't remember."

Another moment passed, and then Sam turned away. "Great. Really helpful. You can remember the numbers on streetlamps or whatever the hell you were talking about. Fine. Let's look."

Rufus ignored the dig and nudged a plastic bag on the floor. It was full of wadded tissues and empty soda bottles. "I guess Jake failed to mention any *X*'s marking the spot in those e-mails to you, huh? In between the keyboard smashes and relationship comments?" Rufus regretted the words even as he said them.

Sam's shoulders straightened, but he was still studying the other side of the room. "What's that supposed to mean? That little jab about relationships."

"Nothing. Never mind. Jake never said anything in an e-mail?"

But Sam was quiet for almost a full minute, and when he did speak, he only said, "I would have told you if he had."

"I know. You have them memorized." Rufus went to the mattress on the floor and warily picked up a blanket, checking underneath.

"And what the hell does that mean?"

"*Nothing*. I didn't mean anything about anything. I'm stating a fact—you have the e-mails memorized." He didn't turn around.

"For fuck's sake," Sam said, breath exploding after the words. He spun to face Rufus. "I can't do this. If you're hung up on Jake, if you... I don't know. I just can't, ok? I like you. I told you stuff I don't tell anyone. I'm too fucking old to be in my own fucking head about whether you're hung up on a dead guy. And, apparently, I'm too fucking old to be cute. And I know I'm the one who said that, so don't—" The words cut off as he tucked his hands under his arms. "I'm really, really fucking overloaded right now. I think I need some fresh air or something."

He staggered toward the window and yanked on the latch.

Rufus's stomach was doing somersaults. He dropped the blanket to the mattress and studied Sam—his back turned and shoulders shaking as he hunched over the window. "I'm not hung up on Jake. Not... really. It sucks, even thinking about him. He made me feel smart and needed, and I miss him." Rufus yanked his beanie off. "But I like you too. And I didn't mean to upset you. I'm still trying to get a grasp on... what sets your tremors off. I'd like to help, if I can."

Sam's breathing was labored, but after a minute, he said in a low voice, "Page one of the Sam Auden freak-out manual: get him something soft, something cool, something that smells like mint or grass or lavender, something with a nice texture. Get him somewhere open, away from people."

Rufus pulled the pack of gum from his pocket and

then leaned against the wall beside Sam. "It's spearmint, but that's close, right?" He held out a stick in one hand, and his beanie in the other. "This isn't really soft, but you *do not* want to touch that blanket over there. Pretty sure Marcus used it as a jerk-off sock."

Forehead to the glass, Sam took a piece of gum, folded it in half, and put it between his teeth. Then he accepted the beanie, big fingers knotting in the wool, his thumb moving restlessly over the ribbing. He closed his eyes. When he spoke, his voice was distant. "So, you have now officially had sex with a guy who needs toddler accessories to keep him from flipping out of his skull." Then he shook his head slowly, forehead still in contact with the window. "I wasn't trying to be shitty. I just—Jake had this whole life that I don't know anything about, and I keep thinking of the Jake I knew. It's messing me up."

Instead of acknowledging that comment, because Rufus felt like he, too, was studying Jake through the looking glass, he asked, "Do you want me to touch you?"

"Shit. I don't know. Yes."

Rufus pressed one hand between Sam's shoulder blades. He moved it up and down a little, but mostly kept it there as an anchor. "You're freaking out about me having sex with a guy like you, and I don't know why you'd be interested in a guy like me. Does that equal us out? Like a math problem?"

"Uh, no. One cute, redheaded smartass does not equal one fucking nutjob."

Rufus smiled a little, squeezed the back of Sam's neck, then said, "Stay there. I'll search the rest of the apartment." He moved off the wall and added, "You can't keep my beanie, though."

"No, I'll help. I'm ok. I just—" Sam laughed, pushing back from the glass, and then he wiggled the beanie into place on Rufus's head. "Believe it or not, I really was in the Army; I wasn't always such a fucking headcase. Tell me where you want me to start."

CHAPTER
EIGHTEEN

Under any other set of circumstances, Sam wouldn't have caved to a technicality. And the redhead had been so goddamn cocky about the bet, so goddamn sure that Sam would lose, so goddamn snide about the place he was going to make Sam take him when he lost. It felt like the whole thing was rigged. But if Sam were honest, Rufus being cocky was actually kind of cute. And technically, Sam had lost the bet—the terms were that Sam would find the pickup first. Which he hadn't. The fact that Rufus hadn't found anything either didn't seem very important at the moment.

Rufus kept the crowing and strutting and, yes, even a little bit of preening to a minimum. For Rufus. They'd parked the junker on the side of the road a dozen blocks away, and then he took Sam west and downtown. As they walked, Sam started doing some mental scrambling. Rufus deserved something romantic; that much was pretty obvious to Sam. But when your entire amorous life fit in a shower stall, what the hell was romantic supposed to look like? Was Sam supposed to buy him flowers? Was there going to be live music, a piano or a violin, something classy, and Sam was supposed to—Jesus Christ, was he supposed to fold a twenty and slip it in the waiter's pocket and ask for something like "Dream a Little Dream of Me?" What the hell did normal people do on dates? The closest Sam had ever gotten to romance was when he let the guy share the hot water before kicking him out.

Not true, a quiet part of his brain said. *Not true, because you packed candles for that float down the Chattahoochee. You bought that piss-poor excuse for a beer that Jake liked. You knotted a lanyard around his wrist, and both of you got chills when you looked up. You kissed him, and that kiss wasn't just about fucking in a tent or blow jobs out by the fire, the heat from the coals scalding your back. That kiss was its own kind of fire.*

But thinking about Jake, thinking about those days when Sam had skated closest to something normal, that didn't help. That didn't help at all. If anything, it increased his panic. What if Rufus wanted Sam to choose a bottle of wine? What if Rufus wanted him to order something off one of those godawful menus where everything was in French? What if Rufus—

Rufus had stopped at a set of stairs that led down from the sidewalk. A door painted turquoise hung open an inch at the bottom of the steps, and a sign in the window said: Central Park Masala. And then below, for those who needed a little help: Indian Restaurant.

"Here?" Sam said.

Rufus looked at Sam with a huge smile. "Want to give

it a try?"

"You won the bet; you pick."

Rufus trotted down the stairs in answer. He pushed the door open and was asking a passing waiter for a table as Sam came down the steps. The restaurant was hardly big enough for half a dozen tables, all with placements for two people. The lights were low, with a warm tungsten glow. There were currently four patrons split between two tables, the one young waiter catering to each, with an older woman overseeing the register in the front and kitchen in the back.

Rufus and Sam were offered the farthest corner table, and even as skinny as he was, Rufus had to contort himself a bit to get into the seat that backed up against the wall without enough space for his long legs. Still, he hadn't stopped smiling. "Smells good," Rufus stated. "Whoa, and check out these tablecloths." He smoothed the tabletop with both hands.

Trailing his fingers down the tablecloth, Sam looked up, looked around, took a deep breath: cardamom and cumin, coriander and ginger. Maybe even cinnamon. No music. No stuffy waiters. He flipped the menu—a single, two-sided affair—and he could read every word. Then he looked up at Rufus.

"Is this ok?"

Rufus picked up his own menu and stared at the listings. "How should I know? I haven't been here before."

"No." Sam forced Rufus's menu flat. "Is this, you know…." When he couldn't come up with anything better, he repeated, "Ok?" Rufus's stare gave him nothing, so Sam gestured. "Are there supposed to be candles? What about wine? Are you going easy on me because I freaked out?"

Rufus wiggled out of his jacket, tugged his beanie off, and said, "No."

"No?" Sam forced his shoulders to come down. "But

I want to take you somewhere romantic. I'll do that thing where you stuff money in, you know." He mimed a jacket pocket.

Rufus's eyebrows went up to his hairline as Sam spoke. Finally, he shook his head and said, "I don't even know what you're doing. This place is perfect, don't you think?" He glanced over his shoulder, up at the lighting, then added, "Low lights, no one around, and we've got our own corner. If I can get my leg under the table, we can even play footsie."

"This isn't some sort of soft letdown?"

"*No,*" Rufus drew out, more firmly this time.

Silverware chimed. A girl at the next table laughed softly and leaned in to say something to the older man she was sharing her meal with. Sam wiped sweat from his forehead and said, "Ok."

They ordered. Or rather, Rufus ordered. Sam contributed a few suggestions, but Rufus made the final decisions, and the list of dishes—curries and chicken tikka masala and lamb vindaloo and dal, on and on like that—made the young man waiting on them grin.

"I guess we're putting him through college," Sam said with a grin. Then he flagged down the waiter and asked for two Taj beers, and the young man's smile got even bigger. "Don't say anything," Sam said to Rufus.

Rufus hadn't stopped smiling, and his expression was the most real and open Sam had seen since they met. "Thank you for this."

"You're welcome," Sam said. "Thank you. For everything. Honestly, I have no idea what I'd have done if you hadn't been seduced by those chips."

Rufus's cheeks got pink and blotchy. He scratched at his cheekbone where one freckle in particular stood out in stark contrast to all the others. "I guess you got lucky. Nearly nine million people in this city, and you happened to drop in on me."

The Taj came, and Sam took a long pull, watching Rufus over the brown glass. "Very lucky," he said when he pulled the bottle away.

They ate. When the bill came, Sam flipped through his wad of cash—his rapidly shrinking wad of cash—and tucked the money under the plate. Then, standing, he held out his hand. With one of his crazy Rufus grins that was somehow both bashful and full-on shit-eating, Rufus took it.

Jake's apartment wasn't far from the little restaurant. They walked, and although the city continued its normal bustle—the breakneck pace of all those people trying to be where they needed to be, get where they needed to get—Sam found himself sliding through the throngs, Rufus guiding him through the press. Horns, shouting, the rumble of a hundred thousand engines idling at red lights—it all became a sound wall in Sam's head, but instead of fighting it tonight, he crashed into it and let Rufus tow him. A trim woman, older, looking like a million bucks, played a mean game of chicken, and she flipped Sam a double bird when he veered at the last second. Even that couldn't shake him. He just floated after Rufus.

Then they were inside Jake's building, Rufus tapping the mailbox, taking the stairs, passing into the relative dark of the apartment. No more waiting; the thought was a pile of gunpowder in Sam's belly. As the door closed behind him, he planted himself and pulled back, reversing Rufus's momentum, drawing the redhead into his arms, turning so that he could bear down on Rufus, pressing him against the door.

He kissed Rufus on the neck. He kissed him on the ear. He kissed his cheek. His lips ghosted over Rufus's once, twice, like testing for heat that could burn. And then he kissed him, really kissed him.

When the kiss broke, Sam brought his mouth to Rufus's ear and whispered, "I think you were going to tell me how hot I am. At length."

Rufus laughed, but it sounded like a shaky exhale at best. "Oh, that's right...." He put his hands on Sam's face and caressed his stubble with one thumb. "You are, quite possibly, the hottest man I've *ever* had the pleasure to stare at."

"Pretty good," Sam said as he moved down, nipping at Rufus's collarbone. "B for effort."

"*Christ*," Rufus gasped before managing, "I finally made the Honor Roll." He gave Sam's hair a tug so he could kiss his mouth again. "I stand corrected—you are *definitely* the hottest man. Maybe since time began."

A little rumble worked through Sam. He slid one hand under Rufus's tee. He wanted contact, yes, but he also wanted to grab. To possess. His hand slid up over smooth skin. His thumb flicked a nipple. "Better, but you know what they say: practice makes perfect."

Rufus gulped like a landed fish. "I think I was absent from school during that lesson." He slid his hands down Sam's back and under the hem of his shirt. "I can't believe you look at me like this. You could get anyone. I bet you do."

The words caught Sam; they suffocated the gunpowder smoldering in his gut. He pulled back and tried to catch Rufus's gaze, and then he kissed him.

"What's my policy on bullshitting?" Sam asked, his thumb rubbing a slow circle along Rufus's areola.

"You don't," Rufus whispered. He gripped Sam's back harder, dug his nails into warm flesh.

"Not things that are important to me. You are important to me. You're smart. You're brave. You're kind. I can tell you the things that would make most assholes run away, and you find a way to make them better. And you are gorgeous." Sam slid down to his knees, rucked the tee up, and planted a kiss on the galactic disc of freckles low on Rufus's belly. "But, gotta be honest, you're lucky you've got all these freckles."

Then he worked the button on Rufus's jeans. The zipper on the fly stuttered on its way down, and then Sam dragged the jeans to Rufus's knees. His hands came up again, stroking over the cotton briefs, heat radiating through the thin fabric. He palmed Rufus once, the cotton wet and bunching under his fingers, and pulled his hand away. Something was running through Sam, something like the tremors that came on him so often now, but different too. Once, outside Bagram, he had watched a bird plummet from the minaret of a mosque, a black arrow diving toward the sunbaked clay, and at the last minute, its wings unfurled, and the feathers were iridescent in the sun as it skimmed the ground, trailing reddish-brown dust like a fighter jet. This, touching Rufus this way, was like that. Sam looked up at Rufus. He slid the briefs down; the waistband had left red tracks in Rufus's fair skin. And then he took Rufus in his mouth.

Rufus knocked the back of his head against the door. A sob tore out of this throat, sounding like protest, like relief, like passion, like desperation. It was a combination of base animal need and an exquisite symphony playing out at the same time. One hand held the back of Sam's head, keeping him close, never letting him pull back entirely, while the other rested on Sam's shoulder, as if Rufus needed distance and didn't know why. Didn't understand why. Maybe was afraid to consider the why.

Sam wasn't exactly watching the clock, but it didn't seem like it took long. He let Rufus run as much of the show as he wanted. When Rufus slacked, Sam took over again. Sam liked giving a good blow job, but he liked the noises Rufus made a lot more. And then, Rufus was clutching at him, whimpering, thrusting. Coming.

When Sam pulled off, Rufus sagged against the door, and Sam braced hands on knees and looked up at him. Rufus's face was blank. Chuckling, Sam ran the back of his arm across his mouth.

"Ok," he said. "I'll take that as a compliment. Come on."

Hoisting Rufus over his shoulder, he fireman-carried him to the sofa, where he helped him stretch out. He tugged the briefs back into place but got rid of the Chucks and the jeans, and then he jostled Rufus until he could squeeze onto the cushions. They lay there for a while, Sam teasing out strands of silky red hair, trying to make it stand up in the weirdest ways he could imagine.

"You alive in there?"

Rufus laughed lightly. "I think so. That was amazing." He looked at Sam. "What about you?"

"Yeah," Sam said with a smile. "I liked that."

Rufus shifted and propped himself up on an elbow. "That's not what I mean."

"I'm fine. Honest. I just wanted it to be about you." Sam raised an eyebrow at the silence. "Come on? Nobody's ever done that for you?"

Rufus looked at Sam once or twice, but the eye contact didn't linger. "Not really."

From the street came the hub and murmur of the city, underscored for a moment by the *whup*, *whup*, *whup* of a helicopter. Sam ran his fingers up the knobs of vertebrae in Rufus's back, hooked the collar of his shirt, and dragged him back down onto the sofa. Then it turned into a mixture of wrestling and forced cuddling, with Sam trying to wrap himself around Rufus and Rufus laughing and trying to get free.

Sam ended up on top, and he leaned to kiss Rufus. Then he stopped. "Oh. Yeah. I'll go brush, I guess."

"I know where my dick's been." Rufus pulled Sam back down and kissed him.

For some reason, Sam was blushing after the kiss. But he kissed Rufus again, out of gratitude. And then he kissed him again. That one was for fun. Then, dropping onto his elbows, he framed his body around Rufus's.

"Bad news: you're officially my captive."

Rufus snorted and said, "Oh yeah? I fight dirty and don't regret it afterward. You really want to test me?"

"I'd be willing to consider an early release in exchange for some information."

Rufus hummed under his breath. "Interesting. Continue."

"One Rufus thing."

Rufus's carefree expression skipped and stuttered. "I already told you a Rufus thing."

"I'm greedy. I want another."

Rufus turned his head and said nonchalantly while staring everywhere but at Sam, "Rufus things are pretty dull."

The helicopter was still somewhere out there, *whup*, *whup*, *whup*ping its way across the whole city, it felt like. Sam tapped on Rufus's jaw. Rufus swatted at his hand. Sam tapped again.

"Cut it out."

Sam tapped again. And again. Until Rufus turned back and looked at him.

And Sam wasn't sure what he saw, but he knew enough to stop. He rolled off Rufus, getting to his feet, and said, "Want to shower?"

Rufus sat up. He grabbed Sam's wrist before he could move out of reach. "Hang on." His mouth worked and his Adam's apple bobbed a few times. "A Rufus thing...."

Three years ago I decided to kill myself. But my building is only four stories—fifty percent probability. So I found a taller one." Rufus laughed, but it was pure reflex. His grip tightened to the point of pain on Sam's wrist. "When I was up there... I decided I didn't want to be the cause of someone else's shit night."

Lowering himself onto the coffee table, Sam locked his free hand around Rufus's wrist, turning them into a chain, Rufus holding Sam, Sam holding Rufus. "Why'd you want to do it?"

"I don't want to talk about that."

"Thank you for telling me. And, so you know, you can always tell me you don't want to talk about something. It's better than trying to figure out if I messed up or if I made you mad." Sam hesitated. "Are you still thinking about hurting yourself?"

Rufus glanced up, his green eyes bright and wet behind locks of disarranged hair. His face and neck were flushed. "Sometimes, I guess."

Nodding, Sam said, "Are you getting help?"

Rufus laughed again, but it was very bitter, and very hurt. "You're kidding, right?" He disengaged from Sam's hold. "I don't want to keep talking about it. I just wanted to tell you another Rufus thing."

"We don't have to talk about it right now. You don't ever have to talk about it with me, not if you don't want to. But you have to talk about it with somebody. Soon. I want to help you. And I care. And there are other people who care too. That waitress, Maddie, or whatever her name was. She cares about you. Jake cared about you. So you don't have to talk about it right now, but we need to get you in to see a therapist as soon as we can. And if you talk about money, I swear to God, I will put you over the arm of this sofa and paddle you until your ass is as red as your hair."

Rufus had begun to protest, was stopped numerous times as Sam kept talking, then offered a brittle smile. "I might like that."

Sam rolled his eyes. "That sounds about right. Christ, what day is it? Friday? I mean, we can try to do this tomorrow, but it might not be until Monday. I don't know. This is a big city. They've got to have walk-in places for situations like this even on the weekend." He glanced back at Rufus. "I'm just thinking out loud."

Rufus jumped to his feet and sidestepped the coffee table. "No. Stop. I'm not talking to a stranger about this."

"Ok. Hey, come here."

But Rufus didn't. "You're making this a huge deal, Sam."

"It is a huge deal." Sam stood up faster than he meant. The coffee table toppled behind him, and the crash climbed the walls of the studio. "You're a huge deal, Rufus. You say stupid things about how you can't figure out why I like you. I like you because you're fucking incredible. And then you tell me you're thinking about hurting yourself. You're goddamn right I'm going to make it a huge fucking deal."

Rufus's face was red now, fists clenched so tight that his knuckles were white, and his breathing came quick and shallow like a small panicked animal. And then, without warning, huge tears rolled down Rufus's cheeks and he broke into a sob. "Please stop," he begged. "I can't—I *can't.*"

"Christ, I'm sorry. I'm sorry I yelled." Sam scrubbed his face, and then he took a single step toward Rufus. "Ok, come here. I'm not going to say anything else. Just come here, I'll be quiet if you'll just come over here."

Sam expected more of a fight, so he was surprised when Rufus immediately closed the distance between them, wrapped his arms underneath Sam's, and pressed himself against the bigger man's body.

"Talking about it makes it worse," Rufus said between hiccups and tears.

Wrapping arms around Rufus, Sam lowered his chin into the red crow's nest. "Thank you," he said. "Thank you for telling me." He kept saying it over and over again because he thought he'd been saying the right things, thought he'd been doing it right, and somehow he'd only made it worse. "You're ok. We don't have to talk about it. We're both ok."

CHAPTER
NINETEEN

Based on the gray-blue light filtering into the studio, rising up toward the loft like incoming tides, Rufus suspected it was close to six in the morning. The sun would cast a whitish-yellow illumination over the city soon, and it'd be the start of a new day.

Another day.

It always came.

Without fail.

It always came because Rufus had never been able to get over the idea of some poor SOB getting called to Rufus's self-made crime scene, their night being fucked after having to shovel his blood and guts off the pavement, only to be left unclaimed with the city medical examiner's office, stuffed into a pine box, and buried with a number instead of a name on Hart Island.

Rufus O'Callaghan didn't have anything in life *but* his name.

So he wasn't going to allow *himself* to take that one last shred of dignity away. Rooftops were still tempting—hadn't stopped being tempting. The city twinkling from far away, beautiful like a siren's song, and the asphalt below the rocks his ship crashed into.

He turned his head on the pillow and studied Sam, still asleep, which frankly surprised Rufus. He had screwed up so hard last night. They'd gone on a real—ok, sort of real—date. And had amazing sex afterward, during which the only sensible thought Rufus had managed to compose was *This must be what it's like to be a prince*. Then he obliterated everything built up between them by telling Sam *that thing*. In retrospect, it probably wasn't the worst truth locked away in his Pandora's box, but it sure as fuck was up there in the rankings.

It'd been enough to scare Sam. And that had scared Rufus.

Only this time, Rufus hadn't cried alone. Sam had stayed with him, held him, kissed him.

Rufus dragged his finger along the mattress, tracing Sam's body without actually touching him. He was a big guy, a strong guy, a handsome guy.

When Rufus was in sixth grade, he'd gone on a field trip to the Met. His mother had actually paid the fee and everything. It was Rufus's first time in a museum, and he'd talked nonstop about the experience for at least a week. He still remembered what it had been like to stand in front of a massive statue of Hercules—naked and youthful, holding the pelt of a lion. All those hard planes and muscles. Most definitely the son of a god. That statue had made it all click for Rufus, even at a young age. Sam reminded him of that experience. Sam was the breathing embodiment of powerful, raw masculinity that'd awakened after being entombed in marble for centuries.

What had Aristophanes written in one of his plays? *The Clouds*, Rufus thought? *A glistening chest, broad shoulders, mighty bottom, and a tiny prong.* Well, minus the small dick—Rufus never could quite understand the Greek's preoccupation with that particular aspect—Sam was a study in the ideal male form.

But it wasn't only the physical that Rufus liked about him.

He trusted Sam like he'd never trusted anyone in his entire life... even Jake. He told Sam secrets he thought he'd take to the grave. And he didn't think twice about turning his back to Sam, because Rufus *knew*, instinctively, Sam wouldn't cut him or cross him—he would only catch him.

Rufus liked Sam's presence. He felt drunk on it. Sam had those little smiles that made Rufus's heart rate speed up, dry wit and limited patience that made him laugh, and a softer, more trusting side that made Rufus feel needed again. And it meant something that Sam was comfortable touching Rufus, when he couldn't bear being physical with anyone else.

Rufus kissed Sam's shoulder, rolled to the edge of the mattress, found his burner in the back pocket of his jeans on the floor he'd dragged upstairs the night before, and got comfortable again as he began typing in the web browser. He'd been awake for a few hours, and in between the self-studies of his own inadequacy and general trauma, Rufus had been thinking hard on what that pickup had been.

The last thing Jake had given him was Chinese takeout and a tongue-lashing for what he had deemed a dangerous decision on Rufus's part to get a job done, but it'd put a real piece of shit behind bars and Rufus had been no worse for wear, so he'd shrugged Jake off. And prior, Jake had bought him that book from the Strand.

Rufus remembered the title, of course. *1001 Buildings to See Before You Die*. It'd been on the bargain rack for three bucks. Maybe Jake bought it for him because he sensed Rufus needed... a reason. Maybe because he knew Rufus would never get an opportunity to leave the city and see those wonders for himself. Or maybe he simply wanted Rufus to shut up about needing to borrow five bucks for a new book and bought the biggest and cheapest thing there to keep the punk occupied.

Whatever the reason had been, Rufus loved the book. He'd show it to Sam when all of this shit was behind them.

Not taking his eyes off his phone, Rufus gave Sam an elbow nudge. "Hey, wake up."

Sam bolted up. "Huh? What?"

Rufus glanced sideways and made a come-hither motion. "Down here, killer."

Wiping his eyes, Sam shook himself like a dog. "What? God, what time is it?"

"A little after six."

"Sleep," Sam said, dropping back onto the mattress and putting his arm over his eyes.

"No sleep." Rufus nudged him again.

"What do you want?"

"Sex, pancakes... oh! I've always wanted a pair of red Chucks. Hey, do you think the pickup item was something wild, like the location of Atlantis?"

A long groan came back as an answer. "No redheads before ten."

"I've been thinking," Rufus continued, rolling onto his side and propping himself up on an elbow. "About Jake's phone."

"What about his phone?"

"Heckler has it. And short of a miracle, I doubt we're going to get it from her. But looking for whatever the pickup *was* or *is* or—it's like looking for a needle in a haystack."

Wiping his eyes, Sam said, "Ok. So…. Nope, I'm too tired for this. What are you saying? We try something else?"

"I'm saying, we're spinning our wheels for nothing, trying to find the pickup without the key information most likely in Jake's phone. So let's focus on the phone." Rufus held up his own and tapped it a few times against Sam's chest. "There are ways to access phones remotely. Clouds and shit, right?"

"Yeah. Right. Like a backup, or something." Sam sat up. "So how do we get to it?"

Rufus mimicked Sam's motion. "I saw Jake on a website a few months ago—CallSpy, I think it was. I broke in while he was at home, and he said he was backing up data so if my skinny ass decided to steal his phone, all his info was safe."

"Well," Sam said, scrubbing his face and staring out over the apartment. "Shit. What are you waiting for?"

"For you to tell me I'm brilliant."

"This is why I said no redheads before ten." Sam pecked him on the cheek, climbed over him, and headed down the ladder. "Get your brilliant skinny ass to work, please."

"Make me coffee!" Rufus called after him. He blew out a quiet breath once he was alone in the loft. Sam hadn't said a word about last night. Maybe he never would. God, Rufus could only hope.

He looked down at his phone and tapped CallSpy into the internet browser. He scrolled down to Forgot Password on the homepage and followed the prompts for breaking into—that was, *recovering*—Jake's account. In the kitchen below, he heard Sam padding around, the sound of his movement soon mixing with the trickle of running water. A minute later, the smell of coffee floated up to the loft. After Rufus had supplied Jake's personal e-mail, a security question loaded.

What was the name of your first pet?

Jesus Christ. *Spot? Skippy?* Shitty pet names popular with children ran through Rufus's mind, but there were too many to consider. Definitely too many to try at random before getting locked out indefinitely.

Rufus got out of bed, quickly dressed, and climbed down the ladder. "What was the name of Jake's first pet?" he asked, joining Sam at the counter.

Sam passed Rufus a mug of coffee. "He didn't have any pets, I don't think. Try 'none.'"

Rufus took the beverage in one hand and typed with the other. "Hmm… no. Try again."

For a long moment, Sam was silent. Then he shrugged. "He didn't have a pet. At least, not that I knew about. Oh, shit. Hold on." Digging through the pile of clothing on the floor, Sam produced his phone, tapping the screen. "What about this?" Turning the phone, he displayed a photo album from Jake's Facebook page. The picture was of Jake standing next to an enormous hog. Overhead, a banner said: *Earlena - Georgia State Champion - 2015.*

"Earlena?" Rufus said, raising a skeptical eyebrow. "All right." He typed it in, then gave Sam a leveled look. "You've got one more shot, handsome. Screw it up and we aren't having morning sex."

Sprawling on the couch, Sam scratched an armpit. "Handsome?"

"Did I stutter?"

"Why are you always salty? No, don't answer that. My future sex life depends on this question?" Hemming,

Sam shrugged. "Pet, pet, pet. Honest to God, I don't know. Maybe when he was growing up, but once we were in the same platoon, we were deployed for too long. He wouldn't have gotten a dog just to leave it—oh. Uh. Ok. Try bulldog. Actually, Bulldog. Capital B."

"Are you *sure*?" Rufus asked.

"That was the name of our camp when we were at Bagram. It's the only thing close to a pet I can think of."

Rufus typed it in. Bulldog with a capital B. He perked up when the browser instructed him to choose a new password. "It worked!"

"Of course."

"Don't get cocky," Rufus warned. He sipped his coffee before giving the account a new password. Once successfully inside, he scrolled through the long list of data Jake apparently dumped into the cloud account every Monday morning. "He's got *a lot* of text messages from the same number. It's not any of my burner numbers…. No contact name either." Rufus looked at Sam. "I'm gonna download it all."

"Now say something like 'They're hacking into the mainframe.'"

"I won't be your *Matrix* wet dream." Rufus tapped at the screen again and then had nothing to do but wait while the download bar inched forward. He set the coffee mug on the desk and walked to the couch. "Hey."

"Well, hey there yourself, stranger."

Rufus hovered over Sam. "Last time you were strutting around in your birthday suit, I got a good-morning kiss."

"You did?" Sam stretched up to kiss him. "Like that?"

Rufus smiled. "Something like that, yeah."

Sam kissed him again, a little longer this time. When he pulled back, his voice was husky as he said, "I wasn't joking about that hack-into-the-mainframe comment.

You've got this crazy, sexy, nerd vibe going on right now. Just try it. Let's hear how it sounds."

"There's something wrong with you." Rufus looked at his phone when it vibrated in his hand. "Ah-ha, success." Rufus moved back a few steps, his brow furrowed. "Hang on… these texts look weird."

Coffee in hand, Sam came to stand at his shoulder. "What?"

"It's strings of numbers." Rufus showed Sam the phone. "This first one looks like military time, but what's the rest of it?"

For a moment, Sam stared at the screen. Then he grabbed his phone from the coffee table, tapped it a few times, and held it out toward Rufus. He had pulled up a maps app, and a pin was dropped not far from where they stood.

"Latitude and longitude," Sam said. "I don't recognize the characters there, though. Chinese, Korean, Japanese? No clue."

Rufus got down into a crouched position and scrolled with his thumb. "Japanese, I think. *This* character means gold, and when it's with these other two, it means Friday. I always remembered that because gold was like payday. Don't ask why I know this."

"I'll try," Sam muttered as he dragged on jeans. "That sounds like a meeting. Day, time, location. Anything else in there?"

Rufus hummed under his breath. "Do you remember old internet jargon?"

"Some."

"It's like cruising old sex ads from Craigslist."

"Let's see."

Rufus held up his phone. "2WF—two white females, yeah? 1BM—one black male. So on and so on."

"1RS." When Rufus glanced up again, Sam's face was stubbly innocence. "One redheaded smartass."

"No need to send a creepy message—you already have me." Rufus got to his feet.

Sam smiled at that, but the smile faded as he turned to the phone. "That's some pretty messed-up shit."

"It corroborates Juliana's story and what we saw at the house in Queens," Rufus said. "Jake was backing up digital copies of requests for people, location meetups, fuck—there's probably costs hidden in these messages too."

"And he's got the numbers those requests were sent from, right?"

Rufus glanced at the phone again, already nodding. "Yeah, it looks like it." He stared at Sam. "The messages weren't coming and going from Jake's phone, though. He was backing up another device into his personal account. So… a burner, maybe?" Rufus's eyebrows shot up at his own revelation. "That's a small tangible item I might have been trusted to pick up."

"So where is it?" Sam said, and then he shook his head. "And do we even want to find it?"

"We have to. Jake was killed because of these messages." Rufus stuffed the phone into his pocket. "But who do we hand it over to?"

"We do what Jake should have done: we make as many copies of this evidence as we can, and we send it to everybody we can think of—starting with Ophelia."

"And Lampo," Rufus continued. "Jake clearly didn't level with him on this shitshow."

"Yeah," Sam said. "Exactly. Why didn't he?"

"If I understood what made Jake tick-tock, maybe he'd still be alive."

From outside, the sounds of the city waking broke the

quiet in the apartment. "You don't really think that," Sam said. "Do you? It's not your fault, Rufus."

Rufus put his hands on his hips. "I don't know why Jake didn't tell his partner, but can we not study a throwaway comment under the magnifying glass? It has nothing to do with last night—just forget about it."

Ripping open the ruck, Sam dug out another of the same white T-shirts and his dopp kit. "Yeah. Forget about it. Forgotten. So where's the phone?" And then he went into the bathroom.

"Sam," Rufus started, following and flexing his tingling fingers. "Let's focus on *this* problem."

He must have heard Rufus coming because he kicked the bathroom door shut. "Focused," he shouted through the door. "One-hundred percent."

Rufus had come up short when the door closed. "Wow. Ok. Well, I'm going to go look for the phone," he called.

"Not without me," Sam said, yanking open the door, toothbrush hanging from the corner of his mouth so he could jab a finger at Rufus. "I'm the one who came here to find out what happened to Jake. I'm the one who's been fucking *focused* on figuring this out. So you can wait five minutes for me to get ready."

Rufus could feel his face flushing. "You're being an asshole again," he warned before fetching his Chucks. "I'm just going downstairs to check Jake's mailbox."

"His mailbox? What the fuck?"

Rufus slipped his shoes on. "That's what I said."

"I'm being an asshole," Sam repeated before retreating into the bathroom again. The door crashed in its frame.

It was painfully clear that last night was still in the forefront of Sam's mind, and Rufus's attempt to shut it down, to pack it into a box and deal with it another time—*never*—was not what Sam wanted to do. *Sam will have to deal, though*, Rufus thought as he left the apartment. Sam might have wanted him to see someone—*a therapist*—and just the idea made Rufus break out in a cold sweat, but there wasn't time for that. Rufus wasn't the priority. Jake needed justice. Those kids needed rescuing. Heckler needed to be wearing a pair of handcuffs for the rest of her life.

Rufus sat on the handrail at the stairs and slid down to the landing below. He considered the idea of a burner phone being the pickup Jake had played hot potato with. It was small and easy to hide. So where would it be safe until he felt he could enter it into official evidence? Where would no one check but his trusted CI—Rufus?

Jake would have given Rufus the address to this secondary apartment and Rufus would have pretended he didn't already know it. He'd have asked Jake were the pickup was, and Jake would have done something like *tap*, *tap*, *tap* Rufus's forehead. Because Jake knew Rufus had a thing about mailboxes.

He slid down the next handrail, then the next, all the way to the ground floor. Rufus walked to the vestibule, stopped at the wall of mailboxes, and took out the lockpick tools from his jacket pocket. He stuck the sharp tips into the lock of 9F and worked the tumblers. Rufus had been so hyperfocused on opening the mailbox, and with the *tink*, *tink*, *tink* of his tools echoing, he hadn't heard the approach of footsteps.

Then a hand wrapped around his mouth and it was too late to scream.

CHAPTER
TWENTY

Fuck Rufus was becoming a common refrain in Sam's head lately. He indulged in a few verses while he brushed his teeth. Through the closed door, he heard Rufus leave the apartment, presumably to check the mailbox—which was what he had told Sam, and that wasn't necessarily the same thing as the truth. And as soon as the thought went through Sam's head, he felt guilty for thinking it. And then he was mad at Rufus for making him feel guilty. And then the fuck Rufus hallelujah chorus started up again. And then Sam decided to take a shower.

A shower hadn't originally been on the agenda, but it moved up the list pretty fast once he thought of it. He smelled like Rufus. Could smell the redhead all over him. And he smelled like Manhattan, which was its own unique funk of sweat and grime and hot garbage. And he even smelled a little bit like Jake, or at least like the cologne that still lingered in parts of the apartment. And all together, combined with the knowledge that, once again, he had screwed up things with Rufus, it threatened to overload Sam.

So he stood under the spray, the water hot, and he soaped up with good old neutral-as-Switzerland Dr. Bronner's, and then, when it was time to rinse, he turned the temperature down by degrees. He didn't want to think about Rufus, so he fiddled with the tuner in his head until he got the Bartman game. Cubs. 2003. He'd been twenty-one, posted at Bragg, and drinking the way twenty-one-year-olds do while he watched his team go for the National League pennant. When the asshole fan in the front row—Bartman—snagged a fly ball moments before Alou would have caught it, preventing an easy out and turning the advantage to the Marlins, Sam had knocked a bowl of peanuts off the bar with his elbow and spent five minutes shouting at the umps—along with everybody else he could think of. It was a good game to replay when he was mad, but he didn't like how that frozen camera still in his head, the one showing Bartman grabbing for the ball like a greedy fuck, kept morphing into a certain redheaded asshole Sam wanted to yell at.

It wasn't until he was shivering under the cold spray that Sam realized he hadn't heard Rufus come back. He turned off the water and stood, dripping. And listening.

Nothing except the *plink plunk plink*.

When Sam rolled back the shower door, it rattled so loudly that he gritted his teeth. He hooked a towel around his waist, dragged his feet on the mat like a dog, drying them enough that he wouldn't slip and fall on his ass, and went out of the bathroom.

"Rufus?"

Still nothing. Water—cold water, because he'd turned the handle all the way to C, hadn't he?—snaked down the back of his neck. Sam fought a shiver.

At the studio's front door, he paused, put his ear to the wood, and listened again.

Nothing, nothing, nothing.

Pulling open the door, Sam stuck his head out into the hall and glanced both ways.

"Rufus?"

Another fat, cold drop slid down his nape; this time, Sam did shiver.

He closed the door and bolted it. How far to the mailboxes? A two-minute walk? Five minutes tops. Five minutes if Rufus waited for the elevator and got stuck because Mrs. Peabody or whoever the hell in 6B got her shopping cart stuck. Five minutes was an absolute outside. And it had been longer than five minutes. It had been double that, maybe triple, because Sam had taken a shower, had played the Bartman game, had sung a few verses of *fuck Rufus*.

Possibilities.

Rufus had finally had enough of Sam, and he'd left. He'd walked out the door never intending to come back; checking the mailboxes had been an easy excuse.

The thought was tempting. After all, guys had been walking out on Sam—figuratively, when they couldn't get away literally—his whole life. And, of course, self-pity was a nice, easy slide.

But, honestly, Sam didn't believe it. Fight or no fight—asshole or no asshole—he didn't think Rufus had been angry enough to leave. Not like this, anyway. And Sam didn't think he'd been wrong in feeling a connection, something real, with the redhead.

And then, in the middle of padding around the perimeter

of the apartment, Sam froze. On the sofa, Rufus's beanie lay discarded. The beanie Rufus wore every time they went outside. The beanie Rufus wore in spite of the brutal July heat. The beanie Rufus wore even though it made his messy hair even messier.

If Sam wanted to, he could believe that Rufus had left because he couldn't put up with Sam. But he wouldn't believe Rufus had left without the beanie. Rufus wouldn't have set foot outside the building without the beanie, not unless he had a very good reason.

Or unless he was forced to.

Dropping the towel, Sam jogged to the bathroom. He pulled on the fresh tee and grabbed his jeans. Socks, too, folded inside out and ready to wear. And then he pulled on his boots and grabbed his Beretta, not bothering with the holster, just tucking it into his waistband in spite of how it felt and pulling the loose tee over it.

He took the stairs two at a time, sometimes three, careening around landings. When he hit the ground floor, his heartbeat ran in his ears at a steady drone.

He had to move more slowly now. He had to be careful.

Rufus was careful, though. And something had happened to Rufus.

As he neared the front door, his steps slowed even more, and all of his attention focused on his hearing: two men arguing outside the building, their voices muffled by the front door; the ding upstairs of the elevator; somewhere in the stairwell, the clap of a fire door slamming shut. Sam's hand crept to his waistband, sliding under the tee, the cool composite grip pebbled under his touch.

And then he could see the front door and the mailboxes.

Nobody.

No Rufus.

Nobody.

Sam checked the mailboxes; J. Brower was still shut. Sam moved to the door, opening it long enough to stick his head out and check up and down the block. No sign of Rufus, although the men arguing were really going at it now, two guys in their fifties, both of them dressed like they were in their twenties, holding a verbal death match: Rihanna versus Beyoncé. He went back into the building because he didn't want to fuck up Rihanna's fanboy.

No Rufus.

And the mailbox? Well, if Rufus had come down here, he hadn't gotten into the mailbox. Whatever had happened—

—they took him, someone took him, Heckler, Lampo, don't be a fucking idiot—

Sam forced the thought away. Whatever had happened, it had happened before Rufus could check.

Then something glinted, and Sam bent down for a closer look. Lockpicks. Sam picked them up; the tremor was worse in his hands now, and somebody had scrambled the tuner in his head. No Cubs games today, folks. Just the staticky need, caught between two signals: find Rufus, and put a bullet in the head of whoever took him.

The static didn't help, though. Static wasn't a plan. Sam tried to get his head back on straight, tried to think. Somebody took Rufus; that was the only explanation. And they took him here, from Jake's building. From his secret second apartment that apparently wasn't quite so secret.

But not Sam.

That was interesting. Why not? Because he was more of a threat? The opposite, Sam guessed. Because he was a joke, irrelevant. They had taken Rufus because they thought he had the evidence Jake had uncovered. They were desperate for it. And desperate people did horrible things to get what they wanted—and they wanted what Rufus couldn't give them.

So, step one: find Rufus.

Great. Great fucking plan.

Step zero: figure out *how* to find Rufus.

Sam's options were limited. He had exhausted his resources in the city, and his options now were to try to do this alone, in a city he could barely survive, let alone navigate. Or he could try to get help.

He thought of Ophelia Hayes's card upstairs. She had shown up at the house in Queens because she was worried about those kids. She had held her ground and shot back when things got bad. She had the Rufus seal of approval, which was worth a lot in Sam's book. Three things that made Sam think long and hard about calling her. He thought about Lampo, too. And he thought about the fact that Jake hadn't confided in Lampo.

Heading back to the stairs, Sam flicked the mailbox marked J. Brower. It was a little thing. A stupid thing. A Rufus thing, and he had a magpie obsession with Rufus things right now. It felt like a way of keeping sane.

And the mailbox door rocked open.

Inside, propped at an angle to fit in the narrow space, was a cell phone in a sealed evidence bag. With Jake's name and signature on the first line in the chain of custody.

Grabbing the phone, he ran upstairs to call Ophelia Hayes.

CHAPTER
TWENTY-ONE

Rufus considered, for a very brief moment, that it'd finally happened.

He had died.

He saw nothing, felt nothing, heard nothing.

And certainly, that's what death was all about.

Nothing.

But it wasn't possible. If Rufus was considering the state of his own deadness, then by that very fact, he wasn't dead. He couldn't be dead and conscious of the condition at the same time. At least, Rufus was pretty certain. Because what sort of shit afterlife was that otherwise, where he existed in a haze of nothing, alone but for his thoughts?

That wasn't even Shakespearean in tragedy. It was just

ridiculous.

Rufus forced his eyes open and then reality came crashing in—an assault on all his senses. He took a shaky breath and forced everything to come apart and break down into smaller pieces so he could study them one at a time and not be overwhelmed by the situation.

Rufus's head hurt. Badly. So he'd been struck.

His vision, as he tried to take in his surroundings, doubled when he focused too hard. Not simply a whack over the head—a concussion, perhaps. Rufus tried again, carefully taking in the room around him. It wasn't that big, and the fluorescent overheads were only on near the door, opposite of Rufus. One lightbulb flickered, and its buzzing filled the silence.

The room smelled too. Musty, like it hadn't been opened in over a year. But more immediate than that was the distinct odor associated with an auto body shop. Metal. Motor oil. Grease. Those little pine tree air fresheners.

Rufus carefully rolled onto his side. He was lying on a sheet of moldy cardboard. He reached out to touch the floor, confirmed it was cement, because what else could be so cold and so hard underneath his bony hip and ass, then belatedly realized there was a large zip tie around his wrists.

That's when all those individual assessments slammed back together, like the north and south poles of magnets in a science class experiment. Rufus scrambled into a sitting position. His breathing was coming quick now, which made his head pound harder. His fingers were already tingling in that telltale manner that warned life was about to get rough if Rufus didn't get control over himself, and quick.

Don't panic. Be smart. Don't panic. Be smart.

Think back, through the pain and fog, Rufus told himself as he tried to recount what happened to have landed him... *wherever* he was. He'd left the apartment and slid down the handrails. Right, because he was going to check 9F, J. Brower. And Sam was still upstairs, still upset.

Rufus felt as if his heart actually stopped beating for a moment. Where was Sam?

He craned his neck to the left, ignored the pain that ricocheted around the back of his skull like a pinball game, and examined the room more carefully. There were stacks of boxes everywhere, old and forgotten. But no Sam. The smell of auto body persisted, and Rufus considered he was in a storage room, maybe on the second floor, above a garage. And maybe Sam was in the garage. Rufus turned toward the lit-up part of the room again and was knocked so hard upside the head that he briefly saw white stars, black spots, then red.

Red?

He was lying on the floor again, with blood dripping from the side of his head and into his eye. Rufus grunted and flopped onto his back with his tied hands in front of him. Looming over him was a big burly motherfucker with a shaved head and nose that'd been broken and set crooked. He probably had a name like Mad Max. No— *Bruno.*

Rufus started laughing. "Aren't you handsome."

Bruno snarled. He reached down, grabbed Rufus by the front of his T-shirt, and yanked him up. "Where's the phone?"

"What?"

Bruno took an unassuming smartphone from his pocket and waved it in front of Rufus's face. "The phone, dipshit."

"That's mine. You're holding it. I don't understand the question."

Bruno cracked Rufus upside the head again, sending him sprawling backward.

The air was knocked from Rufus's lungs and he choked and gasped for breath. He slowly raised his head, watching Bruno through his nonbloody eye as the sonofabitch dropped Rufus's phone to the floor and stomped on it with the heel of his boot.

"That cost forty bucks, asshole."

Bruno unholstered a gun from his side and pointed the barrel at Rufus. "Where's the phone?" he repeated.

"I don't know what—" Rufus bit off the thought. He'd been right about the pickup being a burner, and Bruno the Bulldog here thought he had it, or at least knew where it was. The mailbox. Had Rufus gotten it open before being whacked over the head? No, maybe not, but it was difficult to remember. If he had, though, wouldn't Bruno have the phone? *Yes*. And Rufus would have a third eye.

Maybe Sam found the phone. Rufus had told him what he'd meant to do, after all. That brought him back full circle. Where was Sam? Was he still at the apartment, safe and sound? Did he have the phone and was he giving it to Ophelia, like they'd discussed?

Rufus said, with as steady a voice as he could muster, "I don't have it."

"Don't bullshit me." Bruno forced the muzzle of his pistol against Rufus's cheek, grinding it against his face.

"I'm not."

"You're a liar, Rufus O'Callaghan."

Rufus's eyes grew wide.

"That's right. We all know who you are. Jake's little snitch."

"I don't have the phone! I don't know where it is," Rufus said quickly, and while the latter comment was a lie, the panic in his voice was authentic.

"How long do you think you'll last on Rikers?" Bruno continued. "A day, maybe two, I bet. Until you're gutted and fucked to death. And do you know why?"

Rufus swallowed and whispered, "Because snitches get stitches."

Bruno smiled, and it was an ugly look on an even uglier face. "That's right." He ground the barrel of the pistol into Rufus's face again, only stopping when there was some distant, undetermined sound from outside the storage room. Bruno swore, let go of Rufus with a shove, put the gun in his waistband, and walked to the door. "Don't you fucking move," he said over his shoulder before seeing himself out.

Rufus sat up as soon as the door slammed shut. He reached down with both hands, untied his high-tops, and with a bit of awkward bending, maneuvered one lace through the tight restraints. He knotted it to the other shoe's lace, raised his legs, and started to move them back and forth, almost like peddling a bike. It only took a few seconds before the zip tie snapped and Rufus fell backward from the momentum.

He gingerly got to his feet, muttering, "Should have used handcuffs, you dumb fuck." Rufus patted down his jacket and jeans pockets, but they were empty of everything, even his gum.

The gum that Sam bought him.

And that was all it took to make him well and truly *pissed*.

Rufus moved to the nearest stack of cardboard boxes and began opening them at random, looking for anything he could use as a weapon. All he found were what looked like years and years of accounting documents, customer files, automobile manuals, even some tax returns.

"You goddamn kidding me?" Rufus snapped, shoving a box in frustration and trying yet another.

He found lots of magazines, the sort of shit found in waiting rooms: a year out-of-date and dog-eared within an inch of its life. The box below that was topped with skin magazines covered in greasy handprints. Seconds away from letting out a frustrated scream, Rufus spotted a computer on the floor. It was old as hell—deadweight from the '90s too heavy to use in any practical way as a means of self-defense. There was a keyboard, though. As it stood, that was about as useful as the stained *Playboy*s, but Rufus picked it up, wrangled the attached cable to hold either end like a garrote, and walked to the door. He stood to one side and waited.

There was no sound in the building. There seemed to be no sound outside it either. And without a window to look out, Rufus had no goddamn idea if he was even in the city. He could have been in Yonkers—Poughkeepsie, even.

And if that were the case, Rufus might as well let Bruno take him out now.

The door opened again without any warning, and Bruno entered the room. He hadn't even shut the door before Rufus shouted and slammed the board down, keys first, on the fucker's shiny head. The plastic flexed, cracked, and snapped in two. Bruno, still standing, turned and let out a roar. He lunged at Rufus, who jumped back, dodged, and managed to get around behind Bruno.

Rufus jumped on Bruno's back, wrapped the keyboard cord around his neck, and yanked with all his might. He pulled until Bruno made a choked, wet, gasping sound. Pulled until Bruno clawed at the cord. Rufus kept pulling, even as his hands shook and tears—maybe from fear, probably from rage—streamed down his face. And he didn't stop until Bruno crumpled to his knees and fell flat on his face.

Rufus stood and hesitantly patted Bruno's pockets

until he recovered a handful of zip ties—the sort cops carried nowadays. They were cheaper, lighter, and more efficient than doling out a pair of cuffs for every Tom, Dick, and Jane on the force. He also found a ring with keys—pocketed that—twenty bucks—took that too—then looked around for a place to secure Bruno. A big guy like him, if he regained consciousness anytime soon, might have the raw strength to snap the ties. But that'd be far more difficult if he was zipped to—

Rufus spotted an old water radiator in the corner. Warily, he tied one of Bruno's wrists with a zip tie, then dragged the probably unconscious, hopefully not dead man across the floor. Rufus heaved the big body close enough to the radiator that he could zip a second tie around the first and the heater's turn nozzle. Rufus tugged the pistol free from Bruno's waistband next, holding it pinched between his thumb and forefinger like it was a used tissue. He brought it to the box full of fake tits and slipped it between the pages of a retro *Penthouse*.

Rufus left the room after that. He shut the door behind him, eyed a second door across the hall and to the left, a staircase at his right, and opted to rush downstairs as fast as humanly possible. Sure enough, Rufus entered an empty auto body shop at the bottom of the stairs. Some tools and machinery appeared to have been abandoned by whoever's business had since left the premises. Rufus could almost imagine a For Sale sign posted somewhere outside, but judging by the looks of the place, no one had been interested for some time. There was a small window overhead and to the right that sickly colored sunlight filtered through. Rufus would have to find a way up there. He could break the glass and shimmy out—he was skinny enough—and then what, scale the side of the building? It was better than being stuck in here with Bruno just a floor away. Rufus drew closer, and his heart sank when he saw there were bars on the window.

All right. Fuck the window. Obviously there had to be a door to this garage. Rufus backtracked and found a rolled down metal gate at the far end of the room. He bent, grabbed the handle near the floor, and gave it a tug, but the gate didn't budge. He got on his knees to inspect the floor in the near-dark, and his hands found a padlock. Rufus quickly dug out the keys he'd stolen from Bruno, but none of them matched.

Why bring Rufus to a place as secure as fucking Fort Knox? It didn't make sense—he wasn't worth the trouble. Keep him alive, sure, until they found out where the pickup was, but all *this*? Rufus looked over his shoulder at the staircase, then raised his gaze to the ceiling. There was that second door…. So maybe it wasn't about Rufus? Maybe it was simply convenient to drop him off here, where they were already keeping someone else more important.

Rufus left the garage area and, on the balls of his feet so as not to make any noise, hiked the stairs again. Each step up, Rufus could only think, *Sam must be in that room.* Because Sam came to New York looking for trouble from the start. He'd known Jake, his home address, information about his police investigations, had Juliana's name—and even Rufus hadn't known she was a CI. In that sense Sam had had more information than Rufus ever did. He was most definitely a threat to this disgusting enterprise.

Rufus stopped outside the second door, withdrew the keyring again, and tried the lock. This time there was success. He pushed the door open, and in the grimy light, he saw not Sam, but at least a dozen teenagers and young adults—boys and girls—all races—looking back at him with a particular sort of terror, *a familiar terror*, that made Rufus's heart break.

CHAPTER
TWENTY-TWO

Sam had the gun in his hand when the knock came at the door. Pressing himself against the studio's wall, he drew a bead, visualizing a point chest-high on an average man. Then he called out, "Who is it?"

"Hayes" came Ophelia's voice, slightly muffled.

"Are you alone?"

"Yes. Open the damn door," she growled.

"I've got a gun in my hand. Door's unlocked, but be really smart when you walk in."

A moment, a full moment by Sam's count, had passed before the knob turned and the door was pushed open. Ophelia stood to one side, arm extended to hold the door, and angled to keep her body out of the firing zone. She glanced inside and tapped the holster on her own hip. "Please don't make me shoot you."

Sam let the Beretta drop ten degrees. "Close the door." And then, because he couldn't keep it inside any longer: "They took Rufus."

Ophelia's step faltered. "They *who* took Rufus?" She entered the apartment and shut the door. "What the hell is going on with you two?"

"Whoever was holding those kids in that house in Queens. Whoever's bringing them into the city and making them work. Heckler. Christ, whoever else is involved. And if I had a fucking idea where Rufus was, do you think I'd be sitting here with my dick in my hand?"

Ophelia put both hands up. "Hold up for half a second. First, who lives here?"

"Take a wild guess."

Ophelia puffed out her cheeks while letting out an exasperated little sigh. "Detective Brower? Rufus is tied to him, isn't he? That's why Lampo let him slide yesterday." She frowned and put her hands on her hips. "How do you know Rufus didn't... I mean, he does that, sometimes. For as long as I've known him, anyway—up and vanishes whenever he wants."

"And he leaves a pair of lockpicks on the ground like fucking breadcrumbs? He's been gone, Christ, I don't know. Three hours? I didn't even realize something was wrong until he'd been gone half an hour. Minimum. And then you took your sweet time getting here. We need to find him. They want something, and they think he has it, and they're not playing patty-cake while they wait for him to cough it up."

"Hey, first off, buddy, you need to chill out. I can't just drop my duties because a petty thief went out for a pack of smokes on his new boy toy, got it?"

"Take a look at this," Sam said, holding up the phone

in its evidence bag, turning it so Jake's scrawl faced her. "And tell me to chill again."

Ophelia narrowed her eyes, snatched the bag, and studied the scrawl. "Where'd you get this?" she finally asked, voice dropping low.

"Jake left it for Rufus. Because he couldn't trust anybody else with it. You know what that is? That's your arrest. That's your conviction. That's Heckler and the Wall Street assholes who are paying big bucks for the kids getting trafficked through here. That's Jake's fucking blood, right there in your hands, and if you don't get on board real fucking fast, you're going to be up to your elbows in Rufus's blood too." He was panting when he finished.

Ophelia looked at Sam, her expression like stone. "Rufus is a CI?"

"Yes."

She shook the bag a little. "Yesterday... was this... what Detective Lampo wanted me to find on you two?"

"I think so. This is what Jake wanted to give Rufus. I found it stashed in the mailbox. Hidden in a place only Rufus would look, because he's got a goddamn fetish for those things, at an apartment only Jake and Rufus knew about. You know what? What a fucking waste of time. I'm going to find him myself."

But Ophelia immediately sidestepped and blocked the door. "No, you won't. If Detective Brower trusted Rufus to help him with these exploited children, that's good enough for me. Let's find the little punk together."

"Great," Sam said. "How?"

Ophelia lowered her arm, letting the evidence bag dangle. "Their safe house was Flushing, and Juliana didn't say anything about other locations. I'm thinking they panicked, the evidence in the basement spoke pretty loud and clear." She tapped her chin with her free hand.

"They could have left the city completely, but I'm not sure if they'd chance that with so many kids. Toll roads have speed cameras. A routine pull-over on the highway is how creeps like this end up getting busted. If I was tits-deep in this shit, I'd stick to Queens."

After a moment, Sam nodded. "They brought them in easily enough, and normally, I'd say they'd take them out the same way. But they're running scared. They're scrambling. They don't have the time or the flexibility to do it the way they want. So let's say they stayed in Queens." Sam paused. "How big is Queens?"

"Something like two million residents. But if they're considering going back where they originated, somewhere north to regroup maybe, I'd imagine they'd be lying low near parkways. If they took the Grand Central Parkway, that'd be an easy route out."

"They used a residence before," Sam said. "A single-family structure. That might be what they're comfortable with. Are there houses near the Parkway? Would they try to throw us off with a false start? Maybe they follow the Parkway a little bit out of the city to get some breathing room?"

Ophelia's hand moved from her chin to her mouth, chewing absently on her thumbnail. She winced after a moment, studied the torn-up nail, then said, "It's tough to say."

Tapping on his phone, Sam pulled up a map of Queens and began zooming in. "The house they were in, that was over here. Right? Flushing? And this—this is the Parkway you're talking about? And they want privacy. They want a single-family residence. They're pulling back to get their necks out of the noose. What about here?" He stabbed at a section of the map.

Ophelia moved forward, leaned close enough to see the phone's screen, but was still mindful of Sam's weapon.

"Where—the zoo?"

"I'd like to lock you and Rufus in a room and come back in a month. See if you've gotten all those jokes out of your system."

"Calm down, Hulk. Corona, I get it. But that's an awful lot of doors to knock on. And it's based on nothing but hunches and assumptions."

"Let's hear a better idea."

But before Ophelia could answer, her phone started to ring. Instead of picking up the call, though, she frowned at Sam.

"Answer your phone," Ophelia finally stated.

"I don't have 'Hey Macarena' for my ringtone. Answer your own damn phone."

Ophelia shook her head. "It's not—" She looked at the evidence bag still in her hand. The screen was lit up with an incoming call. No name, only a number.

"Shit," Sam said. And then, knowing how stupid it sounded, he said, "Well, answer it."

"And compromise evidence?" Ophelia protested. "Like hell."

"Through the damn bag," Sam said. "Tap the screen."

Ophelia swore, brought the phone close, and tapped Accept hard through the plastic bag. She didn't speak, instead listened and waited.

"H-hello?"

Sam couldn't help himself. "Rufus? Holy Christ, Rufus, is that you?"

"Oh my God, Sam! You found the phone," Rufus said, sounding near tears. "I called it, didn't I? It was in the fucking mailbox."

"Yeah, yeah, you're amazing. Where are you? Are you ok?"

"I've been better," Rufus said, voice carrying through the bag. "I'm in some sort of abandoned auto shop. I found a sign inside, hang on—Dino's Body Repair. This phone isn't mine. Oh fuck, it's probably being traced."

"Dino's Body Repair. Ok. Are you safe? Can you get out?" Holstering the gun, Sam pointed at the door for Ophelia to lead him to her car.

"No," Rufus replied. "I'm locked inside."

Ophelia shoved the evidence bag into Sam's hand, opened the door, and bolted down the stairs.

"I had to knock a guy out," Rufus continued. "Pretty sure he was left to guard the place. Sam, I think I have a concussion. I keep seeing double."

"Just keep talking," Sam said, because, hell, what was he supposed to say? "We're coming. We're going to be there as soon as we can. Find someplace you can hide." Something wild bubbled inside Sam, like laughter and a scream at the same time. "Channel that inner street rat."

Rufus chuckled. "I would if it was only me and Bruno upstairs."

"What? Who's there? What's going on?"

"The kids are—" Rufus's voice abruptly cut off.

Sam shot a glance at Ophelia as they plunged into the chaos of the street. She pointed at the bag, where the phone's screen had gone black.

The phone's battery was dead.

CHAPTER
TWENTY-THREE

Rufus had gone back into the storage room and lifted Bruno's cell, which had been in his back pocket and not part of his initial pat down. Rufus hadn't been certain who to call for help, but sure as hell not 911. What if Heckler intercepted? What if the brigade Rufus hoped would save his ass were the very people who wanted him dead? He didn't have Sam's number, hadn't bothered to read Ophelia's business card, but he'd memorized the burner number that'd been dumped into Jake's CallSpy account. Sure, it was a longshot, but it'd worked. Sam had found the phone, and the relief Rufus had felt after hearing his voice quelled the panic that had been bubbling inside. When the call ended abruptly, Rufus tried the burner again, but it went immediately to voicemail and he suspected the battery had probably been teetering at zero. It was fine, though. Sam said he was coming, that he'd be there soon, so Rufus had to take it as gospel. Sam had enough information to find him and that was that.

Rufus returned to the kids afterward—and Juliana was right, they were just babies—and told them to stay in the room. Some of them hadn't understood, but a few nodded and others whispered to their friends, relaying the promise Rufus had made them: you're going to be ok. He left the door ajar for the kids and returned to the auto body shop below. He turned off Bruno's phone and left it on a workbench nearby. Rufus didn't actually know if the phone was tapped or being traced, but he wasn't the sort to take unnecessary chances.

Next, he dragged a metal worktable toward the window near the ceiling, his head pulsating and pounding with every screech and scratch of the legs against the cement floor. He pushed it against the far wall under the lone window, and then wiped his forehead. By the time he got it against the opposite wall, his head ached like he'd fallen asleep to Pauly Paul drumming all night long. Rufus climbed onto the table, but even standing at six feet, the window was still out of reach. He hopped down, unearthed a plastic crate that'd give him another foot's reach, and carefully climbed back up.

He held on to the windowsill and looked out the tinted glass. Rufus didn't see any pedestrians. There was a single-family home across the street, a lot under construction to the left of it, but it was the weekend so no crew, and beyond that, he couldn't see shit. Rufus took a deep breath, turned his head away, and slammed his elbow against the glass. It took a few tries, but he finally shattered the window. Rufus pushed broken glass from the frame, grabbed onto the bars, and tried to get *that much more* view of his surroundings.

"Queens," he muttered after a moment of deliberation. He heard the distant roar of engines—a lot of cars—

somewhere to his left. "Parkway…." Not that it helped Rufus all that much, but having a sense of place grounded him. He started to let go of the bars and make to climb down, but a car sped down the street and brakes screeched as it came to a sudden stop in front of the auto shop. Rufus held his breath, but when the passenger door opened, he let out a sob and shouted, "*Sam!*"

Ophelia slammed shut the driver's door and moved around the backside of the car. "Hey, Red," she called.

"I'm locked inside," Rufus called back.

"Did you try a key?"

"Don't be an asshole!"

Ophelia jabbed a finger in the air, but even with the distance between them, Rufus could feel it drilling into his chest. "It's a fucking garage. Are there any tools?"

"I don't—" Rufus glanced over his shoulder into the dimness where shapes of machinery could be made out. "Let me check." He climbed off the crate, down from the table, and moved into the dark corners of the garage.

Rufus found a Craftsman toolbox nearly as tall as himself. He started opening the drawers, the top ones empty but for greasy paper towels and a lone wrench covered in rust. He tried the bottom cabinet next and found an electric hacksaw. He swore under his breath, grabbed it, and carried it to the rolling gate with the padlock. He felt around the wall for a moment before finding a power socket. He plugged the saw in, and it roared to life. Macho man tools were so not Rufus's area of expertise, and he really didn't want to lose a thumb, thank you very much, but Sam was on the other side of that door….

He crouched down and put the teeth to the padlock, and it tore through the metal in no time. Rufus turned the hacksaw off, pulled the lock free, grabbed the handle for a second time, and lifted the out-of-date security gate enough that someone could slip underneath with a bit of wiggling. He gave it another heft, stopping less than halfway when the door got stuck and his head was hurting so badly that he thought he might vomit.

A moment later, Sam squeezed under the rolling door. As the big man came up onto his feet, he took in Rufus with one rapid glance, grabbed him, and pulled him tight. When Ophelia shimmied under the door, Sam released Rufus and said to him, "Took you long enough."

Rufus pointed at the hacksaw. "I'm not a fucking lumberjack."

Sam rolled his eyes and held out a hand for Ophelia. "I guess I got confused. Those big arms. Those jacked shoulders. Anybody could have made the same mistake."

Ophelia got to her feet with Sam's assistance. "Both of you, can it." She studied Rufus. "You're not here alone, right?"

Rufus started to shake his head but thought better of it. "No. The kids are upstairs."

"Where's the guy you knocked out?" she asked.

"I zip-tied Bruno to a radiator in the storage room. He's not dead, but I had to knock him out. It was self-defense, I swear to God."

Ophelia unholstered her weapon and held a hand up. "Don't get all panicky."

Rufus nodded. He squeezed Sam's hand, let go, and motioned for the two to follow him upstairs. He took each step carefully, slower than even twenty minutes ago, because *Jesus Christ*, his body ached and he was so exhausted from the peaks and crashes of adrenaline. Rufus gripped the handrail until reaching the landing, then pointed, ignoring the shake in his hand. "Bruno's in that room. The kids in this one."

Sam moved toward the room where Rufus had cuffed Bruno, opened the door, and went in hard and fast, gun in his hand. From where Rufus stood, he watched Sam through the doorway. The big man moved around the room, inspecting Bruno first and then surveying everything else. After a minute, Sam came back and nodded.

"Didn't believe me?" Rufus asked.

Sam grunted. "Ask me again when you can walk a straight line."

Ophelia moved past the two, weapon at low-ready. She backed up against the wall beside the partially open door, took a quick glance inside, then lowered her gun. "*My God.*"

"I don't know if that's all of them," Rufus said as Ophelia took a step into the room with the kids. "But they're so fucking scared."

Instead of moving to check, as he had with Bruno, Sam just shifted his weight, his eyes restless on Rufus.

Feeling Sam's gaze, Rufus cast him a sideways look. He reached out to take Sam's hand again, but froze when the sound of shrieking metal—the rusted rolling gate—echoed all the way upstairs.

And then came voices and footsteps.

CHAPTER
TWENTY-FOUR

Sam froze when metal screeched below them. His first thought was of the door that they had left partially raised. His second thought was of Heckler—and whoever else she might have brought with her.

When he looked at Ophelia, she said, "The stairs."

Nodding, Sam moved with her toward the stairs. In one hand, he held the Beretta, keeping the muzzle pointed at the ground for the moment—although he didn't think that would last long. With the other hand, he motioned Rufus back.

The stairs were a natural choke point. Sam couldn't do anything about the fact that he had managed to get himself and Rufus—and Ophelia, for what it mattered—trapped on the second floor of Dino's Body Repair. It was a stupid mistake, the result of stupid decisions. One of them should have stayed below and kept watch. Instead, worry over Rufus had led Sam to make mistakes. He hoped they weren't the mistakes that would cost all of them their lives.

The layout was simple: the main floor of the body shop, with the rolling door; a dog-leg staircase, a landing interrupting the steps halfway so that the stairs could turn and come back; and then the second-floor landing, where Sam and Rufus and Ophelia held their ground. The second-floor landing was basically a hallway. On one side of the stairs, it ran for about twenty-four inches before ending in painted concrete blocks. Just a shallow niche, it offered enough cover that Ophelia darted forward and took up position there, her shoulder against the wall. Sam took the other side of the stairwell, where the hallway ran toward the two doors: the junk room where Rufus's buddy was cuffed to the radiator, and the room where the kids were being held. Sam gave Rufus one last glance, waving him back again, mouthing, *The kids.*

Rufus gave Sam two middle fingers, but obediently moved into the room.

Before Sam could do anything else, footsteps came toward the staircase, echoing off the painted concrete. Sam's heart moved into his throat; he thought about hummingbirds. Twelve hundred beats per minute. Hummingbirds had fuck-all on him right then, and most of that had to do with Rufus being in danger. How long had it been since Sam had needed to qualify at the range? Eight months? Ten? How bad had the tremors gotten since then, now that he was off the meds? How likely was he to put a bullet in the linoleum instead of center mass on Heckler? Fuck. He blew out a breath. Fuck.

Below, a figure moved into view. Mousy brown ponytail. Department store pantsuit, accessorized today by some sort of brooch on the collar. Bridget Heckler put her back to the wall as she came up the stairs; she had a gun in her hand.

"Stop," Sam said.

Heckler stopped, but the gun floated like smoke, maybe just five degrees, but it was five degrees more than Sam liked.

"Drop the fucking gun and get on the fucking ground," Sam shouted.

Ophelia was on her phone, her words clipped, concise, voice carrying enough that Sam could pick up her badge number, cross-streets, *officer-involved shooting*, like she already knew which way this was going to go down.

"Calm down," Heckler called back. "Everybody calm down. Rufus? You up there? Am I talking to Sam? That's your name, right? Everybody needs to stay really calm right now."

"Sure," Sam said, finger slick and steady against the trigger guard. "I'm calm. Just like Marcus was calm before you killed him. I said put down that fucking gun."

Rufus, crouched low, crept from the kids' room to call back, "I'm still here. You kidnapped me. I want that on record. Officer Hayes, hear that? I was kidnapped."

Ophelia shoved her phone into her pocket and made a quick motion for Rufus to get out of the way.

He flipped her off too.

"Officer Hayes," Heckler said. "This is Bridget Heckler. I'm a sergeant with Major Cases. Come out here so we can talk. You're up there with two very dangerous men."

Ophelia looked at Sam and Rufus again, but she didn't move from her position. "An unarmed CI was here against his will," she returned. "He's been hurt and needs medical attention. And now you're here, sergeant. Who called you? How'd you know about this place?"

Heckler spoke in a low voice; Sam couldn't catch the words, but the fact that Heckler had brought backup made the odds even worse. Then, lowering her gun, Heckler held up her free hand. "There have been some really serious misunderstandings. I think we can figure this out if we can—"

Her hand whipped up, and she squeezed off two shots faster than Sam had expected. Only reflex and training saved his life. He was already pulling back when her gun came up. The first bullet chipped the corner of the wall Sam was hiding behind. He lost track of the second.

Opposite Sam, Ophelia took advantage of the lull in Heckler's shots to poke her head and gun around the corner and fire once. Heckler swore. Sam couldn't see what she was doing, but he saw her next shot punch into the cement blocks near Ophelia's hiding spot. Steps rang out on the stairs.

Sam knew what Heckler was doing; he would have done it himself if he had to take the higher ground against an armed enemy. Heckler was laying down suppressing fire—a fancy way of saying she was trying to blow their heads off, but she'd be happy with just keeping them from moving or returning fire. While Sam and Ophelia tried to keep from getting shot, Heckler's partner would move up the stairs.

In the next lull, Sam peered around the wall to shoot and then, almost immediately, withdrew again. His glimpse of the stairwell made him swear under his breath: a middle-aged man with a bad comb-over had made his way to the first landing.

Lampo. Fucking Lampo.

Jake's partner had been double-dealing the whole time. For a moment, Sam struggled with overwhelming rage at having been duped. Then, with an effort, he forced himself to focus on the situation at hand. Clinically. Tactically.

Lampo was frozen behind the railing, which offered a modicum of cover, but when Sam shot, he was going to start moving again. Ophelia must have understood, too, because she followed Sam's shot with one of her own.

"Keep coming, fuckfaces," Sam shouted. "As soon as Lampo moves off that landing, I'm going to give him a third fucking eye."

Ophelia's voice was cool in spite of the adrenaline tremor running through it. "Not if I do first."

Sam grinned in spite of himself. He took a few short breaths. On three, he was going to try again, see if he could wing Lampo, or at least flush him out so Ophelia could take care of him. *One. Two.*

Heavy, running steps came from behind Sam, and for a crazy moment, he imagined Rufus rushing him for a bear hug. Sam barely had long enough to glance over his shoulder and register a big, ugly fucker with a nose that had been broken several times in the past. *The guard*, he realized. The one Rufus had called Bruno, the one who was supposed to be cuffed to a radiator. All this flashed through his mind the moment before the guy crashed into him and they went sprawling on the landing.

The impact drove the breath from Sam's lungs, and he tried to suck in air. The guy on top of Sam didn't give him a chance. Grabbing Sam's head in both hands, he raised it up and then slammed it against the thin linoleum—and the concrete underneath.

Sam's world went wavy. Then it went black by degrees, like somebody running his hand on a bank of light switches. Things came back together more slowly, and the mixture of pain and consciousness was accompanied, a moment later, by shock.

Sam wasn't dead.

He just wasn't sure what the fuck was going on.

The shock of red was the first thing Sam was able

to focus on—a beacon of light surrounded by drab nothingness. Then the red took on a face, shoulders, arms— and then it was Rufus on top of Bruno, wrapping his arm around the brute's thick neck and yanking backward as hard as he could.

"Shoulda dropped that fucking monitor on your head when I had the chance!" Rufus screamed, his voice hoarse, broken, incensed, insane.

Bruno let go of Sam's head and tugged hard on Rufus's arm, trying to grapple or fling him off, but Rufus clutched to him like a subway rat fighting for a crust of pizza. Bruno reared back on his knees, struggled to his feet, and gave Rufus another hard shake. But the addition of Rufus's weight threw Bruno off balance and he tipped dangerously toward the edge of the stairs. Rufus let go and fell on his ass as Bruno waved his arms wildly for balance before tumbling forward. The fucker let out a shout as he crashed down the stairs, and then a loud snap silenced him.

Gasping for air, Sam flopped onto his belly. He'd lost the Beretta when he'd hit the ground. Now, he spotted it at the edge of the landing. Eighteen inches, tops. But he was exposed, and the world still hadn't quite settled down after the blow to his head. He was aware of Ophelia screaming, a wordless noise of rage punctuated by another shot.

Dragging himself to the edge of the landing, Sam wrapped his hand around the Beretta. The composite grip was pleasantly cool in his hand; everywhere else, he felt like he had a fever. Heckler must have retreated, because he couldn't see her below him, but Lampo was pinned down on the landing. The balding man swore and fired once at Ophelia, and when she pulled back into her hiding spot, Lampo darted down the stairs.

Sam was ready for him. He shot once, taking Lampo in the thigh, and the dirty cop stumbled, squealed, and hit the wall hard enough that his fancy comb-over flopped to the side and exposed the bald spot. Lampo came to rest two stairs down, still making that squealing noise, his gun forgotten as he clamped both hands around his thigh.

"Oh my God!" His voice was shrill. Hysterical. "I've been shot, I've been shot, I've been—"

The sound of sirens interrupted him.

And then, from Heckler: "Aww, fuck."

The back of Lampo's head exploded as a round from Heckler tore through his skull. Then, from her hiding spot below, Heckler tossed her handgun onto the stairs.

"I'm unarmed," Heckler said. "I surrender unconditionally."

CHAPTER
TWENTY-FIVE

Rufus had never seen so many cops at one location in all his life. The street in Queens was congested with black-and-whites, and uniformed officers swarmed the auto shop like ants at a picnic. Ophelia had Bridget Heckler in cuffs, and Rufus thought, if ever there was a criminal who didn't deserve her Miranda rights, it was her. Because as far as he was concerned, a human being who killed good men, who kidnapped and abused children, didn't have rights. He thought of what Bruno had asked him, about how long Rufus would last on Rikers as a snitch.

A snitch behind bars was one thing.

But a cop behind bars? So long, Heckler.

The kids had been escorted out of the garage, taken in

awaiting buses to the closest hospital where Rufus hoped good cops like Ophelia would be able to reunite them with the families they'd been ripped from. He and Sam were sent to the hospital too—scrapes and bruises for Sam, and Rufus had a mild concussion and needed a few stitches in his head, which required buzzing some of his wild hair to reach the gash, but they were both doing a hell of a lot better than Bruno and Lampo, that much was certain.

Rufus didn't have any idea how big the sex trade was or how many cops were involved in the prostitution of exploited teens, but at least they'd gotten a few of them. And with the cell phone Jake had left behind, hopefully they'd track down all the guilty parties. Jake wouldn't have settled for anything less.

The hospital hadn't officially discharged Rufus, but with the blood cleaned up and bottles of pain killers and antibiotics in-hand, he skipped out before too many more questions could be asked. It was easier that way. A discharge meant more paperwork, and he'd already lied about half of his personal information and was too tired to remember what he'd told the nurses in the ER. Rufus waited outside in the late-evening heat until Sam came out the automatic doors, and then he led the way home.

To *his* home.

"Paper," Sam said as soon as they walked through the door.

Rufus was rubbing the bald spot on his head as he threw the deadbolt. "Paper?" He echoed.

"Yes. And a pen."

Rufus glanced around the studio. "Uh... hang on." He went to the kitchen counter, tore some cardboard from a container advertising Maruchan ramen, then uncovered a pen after a bit more shuffling. He scribbled it a few times against the palm of his hand, got the ink moving, then offered both to Sam. "Gonna write me a sexy poem?"

"Next time you get into trouble, call me directly. Routing the call through an important piece of evidence is just showing off." He jotted the number in quick, hard strokes and passed the cardboard back.

"Oh." Rufus stared at the offering, repeated the random numbers to himself until he'd memorized them, then stuck it underneath a magnet on the fridge. "Thanks."

Sam stepped in, framing him against the fridge, and kissed him.

Rufus returned the kiss. Not exactly energetically, because he was exhausted and wanted to sleep for a week, but enough so Sam knew he meant something by it. "Hey, can I show you something?"

Sam nodded.

Rufus moved to his stacks of books on the left side of the room. He turned the biggest pile to face him, studied the spines, then started digging through the options. He got about halfway through the pile, chose a hefty book, then got to his feet. He brought it to Sam and said, "This is the book Jake bought me."

Sam took it, turned it over, and raised an eyebrow.

"*1001 Buildings to See Before You Die*," Rufus stated. "Three bucks."

Sam turned the book over again. And then again. And then he tossed it on the bed and pinched the bridge of his nose.

Rufus frowned. "Hey, don't throw it. You might bend the pages." He moved around Sam, picked up the book from the tumbled bedsheets, and checked the corners for damage.

"Is that supposed to be funny?"

"Some people dog-ear pages, and some people slap people who dog-ear pages."

"You're going to jump off a building and fucking kill

yourself, so you buy a book about buildings to see before you die. Never mind. I'm too tired. Are you hungry? Maybe we should get something to eat."

Rufus looked back at Sam, clutching the book to his chest. His heart slugged hard against his rib cage, and the stitched-up gash on his head beat in sync. "You said you wouldn't talk about that anymore."

"I said never mind, didn't I?"

"Why are you pissed off? You had asked me what book he bought, and I lied and said I didn't remember. Now I'm showing you because I don't want to ever lie to you."

"Yeah? Because it didn't feel like you were just showing me the fucking book."

"What does that even mean?" Rufus set the book on the bed again.

For a long moment, Sam stood there, hands on his hips. He looked paler than Rufus had ever remembered seeing him; dark hollows marked his eyes. "It means—" He drew a sharp breath. And then Rufus realized Sam was on the brink of tears. "It means you disappeared. Those lunatics had you, and you could have died. And then I get you back, which is a goddamn miracle, and then I have to come here and have you throw that in my face. 'Hey, Sam. Glad you're still around. Might kill myself, but we can't talk about that, we're not going to do anything to make it better.' I almost fucking died today because—because I thought I lost you. Before today, fine, I could say we wouldn't talk about it, I could pretend I was ok with ignoring it. Not anymore, Rufus."

Rufus's fingers were tingling. He wrapped his arms around himself and stared at the floor. At his scuffed-up Chucks. At Sam's boots. At that gouge in the wall that'd been there since one of his mother's friends threw a table across the room. How old had Rufus been when that happened—twelve? Yes, right before Alex Mitchell shoved him down the stairs at school.

Snap.

Pop.

"You don't have any idea what I've been through, Sam," Rufus finally said, his voice hitching. "Sometimes that thought is… it's like a security blanket. It's the only constant I have."

"Ok. You're right. I don't understand. Why can't we go see someone? Why can't we take care of this? You've had a shitty life; join the club. There are people who don't want to lose you. I don't want to lose you, and I don't want you to hurt like this."

"The more you say that, the worse it makes me feel," Rufus said, wiping his face. "I don't want—I'm just going to let *you* down."

A struggle rippled in Sam's face. He crossed his arms and said, "Fine. If you were sick, if you had pneumonia or something, if you refused to go to the hospital, I'd make you go. So I'll make you do this. I'll drag you to a fucking therapist kicking and fucking screaming if I have to. I'll fill out the intake forms myself. You can whine and bitch and tell me you don't deserve to be loved, but you are going. Today. Right now."

Rufus lowered his arms to his sides, his hands balled into fists. Then, very quietly, he said, "Get out."

"No, I told you—" Sam stepped forward, reaching.

"Get the fuck out *right now*," Rufus ordered, his voice rising.

Sam grabbed him.

Rufus punched Sam squarely in the face. He swore, shook his hand, and held it to his chest.

The punch rocked Sam's head back. Sam came to a stop, hands steepled over his nose. The look of shock in his face was almost worse than the look of pain that came after.

Shaking his head, Sam said, "What the fuck am I doing?"

And then he left.

Rufus stared at the front door for a long time. And when he was certain he was totally and unequivocally alone, dropped into a crouch, hugged his knees to his chest, and began to cry.

Sam Auden and Rufus O'Callaghan return in:

A Friend in the Fire
(An Auden & O'Callaghan Mystery: Book Two)

Gregory Ashe is a longtime Midwesterner. He has lived in Chicago, Bloomington (IN), and Saint Louis, his current home. When not reading and writing (which take up a lot of his time), he is an educator.

gregoryashe.com

ALSO BY GREGORY ASHE

Join Gregory Ashe's mailing list for advanced access, exclusive content, limited-time promotions, and insider information.
bit.ly/ashemailinglist

C.S. Poe is a Lambda Literary and two-time EPIC award finalist, and a FAPA award-winning author of gay mystery, romance, and speculative fiction.

She resides in New York City, but has also called Key West and Ibaraki, Japan, home in the past. She has an affinity for all things cute and colorful and a major weakness for toys. C.S. is an avid fan of coffee, reading, and cats. She's rescued two cats—Milo and Kasper do their best to distract her from work on a daily basis.

C.S. is an alumna of the School of Visual Arts.

Her debut novel, *The Mystery of Nevermore*, was published 2016.

cspoe.com

ALSO BY C.S. POE

Visit cspoe.com for free slice-of-life codas, titles in audio, and available foreign translations.
Join C.S. Poe's mailing list to stay updated on upcoming releases, sales, conventions, and more!
bit.ly/CSPoeNewsletter

Made in the USA
Coppell, TX
04 January 2021

47459361R00152